LIMITED WISH

LIMITED WISH

MARK LAWRENCE

47NORTH

Published by 47North, Seattle

www.apub.com

Amazon, the Amazon logo, and 47North are trademarks of Amazon.com, Inc., or its
affiliates.

ISBN-13: 9781542016063 (hardcover)
ISBN-10: 1542016061 (hardcover)
ISBN-13: 9781503946781 (paperback)
ISBN-10: 1503946789 (paperback)

Cover design by Tom Sanderson

Printed in the United States of America

THE STORY SO FAR

Here I present a catch-up for the previous book to refresh your memory and avoid having characters undergo 'as you know' conversations. This is in no way a substitute for reading *One Word Kill*. It is meant to help those who have already read book 1.

Nick is a mathematical genius who lives in London and has turned sixteen between books 1 and 2. He is in remission from an aggressive type of leukaemia. The year is 1986.

Nick's D&D group consists of his two schoolmates, John (handsome, rich, somewhat shallow) and Simon (antisocial, obsessive, has a brilliant memory), plus Mia (witty, imaginative, streetwise) – the girl who became Nick's girlfriend in book 1. Their former dungeon master, Elton Arnot, has withdrawn from the group after the death of his father, a security guard, made him unwilling to risk the rest of his family through continued association with Nick.

Demus is Nick aged forty. In book 1 he comes back from the year 2011 in order to convince Nick and Mia to record her memories so that they can be reinstated after she suffers a terrible accident in the future.

Demus steers Nick and his friends into stealing an advanced microchip needed to complete the memory storage device. During this robbery Demus and Elton's father are killed by school psycho turned would-be drug lord, Ian Rust. Rust also dies. Demus knew who was going to die.

Demus's actions are constrained by the need for unfolding events to match his memories of the time (when he was Nick). If what happens does not match his memories, then the world has branched onto a new timeline and his actions cannot help the Mia he knows in the future.

At the end of book 1 Nick uses the memory storage device to erase his memories of the events during the robbery at the microchip laboratory and of a number of days before that. This is in order to match the gap in Demus's memory and to spare him the detailed knowledge of exactly how he dies in the laboratory.

In order to make sure that Nick's timeline and Demus's timeline continue to be the same, Nick will have to become Demus as he grows older. This means he will have to invent time travel!

One big reason that Nick wants to become Demus is that Demus clearly survives for another twenty-five years. Which is unlikely given the current state of Nick's health.

CHAPTER 1

June 1986

I never expected to die in a punt chase. But actually being in one had rapidly narrowed the odds. Currently fifty-fifty seemed fair. Drowning was a distinct possibility. The pole I was leaning on was a solid sixteen-foot piece of wet spruce. Most of it would have been dry, though, if I hadn't fumbled it into the water in the early stages. The River Cam wasn't even over-my-head deep where I made the turn, but the drunken toffs in the pursuing punt were promising to hold me under. So drowning would probably be listed on the death certificate.

'Faster, boys! We're gaining on the little shit!'

When steering a punt it pays to plan ahead. They make steering shopping trolleys seem easy in comparison. It also helps to have had more than one previous go at punting. Generally it's a leisurely pastime, but when six red-faced third years are intent on 'ducking the oik' it becomes a more hectic, albeit still rather sedate, affair. A car crash in slow motion. In any event I had not planned ahead, and now the bow of my punt was scraping the bricks of the grand building rising directly beside the river.

I call it my punt. In truth all of us had jumped into rental punts and made off without paying. But, ownership aside, it was certainly *my* neck that was on the line.

The boat juddered along, slowly turning parallel to the wall. All I could do was struggle to stay upright on the stern platform while not losing hold of my pole.

'We've got the bastard now!'

Several of the third years were aiding their puntsman along by paddling with their hands, and the great ginger lout in the front lay on his belly over the bow doing the crawl as if he were swimming. Only the fact that they were so drunk had kept me ahead this long. Like me they were all in bow ties and dinner jackets and the puntsman sported a deep purple cummerbund. The ginger giant had originally had a top hat in hand, though that was now floating hundreds of yards behind, the loss only prompting him to bellow even more murderous threats across the diminishing span of water between us.

Just before the 'incident' that set them after me, Ginger had been attempting to impress the ladies by putting earthworms in his mouth. Apparently that's how the upper crust do things at Cambridge college garden parties.

I cleared the wall and leaned into the pole. Get the angle wrong and it digs into the riverbed, leaving you with the choice of either letting go or staying with the pole while the punt heads off. Unlike the sons of judges, lords and merchant bankers in the boat behind me, I had rented my outfit from Moss Bros and I doubted they would take kindly to having it handed back wet. Ahead of us the Mathematical Bridge loomed, an arched affair built entirely of straight timbers. A small but growing crowd of amused onlookers watched the chase over the railings.

'Got you!'

As we passed beneath the bridge the pursuing punt came close enough for Ginger to lunge out over their bow to grab at the stern of mine.

A coldness ran through me and it happened again, that *thing* that had started with the running girl and had been happening ever since with steadily increasing frequency. The coldness wasn't a chill finger up the spine, it was more like liquid nitrogen running through the marrow of my bones. Enough cold to freeze the moment and fracture it, sending a dozen cracks running into the future, a dozen glimpsed maybes, no two the same. In one I was drowning, the surface of the river an impossibly distant two feet above me, the sunlight wavering down through the water, someone's hands locked about my throat. In another I was free and clear, my pursuers capsized in my wake.

Ginger scrabbled at my punt. I won free of my paralysis and stamped on his hand before his wet fingers could find a hold on the platform.

'I say!' declared a chinless wonder from further down the boat. A result of aristocratic inbreeding, no doubt. If only he'd had a monocle he could have stepped straight from the pages of a nineteenth-century edition of *Punch*.

'Grab his pole!'

That got some homosexual innuendos and sniggering, but one of them grabbed it all the same. All I could do was let it go and deliver a kick to Ginger's chest. I shoved off him, hoping to aim my punt at the grassy slope coming up on the left.

Pursued by roars of indignation I ran the length of my punt and made a desperate leap for the bank. I almost made it. The top half of me did, landing on the grass with a thump that drove all the air from my lungs. My legs landed in the water.

To jeers and catcalls I scrambled out onto the path along the bank. My plan was to run. I'm not good at it but fear is a great tutor. My first step on the gravelled path let me know I'd lost one half of my only pair of black shoes. I ran even so, dodging past students and tourists. I made it a good fifty yards along the riverbank before someone tripped me from behind. Rolling over I saw the puntsman with the purple cummerbund looming over me, a tall guy with sharp features and oiled black hair scraped back in a 1920s style. He looked remarkably pleased with himself.

'I'd say it's time for a damned good thrashing.'

I couldn't tell if he really talked like that or if he were playing the role for effect. My hands were bloody and embedded with little bits of grit. I raised both defensively as he drew his leg back like a footballer taking a penalty.

'Fuck off.' She came out of nowhere, a girl in jeans and a black T-shirt, slightly built, strangely familiar, and a head shorter than the puntsman. Without pause she set both hands to his chest and gave him a hard shove. He made an enormous splash. Ginger arrived just in time for a very meaty kick in the balls. He staggered backwards and joined his friend in the wet. I knew how cold the water was. Probably just what he needed between the legs. 'Who's next?'

Apparently none of them were. The remaining four suddenly decided that pulling their friends out of the river was top priority.

The girl helped me up. She really did look disturbingly familiar. 'Come on then.'

And a moment later I was following her into the Queens' College halls of residence overlooking the Cam.

That's how I met Helen.

CHAPTER 2

She never asked me why they were chasing me.

The answer isn't particularly edifying. I'd come unwillingly to the garden party, an open-air affair of the strawberries and cream and string quartets in pagodas sort. Summer dresses and champagne al fresco rather than ball gowns twirling beneath vaulted ceilings. The taffeta and silk would come out next week for the end-of-term May Balls . . . which are . . . of course . . . in June. Garden parties are the warm-up, then it's the balls. Every college seemed to have them and my presence was in demand, at least with the staff if not the students. The party had done nothing to improve my mood, which had already been soured by the phone call I'd had earlier with John about Mia's new boyfriend. I shouldn't have asked, but that wound had yet to heal and I couldn't stop scratching it.

It had been the chinless wonder without the monocle that sparked it off.

'Why, if it isn't Professor Halligan's new pet, hot foot from Moss Bros!'

I would have let that slide. It was largely accurate. I was only at the university because the acclaimed professor had demanded it and sworn to resign if he didn't immediately get his way. And I *had* hired my dinner jacket from Moss Bros. It wasn't dress code for a garden party, but the thing was supposed to segue neatly into an evening do later and many of us had come prepared.

'And the pet's dog,' he added.

He said it just as Henrietta approached. God had given Henrietta the same angular lack of grace he'd given me, along with an unfortunately large nose, and lank hair to frame a face that was nineteen going on forty-five. She also happened to be a genuinely nice person, shy but with a great sense of humour. In addition she had been the only one of the students in my new college to have acknowledged my existence as I hung rather lost at the corner of the quad on that first day. She'd approached me with a 'Hello!', left shoulder slumped in premonition of a handbag from which Kleenex and wine gums would one day be dispensed in equal measure.

Henrietta shared my utter lack of fashion sense, but where the boys had only one option when it came to evening dress, the girls had more than enough rope to hang themselves. And she'd chosen to do the hanging using a rose-patterned monstrosity of a dress with puffed sleeves.

It wasn't the way her tentative smile died on her lips that made me do it. It was the way her face told me that she expected the slap-down and accepted it as her due. I took a champagne glass from a passing waiter and upended it slowly over Chinless's head. At the time I would have claimed I was doing it for Henrietta, but really I don't think I did her any favours. I was just having a bad day. And besides, Chinless was a weedy little guy with a big mouth. What was he going to do? That's when six foot six of ginger worm-eater tapped me on the shoulder and spat his mouthful into my face as I turned.

'Get him!' someone called, and suddenly there'd been half a dozen of them converging from all sides.

'Get your trousers off.'

'What?' I asked. It wasn't that I hadn't heard her or that I didn't understand, I just used the word to buy time.

'You're dripping on the floor.'

I stood at the door to Helen's room on a girls-only floor of the hall of residence. She'd stepped into the carpeted interior and turned to block my entrance. 'We pay deposits on these rooms and the college uses any excuse to keep them.'

I looked up and down the corridor. A tall blonde girl was studying me critically from the far end as if I were a new sort of bug.

'I . . .'

'Your choice,' Helen said with a shrug. 'You can walk home in wet trousers if that's what you want to do. Or come in without them.'

I didn't want to squelch my way home. The material was cold and clung to my legs, and, besides, she was very pretty.

'I just didn't want to get you a reputation,' I said, struggling out of my trousers in the hall. It required as much balance as punting and I came just as close to falling over.

Helen turned and went inside. She had long brown hair with a slight curl at the ends. It swished around her shoulders as she moved. 'You can wring them out in the sink.' She pointed to a cubbyhole near the door.

I followed her in wearing wet Y-fronts and a dinner jacket. The dripping trousers filled one hand and I used my other to wave a cheerful goodbye to the blonde at the end of the hall.

'Nice!' It was her collection of posters I was referring to rather than the room, which was boxy and modern, unlike the antiquated tower room that Professor Halligan had somehow acquired for me overlooking the quadrangle at Trinity College.

She shrugged. 'Better than the Athena wallpaper most of them put up.'

I grinned and nodded. My posters were at least things like Bowie and The Cure rather than Wham and that tennis girl scratching her bare bum, but they *had* come from the Athena chain. Helen's, on the other hand, were bill posts for local gigs by bands I'd never heard of.

'There's a towel.' She nodded to the rail beneath the sink.

'What?'

'To protect your dignity while you wring out your pants.'

'Oh.' It was a very small towel and I was far from sure it would protect any shreds of dignity I had left or indeed hide any future developments. I wasn't even sure I could trust the tiny piece of cloth to stay up while I used two hands to squeeze the river from my underwear.

'I won't look.' She sat on her bed and turned away with a small smile, leaning forward to hit play on her stereo. Marillion started up on the tape deck, the song 'Garden Party' somehow just at the bit where they sing about the joys of punting along the Cam. Chance or design? Was she teasing me?

I wrung out as much water as I could with stinging hands. Helen picked up a large text book and opened it at a marked page.

'What are you reading?' I'd learned that at Cambridge you ask what someone is reading rather than what they're studying.

'Biochemistry.'

I'd expected her to go on for longer so I could use the opportunity to manoeuvre the towel over myself. 'Really?' I prompted.

'You're posh, too. I'm not sure I would have saved you if I'd known.'

'Well,' I said, trying to sound a bit more London. 'Not posh-posh.'

'Private school?' She had a regional accent. Somewhere north. Not quite Liverpool.

'OK . . . yes. But I'm not like those morons you rescued me from. Thanks for that, by the way.' I hitched the towel around my hips with a rather insecure tuck and continued to twist wet clothes over her sink. The water smelled . . . rivery.

'You look very young.' She had turned around and two dark eyes studied me over the top of a book titled *Integrative Human Biochemistry*.

'Ah!' I grabbed at my towel just as it started to slip. My skinny, very white legs were off-putting enough without adding the full show.

'You look very young, too,' I added. She didn't really, but I wanted to put her off the scent.

'I'm seventeen. My school let me skip a year.'

'Well done!' I turned back to the sink, pressing against the edge to help anchor the towel. 'And did you always want to do biochemistry? It sounds interest—'

'So. How old are you?'

I changed tack again. 'I'm sure I know you from somewhere,' I said. She did look maddeningly familiar, but it wasn't like I knew many girls. Certainly not enough to forget one. I hunted for the connection but it remained just out of reach like an unremembered name tickling the tip of my tongue. 'Do you have a twin?'

'No. And you look familiar too. Now answer my question.' She wasn't to be diverted.

'Sixteen.' I didn't add 'just'. My birthday had been a quiet affair in the aftermath of the most insane January of my life. Possibly of anyone's life. The day following it had brought the news that I was officially in remission from my leukaemia, a gift that brought about a smaller and more heartfelt celebration.

'You must be that kid who was in the papers. That's why you look familiar.' Helen set her book down. 'The wunderkind.'

'I guess so.' I shook out my wrinkled and slightly drier trousers. The fall had put a hole in the right knee. The hire shop would not be pleased. 'Look, I'd better go.'

I hated all the wunderkind stuff. Half the tabloids had run with a photo of me caught by surprise at my front door, looking more gormless than I had thought any person could look. *The Sun* had the headline, 'Suicide boffin's son turns Time Lord'. The others were almost as lurid. At least none of them had tied me to three corpses in a microchip laboratory some months earlier. For that I was grateful. I had erased the memory of the incident, but the ghosts of Demus and Mr Arnot still haunted me. And the world might be better off without Ian Rust but I was glad not to remember seeing him die.

'You should hang your stuff outside my window. Be dry in a half an hour with all this sun.'

'I . . .'

'I'll tell you all about biochemistry. I can tell that you're interested.' She gave a grin so wicked that I found its echo on my lips. Her face had a delicacy to it, sharp cheekbones, a narrow beauty. I found it difficult to imagine her felling two of the hooray henrys who had been chasing me. But she had, and she'd scared off the others. I made a note not to forget that.

We actually did end up talking about biochemistry. While my socks, trousers and underwear dangled misleadingly outside her window in the June sunshine I sat in Helen's guest chair with a hand towel to cover my modesty and asked her about the effects of magnetic fields on the human brain. Specifically I was interested in memory, having recently erased two weeks of my own. I didn't admit to that, of course. Neither did I tell her that my last memory before the wipe was of convincing a girl called Mia into a car driven by my older self from the future, and that my next was of finding myself sat beside Mia on a park bench. Or that in my hand had been a note from myself suggesting that I kiss her.

Unsurprisingly, as a first-year student Helen didn't know much about the subject of memory, other than that magnetic fields were known to have a wide range of effects on the brain. She seemed interested though, and promised to ask one of her lecturers who specialised in the neurophysiology of the brain. This was good, because in my room I had two headbands that would erase and record memories, and sometime in the next twenty-five years I had to invent them. If I didn't manage it then I'd get to find out first hand just what the consequences of breaking the universal laws of cause and effect were. It would be a lot easier if someone like Helen invented it for me and let me get on with the thorny issue of inventing time travel.

'So this Professor Halligan is a big deal then,' Helen said, ending our biochemistry tutorial abruptly.

'He really is. If you ask Joe Bloggs in the street for famous scientists they'll give you Einstein and Newton. Galileo at a stretch. Ask for someone current and a small number might know Richard Feynman. After that, if you've picked a more knowledgeable Joe Bloggs, it will be Hawkins or Halligan.'

'Who's Hawkins?'

'Exactly. Anyway, the point is that Cambridge don't want to lose him so he gets away with a lot.'

'The papers said you turned up in one of his third-year lecture courses and caused a riot.'

'It wasn't quite like that,' I said.

I'd been playing around with mathematics since I was twelve. My dad taught me the basics but I'd never been keen. I think it was because he so clearly wanted me to love it like he did. But maths was what kept my father away, it was what sent him around the world to international conferences, what kept him in the university until the small hours, and huddled him over a desk in his upstairs office at weekends. Mathematics was my rival for his affections, and I wanted no part of it.

That was until my dad's suicide.

They said it was fear that put him in the path of that train. They said he couldn't face his cancer, couldn't bear the suffering it was putting him through. Maybe that was true. The doctors had said it was terminal. But when Mother brought home his notebooks from the university they told a different story. A story that almost no one in the world could read.

'My father was a famous mathematician,' I told Helen. 'If that's not an oxymoron. Let's say he was nearly as famous as mathematicians get, a rung below Halligan if you like. He had a theorem named after him and two conjectures.'

'Two what nows?'

'Conjectures. A conjecture is an interesting mathematical state-
ment that nobody has been able to prove or disprove. Fermat's Last
Theorem is a conjecture because it hasn't been proved. The proof he
claimed to have found in 1637 was lost because he said it was too
big to fit in the margin of the page and that he had written it somewhere else. Somewhere that was then lost to us. So it remains unproved.
Anyway . . . it turns out I'm quite good at maths too.'

I rambled on, forgetting my state of undress, the stinging of my
grazed palms, the girl on the bed. Just talking. I don't know what undid
my tongue. Maybe something about her. That unexplained déjà vu and
the way she'd come to my aid. Or maybe it was just knowing that she
wouldn't believe me.

In my father's notes I found that the theorem that bore his name,
and whose proof he had delivered to great acclaim at a conference in
New York shortly before his diagnosis, was flawed. He had discovered
an error in the proof and the notebooks evidenced increasingly desperate attempts to reformulate it. My father had seen it as his legacy. The
thing that would bear his name throughout history once he was gone.
Instead what he'd given the world was a ticking time bomb. Sooner or
later the error would be noticed, the conjecture disproved and forgotten, or proved by someone else.

I think it was that despair that made him take his life. Not the
chemotherapy, surgery and hospital beds. We all have something that's
just too much for us. Everyone does. We may never meet it, but it's out
there, waiting. We all have something that will make us take that same
train my father took.

After his death mathematics became my enemy and I attacked
it hard. It should have been me that my father saw when he looked
for what was going to take his name into the future. Me, Nicholas
Hayes. Not the Hayes Theorem of Topological Compactness. I fixed
his proof for him and proved both his conjectures. I leaked the results

to a professor at Imperial College some years later, offering them up as my dad's unpublished works, found beside his death bed.

'And yet you stayed at school doing O-levels just like everyone else?'

'I wanted a life. You do this stuff out in the open and suddenly that's all that anyone sees. I wanted to muck around, play D&D, meet girls—'

'Those last two are often mutually exclusive.' Helen smiled.

'Anyway, just after Christmas something happened that made me really find my focus. I suddenly wanted to achieve something, make a difference, use the skills I inherited.'

'The cancer?' She came right out with it. Most people hesitate when they say the C-word, just a little, as if they still need to convince themselves you don't get it just by saying it out loud. Like it was one of those demon lords in D&D that are summoned by name. Say *Demogorgon* too many times and he was pretty much bound to show up, but cancer . . . not so much.

I smiled bravely. I didn't want to say 'yes, it was the cancer that made me knuckle down' because it wasn't true. And I didn't want to say 'no, it was a visit from future-me saying I had to invent time travel in order to save the girl who dumped me a month later' because that just sounded crazy. So instead I answered, 'The photographers got to me before my hair grew back properly, which pissed me off at the time, but was a blessing in disguise cos now no one recognises me from the articles they ran.'

I said 'before my hair grew back properly' but it hadn't really. It came back different. It wasn't the only thing to have changed. My friendships had too. But as for the hair, it had grown back finer and more brittle as if it were still busy carrying the chemo poisons out of my system.

'So tell me about the not-riot,' Helen said.

'Well, first I needed to find out who could help me,' I said. 'I spent a week buried in the bowels of Imperial College hunting through dusty science journals in the university stacks. I was supposed to be recuperating. Instead I nearly put myself back in hospital, but I did find out for sure that Halligan was the one I really needed to talk to. His papers were exactly the thing I was looking for. He'd been thinking about the same things that I had and found part of the answer too.

'Unfortunately he's also as close to a rock star as any mathematician is ever going to get. That means he's deluged in mail from would-be collaborators and from other mathematicians with questions. My dad used to get more than he could read and he wasn't nearly such a big deal.' I found Helen easy to talk to. She just stretched out and listened. So I rambled on, falling back into the moment.

February 1986, London

I had known it would be hard to get Halligan's attention. I was still fifteen and I looked it. In a field like the professor's it takes time to prove you really know what you're talking about and he wasn't going to give that time to a random schoolboy.

So, just to begin intelligence gathering in order to plan my approach, I phoned the faculty secretary at Cambridge. I pretended to be a postdoctoral researcher returning from illness and needing to catch up with Halligan.

'Well, you know he hates interruptions, so don't go knocking at his door for heaven's sake!' The lady at the other end sounded alarmed at the very prospect.

'No. I value my life more than that!' Also I had no idea where his office was. 'Maybe I could book an appointment?'

'I can give you the number of his personal secretary. You should probably prepare yourself for a long wait . . .'

'Or maybe just try to catch him at the end of a lecture?'

'Well now, that's quite an art form but you can certainly try, and it might be your best bet. Let me see . . .' I heard her start to leaf through papers. 'His Advanced Algebraic Topology on Complex Manifolds course is almost finished. After that he isn't down to lecture again until the summer. More research and less lecturing – one of the perks of fame!'

'And the next lecture is when?'

More leafing. 'Friday. And I think . . . yes . . . that's the last one.'

'Sh— Dash it!' I tried to sound more Cambridge student and less foul-mouthed fifteen-year-old. 'Friday as in tomorrow Friday?'

'Yes.'

'And where would this be?'

'In the Cockroft.'

'The Cockroft?'

A pause. 'Sorry, what did you say your name was again?'

I hung up. I guessed I was supposed to know what the Cockroft was but it didn't sound like any Cambridge college I'd ever heard of. Though on reflection I could only name about three, and there might be hundreds for all I knew.

'Shit.' So much for careful planning.

I took the 07:10 train from King's Cross. John came with me. I wasn't sure why I'd asked him to come, but as we jolted our way out of London it still seemed a good idea. He was two months younger than me but looked old enough to be a student – annoyingly handsome, broad-shouldered, blond hair somehow naturally coming as close to a quiff as you could get away with at Maylerts.

'Nicky Hayes, bunking off school, never thought I'd see the day.' John gave that easy grin of his.

I shrugged. The way he talked you'd think John was a regular truant, which he wasn't. He played by the rules just like I did, only he always managed to make it seem like he was doing exactly what he wanted to and thereby retained all his cool points.

John pulled out his newspaper. A broadsheet that required at least two seats to unfold properly. In my opinion he rarely read more than five per cent of it, if that, but it was part of his vision of 'grown-up John'. His father always carried *The Times* under his arm, I'd noticed. 'At least you'll have no trouble pulling a sickie.'

'No.' Now that my hair was starting to grow back John had no problem ribbing me about the leukaemia. As far as he was concerned I was cured. The whole thing done and dusted, the only legacy being an easy time of it when it came to getting days off sick. 'I guess not.'

'So, Hooligan—'

'Halligan.'

'You think he can help you with your sums and . . .' John frowned. 'I don't see what's in it for him though? You said Demus didn't tell you how he did . . . all that stuff.'

'Well, I know a few things.' I lowered my voice, though I've no clue why I would whisper about time travel when half the while we were discussing orcs or dragons or spells. 'Like, I know a person can travel back in time.'

'Hell, *I* know that. Do you think he'll want to talk to me too?'

'I speak his language. I need to get on with this. I can't waste the rest of the year with O-levels and then another two years in sixth form.'

'Waste?' To his credit John kept any hurt from his voice but I glimpsed the edges of it around his eyes. He rallied himself. 'You have to stay, don't you? How would you even get into university without exams?'

'I didn't mean to say "waste" . . .' I said. In my small group of friends John had been our star player. He had everything going for him. The looks, the money, the charisma. How he ended up playing D&D with social losers like me and Simon I don't know. But like Elton he was popular enough that any ensuing loss of cool hardly dented his standing. Then all of a sudden I had leukaemia and my future self showed up, pretty much guaranteeing me a hot girlfriend and world-wide fame. At least I assumed that cracking the theory of time travel and then actually making it technically doable would make me famous. Either of those things on its own should be enough for a Nobel Prize and a lifetime of front page news.

When the focus in a group shifts like that it can upset everything. I thought perhaps that our friendship had survived only because John had shrewdly noted that the future Demus had gone bald and then died at age forty.

'Why didn't you ask Mia to come too?' John changed the subject.

'Who says I didn't?'

John rolled his eyes.

'I don't know. It's just . . . Everything is a bit strained. I know you said we seemed good together before *that* night. But now, it's like . . . It's like me and Mia are fated to be together. It's like there's no choice and we know where we're heading.'

'Pressure, dude!' John always said 'dude' as if he were trying it on for size. But he was right. Romance and love can endure external pressure to end them. Being told no just made Romeo and Juliet get serious. But those emotions don't do so well if that pressure is trying to make them happen instead of trying to make them stop. It's like having a gun to your head and being told to laugh convincingly at a joke or you get a bullet.

We exited Cambridge station into the teeth of a cruel February wind. I hunched in my coat, and was for once actually glad of the woolly hat that covered my chemo baldness. John led on with confidence though he had no better idea of the way than I did.

The mysterious Cockroft sounded as if it might have been a public house, gentlemen's club or Michelin-starred restaurant. It turned out to be a lecture hall. We only needed to ask ten different students and waste half an hour walking out of town following fake directions before we found that out.

I got to the lecture sweaty and red-faced despite the cold. John, as ever, looked ready for the front page of a fashion magazine. We were late and a small crowd of students had gathered in the corridor around the open doors to the hall, unable to fit in.

I found myself facing a wall of backs. Worse still, they were talking among themselves so loudly I couldn't even tell if Halligan had started lecturing.

'. . . don't think there's a single third year left in there.'

'. . . half are faculty, and the rest are postdocs and grad students . . .'

'. . . big finale we're hoping!'

I turned to John helplessly. 'He must be airing his current research. Has to be if he's managed to scare off all his actual students.'

'Who are this lot then?' John asked.

'Staff and guys doing PhDs.' I said guys because apart from one severe-looking woman on the opposite side from me every one of them was male. I was definitely not doing the right subject if I wanted to meet women. Still, I had better odds than my father had and they improved each year as the sexism leaked out of the system. 'I guess I can try to catch him when he leaves . . . If there isn't a back door.'

John shook his head. Quick as a flash he snatched the woolly hat from my head, revealing my pale baldness and the straggles of dark hair trying to re-establish themselves. He raised his voice. 'This boy's got cancer! Let him through!'

Half a dozen faces turned our way.

'What?' I hissed at him, trying to recover my hat. 'Don't—'

'Leukaemia! He's got leukaemia. Get him to a seat.' John pushed me ahead of him and amazingly the crowd parted as if I had leprosy. We entered at the back of the lecture hall and moved down through an impossibly crowded walkway with John droning, 'Sick boy coming through.' He even managed to get a row of already intimate spectators to shuffle still closer and allow me to perch on the end of a bench near the front. I was surprised not to hear a thump as someone at the far end was pushed off into the next walkway.

All this while Halligan kept talking, his back to the audience, facing three great whiteboards almost entirely covered in close-packed mathematics. I hunted for the start, squinting to bring the cramped notation into focus.

'Alright?' John asked, crouching down on the steps beside me.

I didn't answer. I tuned him out. I tuned Halligan out. I sat with my knees wedged against the back of the next row and stared. Mathematics is its own language. The language of everything. It doesn't need someone to explain it. It explains itself and leaves almost no room for ambiguity.

I was always good at maths but it wasn't until I started to take the stuff seriously that I began to see the beauty of it. A good mathematical proof is a gem. It sparkles in the same way, and like a diamond it's impervious to time. It takes and multiplies the light of understanding, refracting it through many facets.

The shadows on the flat screen of a shadow play are projections from more complex objects. Our three-dimensional hands can cast a variety of two-dimensional shadows to delight the audience. In the same way there are fabulous beasts that swim in the seas of mathematics. Multidimensional behemoths of incredible beauty that even the best of minds struggle to glimpse. The equations we battle with, the proofs that we use to nibble at the edges of such wonders: these are the shadows cast by those we hunt. And on Halligan's three boards were a dozen or more fragmented shadows, each struggling to assert itself, each a hint at the magnificent tiger he had by the tail. The edge of an ear there, a hint at a whisker here, and in the middle of it, a glimmer, just a glimmer mind, of an eye. A watching eye.

'Nick?' John shook my arm. 'Nick, are you all right?'

I waved him away. It was happening again, the thing that had taken possession of me that night I mended my father's proof and nailed his name to it forever. Somehow I was drifting free of the Nick wedged at the end of a crowded row. The discomfort, the aches, the sweat – none of it registered any more. The equations scrawled across the boards, the statements, corollaries, all of them began to lift free, becoming detached from the blue marker ink that tied them to the surface. They began to take on shape and form, floating clear of their surroundings like the glowing pieces of some vast celestial watch reduced to its components. I rotated them this way, that way, searching for the means to fit the teeth of one equation into those of the next so that one might turn the other.

'That's not right.' It couldn't be right. Deep in the middle board was a piece that would never fit. Unsuited to the task. A cog with no teeth.

'Beg pardon?'

I became aware that I must have spoken, and loudly too. Halligan had turned from his scribbling and strode across the intervening floor so that he now glared at me from less than five yards away. An awed silence reigned in the theatre, the sort of silence that follows the intake of breath on every side. All eyes aimed my way. Everyone waited, fascinated, horrified, eager. All of them knowing that Halligan would destroy me. None of them knowing quite how he would do it.

'Those paths are homotopic in C. In equation 86. The existence of the first homotopy follows from the continuity of the f-functions,' I said.

Halligan's glare narrowed. He was younger than I expected. Maybe thirty, with thin dark hair and a puffy inelegant body stuffed awkwardly into a cheap suit. He had a moustache of the sort you get when you're too distracted to shave. If it weren't for the intensity of his pale blue stare he might have been comical. 'Nonsense.'

He returned to the equation in question and jabbed at it fiercely with his marker pen. 'Nonsense. The homotopy follows from the compactness established in . . .'

He had started to see it. I could tell.

'But . . .' He added a term. Crossed it out.

Somewhere at the back of the hall a small gasp, sharp in the hush. Then an older man's voice, some learned professor perhaps. 'He might have a point, David.'

Halligan spun back towards the audience, teeth bared. I knew what gripped him. That same horror that had taken hold of my father. The understanding that the beautiful edifice you have laboured so hard to create is falling apart in your hands and that even as you try to shore it up you are creating still more damage. He didn't see the packed benches before him. He didn't care that we were watching, or what we thought of his failure. He just saw that golden palace of ideas collapsing one room after another.

'It can be fixed,' I said.

I stood, slowly, not wanting to lose sight of the floating glory that had been revealed to me, the thing of many moving parts, the thing that the equations on the board were mere shadows of. People cleared from my path without needing John to announce my leukaemia this time. Halligan stood immobile, incapable of movement. I passed him, took a red marker, and started to write.

They say that when you learn to type you reach a point where you no longer give any thought to the motion of your hands. You see the paper, imagine the words, and somehow your fingers flicker and the words appear. In the Cockcroft lecture theatre that day I kept my eyes firmly on the shapes I saw rotating slowly in the air. Even as I watched they were fading, their truths growing more elusive. My hands moved and truth appeared on the boards . . . but I gave no thought to the mechanics that put it there. And when at last there was nothing left before me but the board and my ink-stained hands I saw that I had added a river of red entwining Halligan's blue, one supporting the other like the twin strands of a DNA helix.

Nobody in that room understood what I'd done except for Halligan, who was standing in amazement, running his hands around my additions as if they were braille and he might absorb their meaning through the tips of his fingers. Maybe one or two of the lecturers in the audience had caught an edge of the meaning, but the rest were silent simply because Halligan was silent.

'This . . .' Halligan tore his eyes from the board, '. . . is not possible.'

'It's rather wonderful though, isn't it?' I took two more steps back to admire it.

We were two explorers who had advanced further into the unknown than any before us, delving into a realm very few could ever see, discovering and claiming new territory that the human race would own forever after.

Halligan glanced at me and I could see a smile starting to take possession of his face. 'Who are you?'

'Nicholas Hayes.'

He furrowed his brow even as his grin spread. 'I mean . . . who *the hell* are you?' He waved an arm at the boards. There were tears in his eyes. 'This . . . This is incredible.' In the next moment he had my shoulder in a vice-like grip and those pale blue eyes of his bored into mine. 'You're working with me now. You have to.'

And I nodded. 'OK.'

June 1986, Cambridge

'Who's Demus?' Helen asked.

'Who?' I looked up, hauled from my memories of that first trip to Cambridge and back into Helen's cramped little room wallpapered with gig posters and smelling somehow of sandalwood and flowers rather than the odour of stale coffee and old socks that haunted my digs.

'Demus,' she said. 'The fact he died at forty stopped your friend John getting his nose out of joint over you getting famous all of a sudden.' She was sitting cross-legged on her bed, watching me with more interest and more caution than before. 'I didn't understand that bit. You said he was your "future self". Is he someone you thought you might end up like if you weren't careful?'

'Something like that.' I wasn't sure how I'd let that slip out or what else I'd said. I'd been lost in the retelling, sure, but there was more to it than that. Somehow I'd found myself sufficiently comfortable with a complete stranger to let myself fall into honesty. And that just didn't happen, not to Nick Hayes, awkward in my own skin and wearing sixteen years as poorly as most boys do. Definitely not with a pretty girl that I'd just met.

I looked at Helen then. Really looked. Took in her dark eyes, the line of her cheekbone, her small, determined mouth, and suddenly I knew.

'I've seen you before!'

'We go to the same university in the same small city,' she said.

'I didn't finish my story.' I adjusted the towel across my lap, too amazed by her to feel silly. 'The strangest thing about the day John and I came down to see Halligan was that what went on in the lecture hall wasn't the strangest thing to happen to us.'

Helen smiled and watched me. 'So what was this incredible event that put your moment of glory into the shade?'

'You were.'

And I fell back into telling my tale of that winter's day four months earlier.

February 1986, Cambridge

Professor Halligan had wrung every detail out of me, from my telephone number and address down to my mother's maiden name, and sworn that he would have me as a fully fledged student at Trinity College within the week. Finally, and with great reluctance, he let me go. I think if he had had free rein he would have had me imprisoned in a cellar and set me to work immediately.

John, distinctly unimpressed at having been left to cool his heels in a small mathematical library, hauled me off immediately with most un-John-like talk of missing the train and being late.

I hadn't realised how long I'd spent with Halligan. The best of the day had gone and it had been a pretty raw slice of February to start with. A wintry sun watched us with a red eye as John force-marched us up the long road to the station. My breath puffed out white ahead of me. All the shadows seemed to point my way, bare trees reaching.

The girl came running straight at us. I saw her from a way off, heard her footsteps ringing on the pavement. The few people in her way had the sense to move aside quickly. She didn't look like someone that was going to stop. John said something and in that moment she crashed into me. One second she had been fifty yards off and the next almost knocked me to the ground.

'Nick!' She grabbed me by the forearms. 'Help me!'

Even through her terror, even if she hadn't used my name, I would have known that she knew me.

'How?' But I could see it before the word was out of my mouth. Something was coming after her, along the same path she'd taken. It was as if she had left copies of herself strewn behind her, but made of glass or water so that all you could see of them were outlines and a blurring to give away their shape. And they weren't frozen in place where she shed them but chasing her down with the same desperate speed. Dozens of them. Something else was rushing on behind them, right at the back, something that looked like a miniature tornado, again glassy and hard to see, a distortion in the dying light, but full of fury and motion.

'Keep them off me!' the girl panted, hunting in a pocket and dragging out an oversized key. She stumbled past me towards the front steps of the next townhouse.

I stood there with the first of the ghosts racing towards me and the girl climbing the steps to my left. It wasn't the ghosts that left me speechless, or even the silent nightmare of the tornado behind them. It was something about the girl. Something familiar and strange at the same time. As if I'd known her all my life and just misplaced her name. More than that, though, there was something between us I couldn't explain, but that was as real as my skin: the knowledge that it really didn't matter what was coming down the road behind her. I was going to stand in front of it regardless.

I heard the key fumble in the lock as the first ghost reached me. I stepped into its path and it slammed into me. It hit like a wave of icy water, taking the air from my lungs. The next hit and the next, each one jolting into me before I could start to fall. A series of blows that set my mind ringing like a hammered bell, shattering a million images free from memories that couldn't have been mine.

I heard the girl drag the door open. I didn't have time to look, but from the flat blue light that flooded out across the street I knew that whatever lay behind that door it wasn't what anyone would have expected.

'Thank you.'

The door slammed shut with a noise that could have been the full stop at the end of the world. And I was left facing the tornado that was less of a windstorm and more of a swirling wound in the stuff of the universe . . .

June 1986, Cambridge

'And?' Helen prompted after I had fallen silent.

I blinked. I'd been so lost in my story that I'd almost forgotten where I was or that I had an audience.

'And when John picked me up off the street everything was back to normal. The girl was gone and the rest of it he hadn't seen, just me jerking around as if I were having an epileptic fit.'

'So . . . don't you think you might have been? Having some kind of fit, I mean.'

'Well. I guess . . .' I waved the idea away. 'Anyway, that's not the point. The point is that when I first saw you today you seemed very familiar to me. And now I know why. That girl who asked me to save her four months ago. It was you!'

CHAPTER 3

'Those trousers should be dry by now.' Helen stood to retrieve them from outside the window.

'Thanks again, for saving my bacon.' I felt rather foolish now, unloading my unbelievable true stories on her. She probably thought I was mad. If she didn't then she had a severe overdose of gullibility.

'Not a problem.' She tossed me my trousers, then passed over my socks and shoe. 'Apparently you saved mine first.'

'It wasn't you?'

Helen shook her head.

It had looked like her. Different hair and clothes but the same eyes, mouth, nose. Even in that brief moment the girl's face had imprinted itself on my mind. Though how it already seemed familiar was another puzzle to add to my growing store. 'You don't have a sister?'

'I do.'

'Ah—'

'She's nearly thirty and has red hair.'

'Oh.'

Helen turned to face the window. Taking the hint, I hurried to dress.

'You do know,' she said, 'that the bit of your story that really needs defending isn't the part where some girl looked rather like me?'

I zipped my fly. 'You mean the ghosts chasing her . . .'

'And the tornado.'

'. . . and the tornado.' I buttoned up and started to pull on my socks. They were still a little damp and smelled of river. 'I mean, it wasn't a tornado. It was more of a . . . thing.'

Helen turned back to watch me tie the lace on my single shoe. 'A thing.' She nodded.

I stood and shrugged apologetically. It wasn't going how I'd hoped it would. 'Thanks again.'

She smiled that unreadable Mona Lisa smile of hers and said nothing.

I turned to go, limping slightly because of my missing shoe. A moment later I was standing in the hall with Helen's closed door behind me.

'Shit.'

I crossed the hall slowly and banged my forehead against the wall, once, twice, three times. Just hard enough to hurt. I could have played that better. I needed the girl to help me understand what had been happening ever since that first day in Cambridge. Nothing had been the same afterwards. Nothing had been right. And things had been pretty fucked up even before she vanished through that door and left me to deal with her ghosts.

I'd been haunted ever since. And 'haunted' is not a word that comes easily to any man of science.

February 1986, Cambridge

John had got me to my feet and then, unsteadily, into the station.

'What the hell was that?' I collapsed onto a platform bench.

'Some kind of fit?' John asked. 'Too much exercise too soon? Or overworking your brain showing off to the eggheads?'

'I mean the girl and the things chasing her.'

'Things?' John slumped down beside me.

I turned to stare at him. 'You remember the girl, right?'

He nodded. 'The hot girl.'

'And?'

'She was wearing a T-shirt. Which was pretty odd for February, now I think about it.'

'She was?' I had had other things to look at.

'Yeah. Words on it. Something about chilli peppers . . .'

I could tell where John's attention had been. 'And?'

John looked confused, as if 'hot' was really all that need be said. 'Well, she nearly knocked you over.'

'And then?'

'And then you started having some kind of fit and fell over.'

'You saw what was chasing her, yes?'

Again the frown. 'No.' He got back to his feet. 'Train.'

'Woah.' In the act of standing John momentarily split into half a dozen Johns. One stayed sitting, one rose before the others, one held out a hand to help me up, one stooped to pick up a five pence piece from the floor. A heartbeat later they reunited with a snap and there was just one John, striding to meet the train, no hand offered.

I looked down. A dirty five pence piece glinted up at me.

'Come on!' John called.

That night wild dreams followed me home and came uninvited into my bedroom. I wrestled with elusive versions of Halligan's equations, red chasing blue over a thousand boards until the whirlwind came, lifting all the symbols and scattering them like Alice's deck of Wonderland cards.

I woke late to an alarm clock that had elevated itself to defcon 2 and found myself tangled in sheets wet with sweat. All the books had been scattered from my shelves, the main light and the bedside lamp both had their bulbs blown, and in the condensation on the window a thousand equations, one overwriting the next, all in impossibly neat script.

I rolled out of bed with a groan. 'I've seen this film. It's called *Poltergeist* . . .' It wasn't a film I had any desire to live out.

D&D was at Simon's and I'd be late if I took the time to clear up the mess. Ignoring the chaos, I struggled into my clothes. I'd seen ghosts before, though not like this. I'd seen them the first few times Demus got close to me. He'd called them temporal resonances. Echoes in time set off by the supposedly impossible encounter between me and myself, two incarnations of Nicholas Hayes twenty-five years apart and yet together on the same timeline, influencing each other's lives in a closed loop free from paradox.

The only explanation I could think of was that the girl, like Demus, was an interloper from the future, and because I had been the only one to see, and feel, the echoes of her presence it seemed that she must be connected with me somehow. The haunting, though . . . that was new and unexplained.

'Nick! Breakfast!' My mother wasn't saying she'd made me any, just demanding that I make my own.

'No time! I'll eat at Simon's!'

'Crisps and Coke aren't breakfast!' She'd gotten more motherly since the leukaemia but she still wasn't that good at it.

'OK! OK! I'm doing it!' I shook the cornflakes packet on my way through the kitchen and rattled the cutlery drawer. A moment later I was out the back door heading for the garage and my bike.

The garage smelled of spilled oil and spider-dust, all the shadows full of whispering. 'OK! I get it. Haunted.' I grabbed my bike, shoulders hunched against the possibility of a cold hand reaching from the darkness, and hurried out under the sliding door into the street.

'You're—'

'Late. I know.' I ushered Simon back along his hall and shut the door behind me.

'Hi, Nick!' Simon's mum waved from the kitchen.

'Hi, Mrs B.' I waved back and started up the stairs, Simon in pursuit.

John and Mia were at the table in Simon's room, character sheets, dice and snacks at the ready. I pulled a chair out and fell into it, still too hot from my ride. 'Sorry.'

Mia eyed me over the dungeon master's screen, a cardboard wall sporting all manner of game charts and designed to shield her secret notes from players' prying eyes. 'Rough night?'

'Like you wouldn't believe.'

Mia was our dungeon master since Elton's departure. He never said he blamed me for the death of his father. He never gave me dark looks of recrimination. He just said that he had a mother and three brothers left and he wanted to keep it that way. I won't claim it didn't hurt, but I understood. I was a dangerous person to be around. All the stuff I knew about what was to come, and what my friends thought I might know about it, about things that might be waiting for them next week, next year . . . I guess it made me difficult company to keep.

Mia had been the natural choice to take over running the game. She had a devious imagination and a real talent when it came to acting out the roles of the people and monsters we met along the way.

'Where were we?' I asked.

'Still at The University,' Simon said.

The past two weeks' sessions had seen our party of adventurers embroiled in a series of complicated tasks within a mysterious complex known as The University, a sprawling multidimensional edifice whose ivory towers poked into dozens of worlds and whose crumbling halls housed a multitude of eccentric academics, wizards, sages, and enough librarians to shush continents. It turns out that the rivalries between scholars can make orcish blood feuds seem like good-natured ribbing.

'So, what next?' John tapped the map. 'Ideas?' He pushed his warrior, Hacknslay, forward – a plate-armoured giant with a great-sword held in two hands.

Our party hadn't changed. The same alter egos lined up to do battle with all the ills of an imagined world. Still John with his warrior, Hacknslay, an everyboy's mix of hero, cowboy, soldier, policeman and football star. Still me with my mage, Nicodemus, my cleverness embodied, a spell for every occasion, my mind the key to every puzzle. Simon with his thief, Fineous. You didn't have to know Simon for long to understand that choice. A thief comes and goes as he pleases. He slips unseen into the shadows, he scales a wall in a heartbeat and is gone. I'd never felt that I quite fitted into the world or indeed into my own skin, but Simon had all that turned up to eleven. His type of clever was not the sort that understood how other people work, or how to follow the rules of social interaction without seeming like an alien just trying it on for size. All his life he'd dreamed of being able to escape, of just having the shadows wrap about him and spirit him away. Fineous's acrobatics and cat-like grace stood in stark contrast to Simon's overweight lumbering. And that left Mia's character, still a member of our adventuring party but now under her neutral control as the dungeon master, a non-player character or NPC. Her cleric, Sharia, was not an overly pious follower of The Man Jesus, but she was ready to brain an orc with her mace, heal the sick and work miraculous magics against our foes.

'Saving throws first,' I muttered.

My mage, Nicodemus, had tasted the contents of an unlabelled flask two weeks earlier, hoping to figure out what powers the enchanted liquid within might bestow upon the person consuming it. The brew had turned out to be a powerful love potion that had bound Nicodemus and Sharia together in mutual adoration, much to the amusement of our fellow adventurers. Each day of game time we both got to make a saving throw, a roll of the dice that would decide if the effects had worn off yet.

I took a twenty-sided die and threw it. The moment fractured in the way that had happened several times since yesterday's running girl.

I saw a dozen dice roll, two falling to the floor, most coming to rest against Mia's screen.

'Failed.' Mia's voice united all the paths into a single result. I'd rolled a one. She took the die and rolled it back, her character's saving throw. 'Sharia fails, too.'

She reached over to move the lead figures representing Nicodemus and Sharia close together.

'Awwww . . .' said John.

'It's not a joke,' Simon said.

'It is a bit.' I wasn't sure if Simon really knew what a joke was.

'It's serious,' Simon insisted. 'With our magic-user and cleric making cow eyes at each other instead of concentrating, our party is compromised, sub-optimal.'

John pursed his lips. 'It's true. Every time Nicodemus stubs his toe he's getting healing spells while our actual fighter . . .' He laid his finger on his warrior's plumed helm, ' . . . would have to lose an arm to get a Band-Aid off Sharia these days.'

I grimaced. Although the love potion had been something left over from Elton, whose sketched-out plans of The University Mia had taken over and filled in, I couldn't help but feel there was a message from Mia in it. She was asking me how I liked having my choice removed, how I liked romance of the bottled variety.

To be fair the real-world version that we were both stuck in wasn't entirely of my making. After all, I imagine that it's hard to feel responsible for things you did twenty-five years ago, and blaming this on me was asking me to feel responsible for things a much older me was *going to do* twenty-five years from now. And future me was only trying to save future Mia.

On the other hand, knowing that there are an infinity of future mes, and the same for everyone else, makes it harder to care about any particular one of them. This particular future me, Demus, had a special hold on me by virtue of having lived until forty. The doctors had, following my mother's demand for brutal honesty, been brutally honest and at my lowest point were more or less measuring me for my coffin. If I did nothing to untangle my timeline from Demus's then I would be him, and my next twenty-five years were a certainty rather than a long shot. Of course, untangling myself from Demus was difficult to do. In order to jump the tracks of his timeline I needed to actively do something I knew that he didn't do, and I knew precious little about his life. I guess cutting my leg off would do the trick. Unless they could grow legs back in 2010 . . .

Mia's motivations for keeping her association with the particular future that Demus represented were less strong. She would be tying herself to a future where she had a horrific accident in 2011 and the only reason for her not to try to avoid this fate was that Demus had sacrificed his own life to ensure she recovered. I could see that it was a heavy thing to lay on someone. I wouldn't blame her for making her own future. But the only thing she knew about the future in question was that she and I were together in it. And so the only way she could avoid it was to avoid me. Which incidentally would take away my guarantee of recovery, leaving me open to the leukaemia taking a second bite and dragging me down for good.

As I say, it was a heavy thing for Demus to lay on us.

'Nick?' Mia said my name as if she'd said it before and been ignored.

'Sorry, yes?'

Mia frowned. She'd come wearing her Goth-girl war paint – white skin, thick eyeliner, black nail varnish. 'You OK? John said you had some kind of fit yesterday.'

'John should keep his mouth closed.' I was tired of being thought of as sick. I was tired of her thinking that if she left me she took my health with her. Even if it was probably true.

John gave a snort. 'Actually I said you met a girl. Then fainted.'

'She wasn't just any girl,' I said, and Mia arched a brow. 'I mean, weird stuff has been going on since I met her. I had crazy dreams.'

John shot me a look that said, *Really?* and added, *You do realise you're hanging yourself out to dry?*

'Not like that, you idiot. She was like Demus, only different. I saw time echoes of her and I'm getting these after-effects where every now and then time kinda fractures and I can see a whole bunch of possible futures.' I folded my arms and leaned back. 'Also I'm being haunted.'

'Haunted?' Simon edged his chair from mine. Despite his logical mind Simon had never coped well with the supernatural. We started watching *Nightmare on Elm Street* on video one time. Managed to get about fifteen minutes into it before Simon turned it off and refused to see any more. He had nightmares of his own for weeks after.

'Not spooky haunting,' I said. 'Books moving. Mathematics on the windows.'

'I call that pretty fucking spooky,' Mia said.

'I mean not skulls and fiery eyes and blood dripping down the walls spooky.'

'Not helping.' Simon moved his chair another foot away from me.

'Anyway, there's not much I can do about it unless she shows up again. So let's play!' I rolled my D20 out ahead of the figures representing our group, just to indicate we should get on with it. I got a one.

'Do that again.' Simon frowned. He had a scary mind of his own did Simon. He would, if you asked him, and sometimes even if you didn't, run backwards through all of the dice rolls in a game. I was afraid to ask if he remembered them any further back than that. The idea that his mind might be clogged up with the results of all the dice rolls I'd ever made was one that I found rather disturbing. 'Go on, roll it!'

So I did. I rolled another one, the third in a row. 'As I said. Haunted.'

'I'll be rolling for Nick until he's exorcised.' John claimed my dice and rolled them all together, getting the usual scattered results.

The game got started and soon enough we were wholly focused on the world Mia unfolded for us. She lacked some of Elton's sneakiness but made up for it with dramatic flair, proving herself quite the actress when it came to portraying the array of strange characters strewn between us and our goal.

In the vast university our group had fallen into, literally fallen into –
but that's another story – there were many seats of influence. The academics researching the fundamentals of magic wielded little destructive power
themselves, but the mages and wizards who exploited their discoveries in new
spells were very protective of these great thinkers. All of them had defences in
place, from those who spent their lives amid grey oceans of dusty scrolls glu-
ing together pieces of arcane law with their own genius to create something
new, to the wild-eyed and scorch-marked alchemists tinkering with dangerous concoctions in fire-proof bunkers. In addition, between these great and
often rather impractical minds and the outside world stood the hard-nosed
business acumen of the guilds. There were five of these ancient organisations,
each seeking to turn the discoveries of the scholars and potion-makers into
commercial products that could, and did, suck into The University's many
coffers sufficient gold to make dragons look like paupers.

In addition to being a seat of learning The University was effectively a
prison, one that we had repeatedly failed to find our way out of. The only
safe way to leave seemed to be to graduate, and that took money. Lots of it.

The task that our thief, Fineous, had signed us up to was part of
our effort to raise the money needed to buy our degrees and thus win
us an exit. He described it as a spot of industrial espionage. We were
to infiltrate the notoriously dangerous laboratories of one Mercuron
Burnwit and recover samples of his most recent experimental potions
along with whatever recipes we could steal. The guild employing us
would feed any such information to their own alchemists. The guild
financing Mercuron, on the other hand, would feed any such intrud-
ers to their sharks. For a large bonus we would return with Mercuron
himself so he could find new employment with our paymasters.

It had grown dark by the time we stopped. I'd rolled seventeen ones on
a whole range of different dice and we were currently being pursued

around a vast library containing nothing but books that detailed a particular family of blue moulds. The librarian in charge of this repository of mouldy wisdom was a towering mechanical monstrosity with steel quills for claws and a seemingly endless supply of silence spells that left my magic-user unable to speak any of his spells, or indeed to curse his luck while sprinting away.

We tidied up quickly, dice into boxes, boxes and books into bags, Coke cans in the bin. Mia was the first to leave.

'See you.' She paused at the door for long enough for me to open my mouth but not long enough for me to speak. Did she mean see you next weekend . . . or see you in the week? I wanted to see her before our next game session. Hell, I wanted to see her every night. I'd never had a girlfriend before and Mia was ridiculously beautiful, which would have been more than enough motivation in itself if I'm honest, but I really *really* liked her too. She had a wicked sense of humour and endless imagination. So yes, no question, I wanted to see her. But every time I gravitated to the heavy black phone in the hallway of our house I felt Demus's hand on my shoulder. I imagined myself talking into the receiver, not knowing what Mia was doing at the other end of the line, with me making those awkward dry-mouthed opening lines, acutely aware that my mother was probably listening from the living room. I imagined myself talking and knowing that every step Mia and I took towards each other was binding us to an already determined future, one to which we both had obligations. I didn't know much about love but I didn't think that was the way it grew.

John followed Mia out. They were both gone by the time I'd bagged my stuff and reached the front door. Simon came out as I unchained my bike from their railings. And Simon never left the house without good reason. Not even if he wasn't going past his front gate.

'You're calling it a haunting?' he asked.

'Well, what would you call it?' I stowed my bike chain in the saddlebag.

'Science,' Simon said.

'OK,' I agreed. 'But the bit where books are moving around at night . . . that's pretty haunty, whatever the reason is.'

Simon nodded. 'The stuff with the dice though. That's more like a statistical outlier.'

'Um . . .'

'I mean, it's very, very unlikely rather than defying the laws of physics as we know them.'

'I guess.' He had a point. The books and the writing on the window were impossible for me to explain. The dice rolls on the other hand . . . on one level they didn't need to be explained. They were a possible but incredibly unlikely event. 'Does it matter?'

'Maybe not. But if something has messed up the laws of probability for you . . . if you are now a statistical outlier, a one in a trillion . . . then what else might be waiting for you out there?'

'Like?' I had some unpleasant ideas of my own. I thought I'd rather hear Simon's.

'Statistically unlikely events. Like being struck by lightning, or murdered, or hit by a meteorite, or run over by a car full of clowns, or—'

'Alright! Alright!' I wheeled my bike through the gate and mounted it. 'So, what do you suggest I do?'

'Put your lights on for one thing.' Simon reached forward to turn on my front bike lamp, which I'd forgotten about. 'And be careful out there.'

'I . . .' This was the closest to friendly concern I'd seen from Simon in the whole time I'd known him.

'I'm not having you die and leave us stuck in that damn library.'

CHAPTER 4

June 1986, Cambridge

I left Helen's hall of residence by the main entrance and as I set my shoeless foot to the concrete path it happened again. That fracturing of time which, like the haunting, had occurred sporadically over the intervening four months suddenly flared into action. I saw the next few seconds play out in more than a dozen ways, but in all of them a heavy flowerpot hammered into the spot that my next step would take me to. In almost all of them the flowerpot smashed into my head, shattering my skull.

Simon had been right. Ever since the girl and the ghosts a series of very unlikely things had been happening to me. I'd become a statistical anomaly. And, just as Simon had guessed, they weren't the good kind of unlikely. I won no lotteries, caught no falling babies. Instead I faced one bizarre accident after another. The only thing that had saved me was that on each occasion time had fractured, showing me a possible exit, and fortunately I'd always managed to take it. In the case of the exploding chip shop I had been set on fire and cut by flying glass, but only a little bit.

I dropped and rolled to the left. It required swift but not inhuman reflexes, and would have been totally impossible without forewarning. The plant pot hit the ground and sent out a hail of ceramic fragments.

Several shards hit the back of my Moss Bros dinner jacket, followed by a shower of wet compost. I clambered painfully to my feet to see a blonde girl, possibly the one who had watched me in the hall, leaning from her window three storeys up with a sheepish expression. 'Sorry!'

I limped away. Life as a statistical anomaly had already taught me not to waste time on recriminations. Of more immediate interest to me was the fact that both immediately before and hard on the heels of meeting Helen, the phenomenon that had started with the running girl and that was absent on most days had shown itself again. No matter what Helen had to say on the subject there was a connection here. I could stay away from her and hope that the effect faded back to 'normal' levels again, or I could pursue the connection and risk more unlikely deaths in the hope of finding an answer.

Either way I was done looking like a penguin. I just wanted to get back to my room and change into some normal clothes that didn't smell of the River Cam.

Trinity is one of those colleges that draws tourists by the thousands in the summer months. It has the iconic sort of Oxbridge architecture that features in *Brideshead Revisited* and *Chariots of Fire*. It's hard to get more Cambridgey without a punt beneath your feet and a straw boater on your head.

The room that Professor Halligan managed to secure for me was, at once, both immensely sought after and deeply unpopular. It was sought after on account of allegedly being part of Isaac Newton's rooms when he was a Trinity student, or perhaps his butler's room . . . I was never clear on that. But it was unpopular owing to it being positioned directly over the porters' lodge. The night porter, Mr Chardwick, a man with mutton chop sideburns, looked to have stepped straight from the pages of a Dickens novel and had zero tolerance for parties, loud music or anything else that might possibly infringe the long list of college rules, some of which appeared to date back to the reign of Henry VIII.

I crossed the great court in blazing sunshine, white-winged butterflies rising around me with too much energy for the day. Students idled in the shadows, strains of Vivaldi or Iron Maiden reaching out from various windows according to taste. I slipped through one of the main doors and hurried along the corridor, up a flight of stairs, along another corridor. I tried to reach my front door unseen, but there's always someone hanging around in a college hall of residence. On this occasion it was Crispin Waugh who spied me through his open doorway as I passed.

'Lose a shoe, Hayes?' Waugh claimed a famously witty novelist as a relation, but his own wit seemed to begin and end with offering up the obvious as though it were a question.

'No, I went out barefoot but was lucky enough to find a shoe.'

'Run along, you little oik.' Waugh waved me away. He was the typical 80s Cambridge student, a generation late to the unchallenged privilege party and deeply troubled by the idea that the 'rights' his family's wealth and station accorded him were visibly eroding at the edges with students from comprehensive schools and the working classes starting to appear on the benches of lecture halls. From the lofty heights of his Eton education my position in the lower reaches of the middle class seemed to make me one with the children of factory workers to him, or perhaps it just pleased him to treat me that way.

I reached my door and fumbled the key into the lock. Waugh moved in the same social circles as the puntload of aristocracy who had been chasing me earlier. My life was complicated enough without inviting more trouble into it.

Moments later I collapsed face-first onto my bed and lay there unmoving while the first strains of Blue Monday swept out of the ghetto blaster beside me at a volume judged loud enough to annoy the porter but not sufficiently loud to make him climb the stairs to silence me.

I groaned. My body still felt the damage from all those chemo sessions, even months down the line. The day's efforts had left me aching and bone tired. I lay for a minute unspeaking. Then another.

'I organised your bookshelf.'

'Fuck!' I leapt up at the sound of the unexpected voice, then slumped again as I realised who it was. 'Simon . . . I'd forgotten you were here.'

Simon sat in one of the large over-stuffed armchairs that had come with the room. I'd say he was hard to spot in its embrace but that would be letting myself off the hook. Simon, being somewhat overstuffed himself, was fairly visible. I'd just missed him.

'How was the garden party?' Simon had refused point-blank to go with me. His mother had frogmarched him to the train saying that it would do him good to give Cambridge the once-over, since he would probably be coming to the university to study mathematics in two years' time.

'Awful.' I didn't look up from the bed. 'And it's the Master's thing next. You're coming to that.'

'I don't want—'

'You're coming. It's not a party and there won't be any girls.' I wasn't completely lying. It was a soirée rather than a party, and girls would be in a minority as they were at almost every Cambridge student gathering. 'The Master invited you himself!'

'The Master as in—'

'No, not as in *Doctor Who*, although it would be rather handy to have a chat with a Time Lord right about now.' Simon sometimes let the line between imagination and reality blur. It was a touch worrying but usually short-lived. 'The Master as in Sir Andrew Huxley, Master of Trinity College. He also happens to be a Nobel Prize-winning scientist and the half-brother of Aldous Huxley, author of *Brave New World*, a man who famously spent a fair bit of time pondering the future!'

'And Sir Andrew invited me?'

'Yes,' I lied. Getting Simon to any social function involved lying. A lot of lying for a party, a modest amount for a soirée. Actually, Sir Andrew had invited me. I guess, having been leaned on by Professor Halligan to admit me, the Master wanted to see what kind of oddity he had acquired. 'So, you're coming then?'

A long silence ensued. I may have fallen asleep in it.

'OK, I will.'

Simon's voice startled me out of my doze.

'OK?'

'I'll go.'

'Hoorah!'

'We should get ready,' he said.

'It doesn't start until seven. I thought I'd just lie down for a bit first.' I kept my face firmly in my pillow.

'You've been doing that for hours though.'

'Nonsense.' I tilted my head and cracked open an eye. The sun was no longer streaming in through the net curtains. I patted the bedside table hunting my alarm clock. 6:52. 'Shit! Shit!'

The bed proved narrower than I remembered and my roll to the side dumped me unceremoniously onto the floor. 'Shit.'

I got up, shrugged off my dinner jacket, and began fumbling with the button of my river-soiled trousers. 'Shit. You've just been sat there watching me sleep?'

Simon shook his head. 'Only for the first hour. Then I slept for a bit too.'

'Crap. We need to move.'

'I thought it was fashionable to be late,' Simon said.

'Halligan told me to get there early. Wants to show me off or something.' I cast an eye over Simon. He was fairly smart, which was good since none of my clothes would fit him and I had precious few that came anywhere near smart anyway. Simon's mother had convinced him to come by framing the visit as practice for future university visits and interviews, so Simon had taken her at her word and worn his interview jacket and tie.

'So what happened to you?' Simon asked as I kicked off my shoe. 'And where's your other shoe?'

'I met her,' I said. 'That girl. The anomaly.'

'You're sure?' He frowned. 'You saw her for what, five seconds, four months ago.'

I straightened up, trousers still around my ankles, and looked past Simon to the shadowy half of the room behind his chair. My bookshelves were empty, all the books now standing on their pages, half opened, their spines to the ceiling, like a scattered range of tiny mountains. 'Yeah, I'm sure.' I kicked the trousers off and walked over to stand among the range of mountainous maths books. 'Unless this is how you organised my books while I was out?'

After the business of the books moving while we both slept there was no way Simon was going to stay behind by himself. We got to the Master's soirée a mere ten minutes late and inserted ourselves into the mixed crowd of staff and select students. It was supposed to be a black tie affair but I was happy for them to throw us out if they wanted to adhere to the letter of the law.

The day's heat had lingered and the soirée was held in the open out on the Fellows' Bowling Green before the old King's Hall, a part of the college that looked positively medieval, and actually was.

Waiters – probably students earning some spare cash – circulated with silver trays sporting canapés and champagne flutes, and a long buffet table had been laid out with more silverware on white linen. I looked around for Halligan but saw no sign of him. He wasn't any more reliable than I was when it came to appointments and meetings. His secretary joked that since the two of us expended so much brainpower on the subject of time we should be better at keeping it. My answer was that we were working on ways of making it so that we didn't have to. Time would eventually dance to our tune rather than we to its.

Simon and I gravitated towards the buffet table. Free food has an allure all its own. We stood there, both of us too uncomfortable to really tuck in, gazing over the arrayed elite – the sons and occasional daughters of old money: confident, well groomed, erudite. I felt out of place, a dirty schoolboy at the opera. Simon looked rather like I felt. Both of us wondering how long we had to stay before we could retreat to the safety of my room. The fact that my room was haunted was probably all that was stopping Simon making a break for it right away.

'Hello, Nick.'

I spun around, arms raised defensively. Helen stood there, champagne glass in one hand, jeans and T-shirt replaced by a flowing evening dress, a work of blue silk that made her look twenty-five rather than seventeen. With a talent any chameleon would envy, Helen had transformed seamlessly from someone who could be selling Goth and punk clothes from one of those alternative shops on London's King's Road to an English rose who looked as born to privilege as any of the Master's guests, and from whose painted lips you might expect to hear about her Swiss finishing school or Daddy's new yacht.

'Er . . . hi.'

'Look at these tossers.' She spoke in a low voice through a smile. 'It's like leafing through the pages of *Who's Who*. Takes a bit of getting used to. I might be the only one here from a state school. Present company included.'

'I . . . uh.' Something about her dress had stolen the words from my tongue. I would say that all my cool deserted me, but I'd never had any in the first place.

'Keeping dry?' she asked, her grin teasing now.

Beside me Simon looked up at the sky with a puzzled expression as if expecting rain.

'This is my friend Simon,' I told her, glad of something to talk about. 'Simon, this is Helen. I met her earlier today just after falling in the river.'

'Oh.' He stuffed a miniature sausage roll into his mouth. 'The anomaly.'

Helen narrowed her eyes. 'What did you just call—'

'And here's our own little celebrity.' A voice that managed to be both loud and bored at the same time cut across her. Crispin Waugh broke through the crowd trailing a number of slightly drunk-looking friends behind him, typical of the breed. 'Our darling of the tabloids. Grubbing for fame and playing with his sums while greater minds consider deeper matters.' Waugh was reading PPE, a popular choice among the toffs. Politics, philosophy and economics. Much of the diplomatic service comprised old Etonians who had read PPE at Cambridge. Their backsides warmed a fair length of the benches in the House of Commons in Westminster too. It was the philosophy that they liked to roll out on social occasions though, finding that it demonstrated their intellectual superiority most effectively. Waugh reached for it now, standing face to face with me, a sardonic smile hanging from the corners of his mouth. 'Popularity with the masses is so tacky. I heard that the *Daily Mail* want to dress you up as Doctor Who for their next piece, Hayes.' Waugh shook his head, sorrowfully. 'As Schopenhauer said to Hume, "The man who performs for fools is always popular."'

'I doubt it,' I said.

'And what would a creature like you know about it, Hayes?' He was almost nose to nose with me now, still affecting disinterest, but there was no hiding the malice in those pale blue eyes of his. 'You're an uneducated little worm, a jumped-up schoolboy yanked out of the classroom because of some freakish ability to push numbers around the page. There's no real learning in it, no culture. What does a little toad like you know about Schopenhauer?'

'Well . . .' I looked at the ring of hostile faces, at Simon studying his shoes, at Helen, her face unreadable, seeming as likely to laugh at me as to deck Waugh with a punch to the mouth. 'Well . . . I know that Schopenhauer was born twelve years after Hume died in 1776 and is therefore unlikely to have ever said anything to him. I also know that you got the quote wrong and that it is actually, "The person who writes for fools is always sure of a large audience." And I know that the main thing Schopenhauer and Hume share is that their first books sold pitifully, which likely explains the sentiment.'

Waugh's mouth worked, but for a moment nothing came out. I knew he considered himself an expert on Schopenhauer and was supposed to be doing some sort of thesis on the man. The thing is, though, that it's very easy to appear to be an expert on something that hardly anyone knows about.

He sneered, finding something to say at last. 'Go back to your equations, Doctor Who! Leave the big questions for the philosophers.'

'"Every man takes the limits of his own field of vision for the limits of the world."' I shrugged.

Again the sneer. 'What lolly stick did you read that off?' He turned to his cronies. 'Gentlemen, I present Nicky Hayes and the wisdom of fortune cookies.'

'Actually Schopenhauer said it. Those were his exact words.'

Waugh turned back and the look in his eye told me he was coming at me with more than words this time, but a moment later Professor Halligan found his way to the table, deploying sharp elbows, and Waugh retreated into the throng with his friends in tow.

'Ah! Nick!' Halligan clapped a hand to my shoulder. 'Good, good, I caught you.'

'Professor. Sorry I was late. I had—'

'Never mind, never mind.' He waved my excuses away. 'I was late too and now I've got to go. *Tempus fugit*, as they say, *tempus fugit*.' He grabbed a handful of vol-au-vents from the nearest plate. 'Come to the Winston Lab tomorrow at ten. I have something to show you. Something remarkable.' He retreated, cramming his mouth with pastry and making the rest of what he had to say hard to decipher. 'Don't be late this time.'

'I see being Nick Hayes is a full-time occupation,' Helen said beside me. 'And you're a student of philosophy now? When did that happen?'

'Ah. Well, not really. But when you're on chemotherapy you do tend to do a bit of navel gazing. In between throwing up anyway. Why am I here? What's life all about? All that type of stuff. So I read a bit. And it turns out that "a bit" is enough to win an argument when your opponent is a dick.'

'Can we go now?' Simon asked on my other side.

'Hello, Simon.' Helen leaned across me to wave at him. 'Nick's told me nothing about you.'

Simon immediately looked at his shoes again and muttered, 'We shouldn't be talking to her.'

Helen narrowed her eyes, not at Simon but at me. 'You might not have told me anything about Simon but you appear to have told him something about me. Why shouldn't you be talking to me? And why are you calling me "the anomaly"?'

'You're causing time shocks,' Simon said, unhelpfully. 'And moving books around in Nick's room.'

Helen raised a brow. She really was outrageously pretty. Dark curls framed her face, one stray strand curving beneath the sharpness of her cheekbone. 'I am, am I?'

Simon replied with a vigorous nod.

'I'm moving books in your room?' She looked at me, amused. 'Am I having any other odd effects on you right now, Nick?'

She was. A dry mouth for one thing, and other things I wasn't going to mention, but nothing like Simon meant. 'No.' I shook my head.

'Well, you're both scientists. Maybe you need to gather more data . . .'

That sounded close to an invitation to me. My mouth grew drier still as I tried to gather the courage to use it to ask her out.

Helen turned away before I managed to get the first word past my lips. One of the biggest guys I'd ever seen was approaching, moving through the crowd like an icebreaker, head and shoulders above nearly everyone. He looked rather like John – blond, broad-shouldered, handsome, confident. But a John on steroids. John if John were captain of the rugby team. And not the school team, the national one. Heads turned as he passed. All the women watched him. Quite a few of the men too.

'Who's that?' I murmured.

'Piers Winthrop,' Helen said. 'My boyfriend.' She glanced back at us. 'I have to go. Nice meeting you, Simon.'

And she was gone in a swirl of skirts, bound for the arm of Captain Fantastic.

'Can we go now?' Simon asked.

'Yes.'

CHAPTER 5

An electronic beeping hauled me from the depths of my dreaming. By the time my flapping hand had managed to silence the alarm clock all memory of whatever had been entertaining my sleeping mind had been shed, water from a duck's back, leaving just fragments. A dark brown strand of hair curving beneath a cheekbone. Helen then. Helen had been in my dreams.

'It happened again.' Simon's voice came from beneath the heap of bedding across the room.

On the floor between the two of us my books had been arranged in a series of short, twisting towers. Both the armchairs had been turned upside down. And the three balding tennis balls that had been left by the previous resident had been moved from the windowsill to my bed-side table. Also, one of them had been turned inside out.

'Crazy . . .' I picked up the inverted tennis ball, its surface smooth and black. 'It has to be to do with other timelines coming too close to ours. Isolated events leaking between them and our timeline.'

'But it didn't happen around the anomaly this time.'

'Helen,' I said. 'She has a name.'

'Helen.'

'No.' I set the ball down and reached for a T-shirt from the clothes heap by my bed. 'Curiouser and curiouser!'

'What's for breakfast?' Simon emerged fully clothed from the mounded covers on the floor.

'A brisk walk to the Winston Lab. And we need to be away from there by one if we're going to catch the train.' On Fridays I caught the train home for the weekend. Mother considered sixteen too young to fly the nest completely and it meant I could keep going to the D&D sessions at Simon's house.

'But breakfast . . .'

'You're welcome to stay here and make some. Kitchen at the far end of the hall, bread and peanut butter in my cupboard just behind you.'

Simon glanced around at the room as if wondering whether he might be the next thing to be turned inside out. 'I'll come. Mum says I need a diet and exercise.'

We marched to the Winston Lab. Well, I marched, determined to be on time for once, and Simon dawdled, gawping at the city, which admittedly is rather grand the first few times you see it. The walk took us out of the pretty parts and turned out to be much longer than Simon had anticipated. He started to get mutinous and ask about buses. I suggested I could borrow a bike for him. That got the silent treatment.

'So, what is this place?' Simon asked as we finally approached.

The building looked more like a space-age warehouse, but a discount one – *Blade Runner* rather than *Star Wars*. A low-roofed building with plastic sidings, loitering on the edge of an industrial estate.

'It's a private lab funded by . . . someone.' I didn't know who. 'Anyway Halligan knows an experimentalist, a big name from the uni, who does some of his work there.'

'But your stuff is all theory. You don't get your hands dirty.' Simon shuddered. His own interest in maths stemmed from a revulsion for physical labour of any sort, and that extended to physics practicals as well. He was fine manipulating the equations of gravity to solve problems, but ask him to hang a pendulum and measure its period and Simon got as truculent as if you'd suggested he retile the bathroom.

'I'm afraid I'm going to have to roll up my sleeves at some point. It's not a page of equations that sends Demus back to us. It's some massive construction that drinks electricity like a dozen capital cities with all the lights on.'

The place had a locked gate, and no fewer than three hefty security guards came out from their hut to eye us through the chain link fence. In my limited experience laboratories didn't have security. You could walk unchallenged into any of the university labs as long as you looked the part. These guys weren't messing around though. No pass no entry. They wouldn't even open the gate to discuss the matter. We didn't get through until Professor Halligan himself came out to sign us in. He suggested that Simon wait outside, and I suggested he get a new research assistant if he was going to be like that. Halligan clipped the security badge on to Simon himself, and on we went into the cavernous warehouse.

If George Lucas wanted to make a fourth *Star Wars* film then the Winston Lab would have been a great place to start filming. Huge pieces of equipment littered the space, strewn across an acre of concrete floor, arranged on benches, draped over scaffolds. Power cables ran hither and thither like the confusion of roots in a mangrove swamp. Things resembling half-built rocket engines rested beside curved electromagnets that looked capable of picking up a locomotive. A bank of computer terminals glowed near the middle around a closed hut that presumably housed a mainframe.

'Wow.'

'Wow,' I echoed.

'I'll show you "wow".' Halligan waved us on, his enthusiasm lengthening his stride to the point where Simon almost had to jog to keep up.

Halligan wove a path around various benches and partitions, nodding to the scattered researchers at work in ones and twos. The white-coated academics were almost lost in the organised chaos of the huge lab. Occasionally the professor would wave at one or other piece of equipment. 'A capacitor bank. We use that. And those loops are for measuring stray magnetic flux. Those over there monitor the power flow. That thing's been here years. An old Tesla-inspired experiment trying to make ball lightning.'

A man who looked old enough to be the famed Nikola Tesla himself stood soldering away beneath the metal tower emblazoned with HIGH VOLTAGE signs. Wildly asymmetric tufts of white hair and a stained lab coat completed the image, making him a walking mad scientist cliché.

Halligan took us into an area surrounded by its own chain link fence and with its own security guard. Within this inner sanctum, hidden from external view by extra-tall office partition screens, he introduced us to his experimentalist colleague.

'Nick, this is Dr Ian Creed. You'll be familiar with his work, of course. Dr Creed, Nick Hayes – the remarkable young man who can take a good share of the credit for this breakthrough. And this is his . . . uh . . . friend, Simon.'

Dr Creed looked me over with an intense dark stare. He was a short man, a little older than Halligan, maybe in his forties, with black hair and a thick black beard untouched by grey. If you took off the lab coat and set him in a sou'wester he would have fitted in fine on a trawler. 'Come and see this.'

Clearly, that was all the welcome I was going to get. I shrugged and followed. He led us through a small maze of partitions, neglecting to mention the cables alternately positioned to catch the ankle or the throat of anyone much over five foot. The grand reveal was a large bench set around with heavy electromagnets. On the bench was a Perspex box big enough to hold a car engine, and in fact holding something much more complex.

'It's an atomic clock.' Creed gestured at the monster of tubular steel and aluminium cylinders inside the box. 'The computers outside pulse the electromagnets in the sequence determined by your variant of the

Violander equations, cycling phase and beat frequency while building the amplitude in waves.'

'Can you do a run for Nick?' Halligan sounded as excited as a schoolboy with a new Atari.

Creed frowned. 'I can show him the results . . .'

'Oh come on, Ian! This is as much Nick's baby as ours.'

Creed's frown deepened. 'Those capacitors take nineteen hours to recharge and each cycle degrades the—'

'I've talked to Guilder-Johnson.' Halligan offered a broad smile. 'Funding going forward is not going to be a problem, Ian.'

Creed shrugged, then shouted at a remarkable volume, making both me and Simon jump, 'Run the sequence!'

Someone outside clearly heard. The sound of a heavy lever being manually thrown was followed by a low hum and a creaking as powerful electric currents began to magnetise the chunks of iron set all around us.

'I guess I should have checked that none of you have a pacemaker,' Creed said. He reached out to tap Simon's digital watch. 'That's not going to work any more.'

The hum built to a pulsing whine and the huge magnets began to rock in their housings.

'How come the atomic clock still works?' I raised my voice over the increasing noise.

'Shielding,' Halligan said.

'Very costly shielding,' Creed added.

My vision started to blur. My teeth ached.

'I feel . . . strange.' Simon held his hands out before him, staring at his fingers.

I felt it too, a weird kind of pressure, as if my consciousness were breaking free of my body.

'Temporary effects of the magnetic fields!' Creed shouted over the rattling, buzzing roar. 'Different for everyBODY.' Suddenly the racket cut off and he was shouting into silence.

Creed walked forward and set his hand to an old-fashioned cold cathode numerical display of the sort that liquid crystal had made obsolete. Presumably it weathered the magnetism better. He flicked a switch and the number 0056 appeared in flickering red.

'Incredible!' Halligan clapped a hand to my shoulder. 'That's the best so far.'

'Fifty-six what?' I asked.

'Fifty-six nanoseconds' difference between the clock in there and the clock on the far side of the lab,' Creed said.

'You slowed time down in that box?' Simon asked.

'We sped it up!' Halligan declared. 'Which is even more remarkable!'

I tried to look impressed. It really was remarkable. Earthshakingly remarkable. We were rewriting physics! On the other hand it was just fifty-six nano seconds and in the wrong direction, and I'd already seen a man come back from twenty-five years in the future . . . and the man was *me*. So I was the toughest of tough audiences for this kind of thing.

'Nice,' I said. 'I'll get back to my desk on Monday. There might be some useful tricks to be squeezed out of the Andretti-Vesentini work on separation of cohomology groups of coherent sheaves.'

Halligan opened his mouth. I cut him off. 'But right now I have a train to catch.'

'A train?' Creed looked bewildered. 'I don't think you understand. We've just—'

'I do and it was great!' I started backing along the exit maze, remembering to duck the first set of powerlines. 'We really do have to go, though!' My hard stare finally got Simon to begin moving in the right direction. 'Thanks again! Really impressive! Really!'

Halligan glanced at Creed, shaking his head. 'He's too young. The young have no frame of reference to understand how momentous something is.'

I turned a corner and lost sight of the two of them huddled over the timer.

'C'mon.' I grabbed Simon's arm. 'Or we'll never get out of here.'

We started to hurry, pursued by Halligan's raised voice. 'Everything will change now. Mark my words, Nick. Everything will change!'

We made it through the inner sanctum and across the cluttered expanse of the outer laboratory. The security guard at the main door unlocked it using a combination on a keypad. As he opened it I saw Helen outside, just ten yards away across the bare tarmac that lay between the lab building and the exterior fence. She was watching the door, her expression unreadable.

Immediately alarms began to echo in the cavernous lab behind me. Something anchored my gaze to Helen though. Maybe the intensity of her stare, or the way she didn't look quite the same as last night. Her hair was different. Also the air between us seemed to shimmer.

'Nick!' Simon physically hauled me round so that I was aiming back the way we had come. Almost every bench was lit up now, every light on every piece of equipment blazing. Warning lights flashed back and forth across the drained capacitor bank that had supplied the power for Dr Creed's demonstration. It should take nineteen hours to refill but instead seemed to be sparking with stray energies. The computer terminals on the other side of the inner sanctum glared, then died, blue smoke rising from them. In one sudden burst of brilliance all the overhead lighting burned out and glass fragments showered down into the patchy gloom. And in the next moment lightnings began to writhe over the outdated Tesla tower, searing blue-white snakes of electricity etching themselves across my retina. Suddenly one knotted itself and instantly a pulsing violet ball of lightning hung there. Then another, and another, and another, all beginning to drift out above the benches buzzing like angry hornet nests.

I blinked and the afterimages were not the usual random flashes but the shapes of people, converging on me.

'Run!' I shouted.

'We . . . we need to help them.' Simon wasn't given to heroism, but when it came to it, he wasn't one to abandon people in need. Unless it was in a D&D game, and then he totally would.

It was my turn to do the grabbing. 'I'm causing this. We need to get away.'

Out in the daylight I saw the ghosts as I had seen them when Demus first approached me. Grey shapes taking on more detail by the moment. People I recognised – Helen, Mia and John. Simon was there, his ghost cowering as if from the heat of a conflagration. My older self, Demus, trying to tell me something but making no sound. Even the psychopathic and thankfully dead Ian Rust who had carried the severed head of a man as he stalked us through London. And others, unknown figures advancing behind the ones I knew: men in suits, moving with purpose. I ran through them all, trying to keep the flesh-and-blood Helen in sight. She was sprinting away with not so much as a backwards glance.

The electronics that kept the outer gate secure had been scrambled and I opened it without permission. The guards, already emerging from their hut, hesitated, unsure whether to pursue us or see to the emergency in the laboratory. The gap we managed to open between us and them decided the matter and they hurried off to help their employers.

'Where is she?' I turned the corner into a residential street. I'd seen Helen run this way just thirty yards ahead of me. I spun in a full circle. 'Where?'

Simon came up breathing hard and grateful for the chance to stop. 'We lost her?' He didn't sound upset.

'She must be hiding.' The end of the street seemed too far for her to have gone before I rounded the corner.

'Why . . .' Simon heaved in a breath. 'Why are we chasing her?'

'She caused all this.' I waved towards the Winston Lab, now out of sight.

'I thought you said you caused it.'

'We both did. Her and me. Together.'

Simon looked doubtful. 'She stood right next to you last night and nothing happened.'

He had a point. The fruit punch hadn't boiled. No champagne glasses exploded. Not so much as a hint of a ghost.

'Why did she run then? Why was she even here?'

'Well, the place sort of exploded a bit,' Simon said. 'I would have run.'

'Come on.' I led off. 'Perhaps we'll see her on the way to the station.'

'Are you sure we shouldn't, you know, go back and help?'

'And maybe set everything off again?' I shook my head. 'They had plenty of guys there to help clean up.'

Simon hesitated, then followed. 'I guess.'

We reached the station in time for our train to London and without sight of Helen. On the walk there Simon had almost convinced himself that the bizarre effects had been a result of Dr Creed's experiment. Some kind of aftershock. He hadn't seen any of the ghosts, just the light show.

'You're sure it was Helen?' he asked, as we took our seats in one of the second-class carriages.

'Yeah . . .' I was ninety per cent sure. Her hair had been different, but girls do that.

'Who's Lady Gaga?'

'Who?'

'Lady Gaga,' he repeated.

'Dunno. It sounds made up. Why?' The train began to pull away in a series of lurches.

Simon shrugged and watched the scenery slide past the window. 'She had it on her T-shirt.'

I echoed his shrug. Simon had an eye for details and a memory that never let go. 'Just some new band, I guess. She's really into those.'

CHAPTER 6

On Saturday Simon pulled his front door open, leaving my attempt to knock swinging at empty air.

'There's something important you should know,' he said. 'We've got a guest character this session.'

'And . . . ?' I followed him into the hall.

'And things are going to get really awkward.' Simon started up the stairs.

'Because . . . ?'

'It's a paladin!'

A perfect holy knight, champion of all that's lawful and good. I could see how that might inconvenience Simon's character, Fineous, who specialised in theft and the occasional spot of backstabbing, both the treacherous and the fatal kinds.

I followed Simon into his bedroom where John and the new guy already sat at the table opposite Mia, who was still unfolding her various books and maps behind her foot-high cardboard screen.

Our new player smiled at me pleasantly enough. His dark, possibly permed, hair was piled forward, sweeping across his brow like a New Romantic pop star. The face below was just a touch too fleshy to pull off the look, though he had made an effort with some eyeliner. A lavender shirt with a broad collar completed the ensemble. He reminded me of a boy that Elton had got off with at the Arnots' party where I first kissed Mia.

I took a chair and sat, leaning down to get the stuff I needed from my bag.

'This is Sam,' Mia said.

I sat up at that. 'Sam as in . . .' I couldn't stop the words escaping. Sam as in her new boyfriend Sam. Sam as in the seventeen-year-old star of three TV commercials. Sam who attended the same school of performing arts that the eldest of Elton's brothers went to. Sam who could have dated any number of hot dancers but instead had taken 'my' Mia . . .

'Mia's boyfriend,' Simon said, taking the last seat.

Next to me John rolled his eyes. Clearly Simon had been briefed to forewarn me in order to minimise the upcoming awkwardness, and in Simon's world that had meant warning me about the paladin and the thief rather than the fact my ex-girlfriend had invited her new boyfriend to play D&D with us.

'Right,' I said. What I wanted to say was *what the hell were you thinking*? 'Right,' I repeated.

'So.' Mia tapped the table with her pen. 'The party – the group of adventurers – have been stuck in this multidimensional complex known as The University for several months. Sam, your character—'

'Sir Algernon de Pommefrite!' Sam declared dramatically.

'Sir Algernon,' Mia acknowledged, 'has been released from a sarcophagus in Mercuron's halls of experimentation.'

Simon had been extremely proud of defeating all the locks both on the sarcophagus itself and those required to reach the inner laboratory. The fact that it contained a live paladin rather than a dead king mounded with grave goods was perhaps Mia's way of telling him that *crime doesn't pay*. The fact that the paladin was now being played by her boyfriend was Mia's way of saying something else. I wasn't quite sure what.

Possibly, *fuck you*.

Our current mission in the game was to find Mercuron while evading or killing the guards set to watch him by the guild who backed his work, the Guild of the Hidden Eye. We were to convey our employer's relocation offer to him and convince the old alchemist to transfer his loyalties to the Guild of Golden Truths – either that, or just steal his work. If we brought him back with us, the task would earn us enough gold to finally purchase ourselves degrees and graduate from The University. Which appeared to be the only way to leave while still carrying the same number of vital organs that you entered with. I couldn't see that towing a self-righteous paladin around with us was going to make the job any easier.

Simon slipped a note to me under the table. *Can I kill him?*

I gave a small shake of my head, though I thought I would probably regret the decision.

It took about five minutes to regret the decision. Sam clearly considered the game an audition for some TV part and threw himself wholeheartedly into the role assigned to him. He was irritatingly nice, unbendingly honourable and subject to frequent dramatic flourishes that a lesser man than me might have called ham acting.

Sir Algernon even objected to us killing the alchemist's guards, despite the fact they might be better described as prison warders. Fineous's plans to creep around the shadowy margins of one abandoned feast hall, then backstab the particularly huge guardsman defending the far door proved to be a sticking point.

'But, my dear Fineous!' Sir Algernon declared in an overly loud voice. 'Surely you are a trespasser here, an interloper, a miscreant. You have broken and, sir, you have entered. How then, prithee, is it just that you attack yon gentleman without provocation or even warning?'

I looked longingly at the place on my character sheet where the traces of the erased Power Word Kill scroll could still be seen. 'We may have entered in a . . . non-traditional . . . manner, Algy, but you were kidnapped and subject to involuntary medical experiments. Which in my view makes the whole organisation that kept you here guilty of . . . um . . . war crimes. So that man at the end of the hall is guilty by association, and Fineous is merely proposing to serve justice to him.'

'Vigilante justice!'

'Of course, we could just put you back where we found you,' I said, on behalf of my mage, Nicodemus.

Mia narrowed her eyes at me.

In the end we had to compromise by approaching openly and giving the guard the opportunity to surrender. Which of course led to a bloody sword fight that John's warrior and the paladin barely survived.

The real trouble would start when we found Mercuron. The guilds regarded the alchemist and his fellow scholars as unruly geese of the golden egg-laying variety. Both the carrot and the stick were employed to keep them on side. As ever, when mountains of money were involved, things got dirty fast. The stick could be simple threats, fear and intimidation, but frequently included finding dirt in their backgrounds with which to control them, or capturing family members to hold as hostage. We had a sealed scroll – for use in emergencies only – that contained dark deeds from Mercuron's past that he would definitely not want to have made public. And when you considered that Mercuron's present included vivisecting holy knights, then it took quite some imagination to think up what might be written on that scroll. In any event, having Sir Algernon standing over us would make turning the screws on Mercuron rather tricky.

'Hoorah! Victory! A veritable victory!' Sam clapped John on the shoulder, oblivious to the fact that both their characters were walking wounded now.

I pursed my lips and rolled my dice. All ones. While waiting for Sam's speechifying to end I mused about making money from my talent at rolling a one on any die. Maybe at a casino.

Finally Sam ended with a 'What ho, chaps!' and advanced his paladin through the now unguarded door. I had to hand it to him, he had great skill at staying in character. At least when the character was a dick.

We stumbled on in this manner until Simon's mum mercifully made us break for lunch. She took orders for drinks. Sam announced that he only drank lapsang souchong, which turned out to be a type of tea rather than a village in Tibet. He produced a teabag from his pocket and offered to go down to supervise the brewing. John, Simon and I breathed a collective sigh as he left the room hard on Mrs B's heels.

'Sorry,' Mia said, as the footsteps on the stairs faded. 'He kind of insisted on coming.'

'No problem.' I waved it off, then lied, 'I like him.'

John nodded appreciatively. Simon's look was blank amazement.

'Anyway,' said Mia, moving on swiftly, 'I had a reporter asking about you at my aunt's flat. How he found me there I have no idea.'

'About me?' I thought the story was old news now. And surely Creed and Halligan's experiment was secret for the time being. Not much point to all the security guards, locks, fences and partitions if not.

'About you.' Mia nodded.

I tried to concentrate. It had been easy when she was the GM creating the world around us, throwing monsters and mayhem our way. But now it was hard not to see her as what she was, the only girl I'd ever kissed and beautiful to boot. I'd been trying to be an adult about the whole thing, throwing myself into my work with Halligan, but with her in front of me I just felt lost. I wasn't an adult and, besides, from what I'd seen it's a rare adult who's 'grown up' about a break-up.

Ours hadn't been an angry break-up, just a sad, strained one where the chemistry between us had been ground down beneath the heavy heel of destiny's boot. I wanted her back. I could still feel her last kiss on my lips, and it lit me up the same as it ever had. My heart hurt. Literally hurt, as if it were being pulled along the line joining it to Mia's by some force hitherto unknown to science.

'Nick?' Mia had been speaking and expected some response.

'Sorry, what?'

'I mean . . . he was asking about Elton and Elton's dad. Where the hell would he have got that from?'

'The reporter?' A chill displaced the warm feelings Mia had been causing. 'What about Elton's dad? No, wait, don't tell me.' I couldn't know the details of what happened the night Elton's dad had died. Demus didn't know them, and if I wanted to be Demus I couldn't know them either.

'Anyway, I didn't like him,' Mia said. 'Dark-haired man, wiry, with a sharp face. Had a hard look to him. Reporters are supposed to have the common touch. This one looked like he got his stories using thumbscrews.'

'Police?' Simon said.

'Nah.' Mia shook her head. 'They would just ask.'

'Private eye?'

'Hired by who?' None of the Elton's family would do that.

John rapped the table with a die. He looked troubled. 'Mother bought home some woman from the art gallery a couple of weeks back. She invites the ones that look as if they might spend a lot of money.'

'And . . .' I said.

'And this woman seemed more interested in speaking to me about you than she did in speaking to my mother about art. I remember it because she was really insistent. Also she was young and quite hot.'

I shook my head at John's rather shallow insistence on categorising half the population as hot or not hot. 'I wonder—'

Sam returned with a tray of drinks and I decided to keep my wonderings to myself. He sat beside me and handed me my Coke and a glass. I grunted my thanks and reminded myself that I was seeing him through the sourest of filters. Clearly, Mia liked him, and he probably wasn't as much of an arse as I wanted him to be. It wasn't as if he'd chosen to play a paladin, after all. It was Mia who threw that spanner into the works, and it was basically her job to do that sort of thing. Then Sam opened his mouth and began channelling Sir Algernon over the unpleasantly sharp aroma of his lapsang souchong, and I went back to hating him, all my mature rationale up in smoke.

'What time is it?' Mia glanced at the window with a frown. The sky was paling, orange in the west.

'I don't know.' Simon was our timekeeper. He was supposed to call a halt at eight. 'Someone broke my watch.' He gave me a dark look.

'Crap, it's nine already!' John consulted his expensive Omega-something.

Mia called it a day. We'd been at it nearly twelve hours and despite a number of close calls, none of us had killed Sam or his character. She and 'Sir Algernon' had a party to go to. She thought she could get us all in if we wanted. Simon declined on principle. I declined on the basis that I didn't want to spend the night nursing a can of Fosters and watching Mia smooch Sam. Also my mum would object, and remind me that I was only just sixteen and recovering from serious illness. John said it sounded like fun and would go along. I expected he'd need a stick to keep the girls off him. Ever since that first party at the Arnots' house, John seemed incapable of walking down the street without getting a new girlfriend. He got one while walking past a girls' college on his way home and another on the train to school. None of them lasted more than a week or two, but still . . . I had no idea how it happened.

Simon came out to watch me unchain my bike. Shadows filled the street; the summer sun lingered only on the rooftops. I had one of those moments when you become suddenly hyper-aware of your surroundings. A car went past and birdsong filled the space it left behind, a sharp complexity of tweets and trills, pretty little threats levelled against all the world. The wind in the leaves, ten thousand almost separate sounds. All of it underwritten by the ever-present rumble of distant traffic. I stood with the chain in my hand, noting every gleam and glint from the cars lining the street, seeing the green flutter of the stunted cherry trees planted at twenty-yard intervals, and the houses themselves, bland 1940s terraced homes slowly succumbing to double glazing and central heating.

'It's all going to change,' Simon said.

'Yes, I imagine so.'

'Us too,' he said. 'This work you're doing. Everyone is going to want a piece of you. And now it's experimental, too, everyone is going to want a piece of that. How much do you think all those computers and capacitor banks and atomic clocks cost? And it seems like they're going to have to buy new ones after today . . . You heard your professor though. Money isn't going to be a problem going forward. Who do you think is providing that money? If it was me handing it out, I'd want to safeguard my investment as much as possible.'

'Safeguard how?' This was more interest than Simon had taken in the actual world for an age.

'You, Nick. All this rests on you. What if you decided to stop? What if you went off to farm yaks in Tibet or . . . got another girlfriend . . . or something else crazy? If someone is putting in millions then they can't afford to let anything happen that stops you producing.'

'So this reporter that went to Mia's . . .'

Simon shrugged. 'Just watch yourself. And follow the money.'

I got about a mile from Simon's house, thinking about what he'd said, before I realised it was *me* that was being followed. It didn't take any great feat of detection on my part. The black BMW came up right behind me and flashed its lights. I glanced over my shoulder but couldn't make out much of the driver through the gathering gloom. A man with dark hair. Mia's 'reporter' had had dark hair . . .

I swerved off the main road into a side street, half-thinking that the driver was just trying to get me out of his way. But no, the BMW turned off too and flashed its lights again. Was it the guy from Mia's, some other investigator or clandestine agent . . . or just a common or garden murderer who'd happened to pick me for his next victim? Despite my status as a statistical outlier, my bizarre series of near-fatal accidents had yet to include any deliberate attempts at murder.

'Shit.' I veered between two parked cars and mounted the pavement, yanking on the handlebars to hop the curb. Now at least I had a screen of parked vehicles and the occasional tree to stop the driver squashing me so easily.

I had no hope of outrunning the pursuit so I played to my mode of transport's strengths instead. I stopped and wrenched the bike around, one foot on the ground, before heading back the way I'd come. Behind me, the possible-reporter possible-murderer started on his three-point turn.

I made my next turn before the car re-emerged on to the main road. He couldn't have seen where I went, but somehow those headlights appeared behind me before I'd made it to the next corner. Fear started rising through me, lending fresh energy to tiring muscles. What if it really was a murderer? Far more unlikely things had been happening to me lately. A falling flowerpot might be no less fatal, but somehow it lacked the horror of a man with a knife who wanted to hurt me.

I needed to lose him, but my options were limited. I didn't know the area well enough to find an alley that might fit a bike and not a car, or some useful patch of waste ground where two wheels would fare better than four. I could turn into someone's driveway and crouch in the dark. But then I'd be trapped if he found me.

It's funny how fear squeezes common sense from your mind and freezes you into a narrow set of paths. There were plenty of ways out of my dilemma. I could literally have knocked on any of the scores of front doors I was passing and asked for help. I could have abandoned my bike in a driveway and escaped across the back fences of gardens. I could have doubled back endlessly until he got tired of turning.

Instead I aimed for what I knew. Somewhere I would find other people. Nobody gets murdered in public, right? I would have gone for the McDonald's on the Redland Road high street but my legs were failing me. Sweat-soaked and panting, I steered a course for the much nearer Tony's Cabs. From the outside, the place was a blank white door in a featureless wall. It lay several blocks back from the high street in a road half-occupied by rundown houses and half by tiny businesses, most of which seemed to have been mothballed years ago.

A swift double-back and a final burst of speed got me there, out of sight of my pursuer. I let my bike clatter to the ground outside and ran up the trio of concrete steps. The door sat beneath a neon sign where only the 'T' worked, and gave access to a tiny room sporting a grille window where you could allegedly order a cab, though I had never seen anyone do that, and three slightly beat-up video machines. I'd dropped several hundred pounds' worth of ten-pence pieces into those over the past few years. They had a street fighter game where bashing 'foot sweep' repeatedly would get you through the first five one-player enemies, an elderly Pac-Man machine with a tiny screen that fuzzed at the edges and Robotron: 2048, my favourite, in which an insane number of robotic foes would flood the screen from all sides and electronic mayhem ensued.

Empty. Tony's was never empty outside school hours. All that changed was the age of the kids slotting their coins into the machines. Right after school it was the ten-, eleven- and twelve-year-olds. At 3 a.m. on a Friday night it was drunk eighteen-year-olds coming back from parties, trying in vain to summon the hand-eye coordination to play the games.

'Hello?' There wasn't even anyone in the taxi office behind the grille.

A squeal of tyres outside. A car door slamming. I cast about wildly for some other exit as if Tony's might magically have grown an extra door since my last visit. In desperation, I threw myself at the door I'd come in by and wedged myself against it. Someone outside pushed hard. I held firm but not firm enough to support the illusion that it was locked.

'Hey—'

Whatever else the man outside had to say was lost beneath a wave of electronic sound, as all three arcade machines behind me started up new games as though someone had just fed them money. I pushed harder against the door and seemingly the music from the machines swelled in proportion, growing louder than any design spec had ever called for. Already frenetic games scores grew into wild, discordant assaults on the ear.

The push from outside became a shove that jolted the door open an inch or two. I set my back to the wood and drove into it, heels skittering across the tiles. The whole of Tony's was lit now with sliding colour, as if the game screens had become projectors. Fuzzy Robotron robots swarmed across the walls overlaid by Pac-Man and his dots.

The man outside was shouting, but all I caught was my name. The street fighter game blew first, the screen going black, acrid smoke rising from the back vents. Robotron went with a pop and an ominous sizzle. Venerable Pac-Man was the last to go. The game screen cracked, something in the casing sparked, and silence reigned.

I sat with my back to the door, gasping. The lights had all died too. I could see nothing.

'Open the door, Nick.' There was something familiar about the voice.

'Who are you?'

'Take a look.'

I stood slowly, taking care not to release the door, then edged to the side and allowed it to open an inch. Pieces of thin, curved glass littered the steps, catching the orange glow of the nearest streetlight. The neon sign had fared no better than Tony's arcade games. A black-haired man in a dark trench coat stood at the foot of the steps, his face in shadow.

'Who are—' I bit off the question as ghosts began to fill the gloom. Echoes of scores of teenagers streaming through us both, up the steps, coin-laden and eager, down the steps with empty pockets and reluctant feet. The echoes of taxis coming and going. Pedestrians passing by. The man stepped back, letting the street lights illuminate him.

'Demus!' I gasped. 'You have hair!'

CHAPTER 7

'You have hair!' I repeated. It had been an enduring worry ever since our first meeting. I know it's pretty shallow, given that the other things to worry about had included my imminent death, my death at age forty, Mia's survival and how to twist the fundamental laws of physics in our mutual favour. But still, young men are vain, emotionally delicate creatures, and the idea that I would be the owner of a shiny head by 2011 had plagued me. When would it start? Was the chemo responsible? Would I be bald from now on? The intervening four months had seen a tentative return after the chemo hair loss, but I still worried how long it would last. 'Wait . . . does that mean you're not Demus? You're *another* me from the future?'

'I hope not.' The man who might be Demus frowned and touched his head as if to check it was still covered. 'But stop telling me this stuff. You may have already met me in your past, but that's *my* future.' He crossed to his car and opened the door. 'Come on.'

A shout came from back in the cab control room. 'The lights are all out!'

'They're not going to be pleased.' Demus went round to the driver's door. 'They replace Robotron with a fruit machine. I can tell you that for free. And you never find another one, though eventually there's an emulator on the internet.'

'A what on the what?'

Demus shook his head. 'Quick!' he said over the BMW's roof, and got in.

I went to the open passenger door. 'My bike . . . oh . . .' On the seat there was a roll of ten pound notes two inches thick, held tight with a rubber band. 'I guess I could buy a new one.'

Demus drove about a mile, slowly and without speaking. The car's lights pulsed and flared, the wipers went into a frenetic burst of activity and then froze, the engine sounded far from happy. Even the street lights brightened as we passed by, and the whole time ghosts, or time echoes as Demus liked to call them, streamed behind us like dirty smoke.

By the time he pulled over in a street not far from my house, the weird effects were starting to lessen.

'This is some crazy stuff, right?' He stared through the windscreen at the fading ghosts, his face a mask of amazement.

I said nothing. I knew that he could only say what he remembered himself saying when he was me. What he did here should have no bearing on the future he came from or the past he remembered. But somehow, the endless paradoxical loop of self-modifying conversations and action that should just throw us on to a new timeline had been frozen into this particular incarnation that he did remember. And if he played his part, then what he did here in his 1986 could change what happened next in his 2011. If Demus went off script, that would just start a new timeline and whatever changes he made would still affect *a* future, but not *his* future. And that would be a big waste of the sacrifice he made by coming back to die.

'So,' Demus said. 'This is a bit of a disaster. I was supposed to arrive in January . . .'

'What?' I asked, aghast. 'You don't remember this?'

'None of it.' He shook his head. 'Some kind of calculation error.' He looked mortified. 'This is terrible . . .'

'Can't you . . . just go back some more?' I asked. 'I could wipe this memory and everything is fixed. No harm, no foul.'

'It's more complicated than that, Nick. A lot more complicated.' He still looked grim. 'But yes, we could salvage something. Mia can still be saved. First, though, I have to understand what went wrong with my calculations.'

'So.' I frowned, trying to puzzle through it. 'Why come to me at all? If you hadn't sought me out then you wouldn't have made any memories you didn't have. We shouldn't be talking at all!'

'I didn't come straight here. I'm not an idiot.' He rolled his eyes. 'There's no point me trying to jump back to January until I understand what went wrong. I've set up a lab and worked on the problem. And the problem is you. Something to do with you. If I can find out what's going on, and fix it, then I can aim myself at January for our first meeting.

'Remember, I haven't got there yet, so all I know about how things go down is what I remember from your side. And that means all I know is what you allowed yourself to remember. I don't know the details of what happened in that microchip research lab, because you made yourself forget them. Though that fact, of course, lets me know that we got the chip that we needed to work the memory eraser.' He still sounded worried.

I looked at him, the older me. I hadn't expected to see him again, at least not for another few decades as he slowly began to make himself known in the mirror every morning. I'd thought to see him looking back at me with that air of mild surprise and disappointment old men must get every time they see that the face they present to the world is no longer the one they think of as their own. He watched me back for a moment, perhaps remembering what I was thinking.

'This thing with the lights blowing,' he said. 'All this stray energy floating around us, overloading circuits . . . it shouldn't be happening. It's not in the equations. It's part of the problem.'

'Well, it keeps happening. You must have got pretty close to us in Cambridge to have caused that big blow up at the Winston Lab.'

Demus's brows rose towards his hairline. He shook his head. 'I've not left London.'

'OK . . . but you must remember the reason for it. Either you remember the reason or we never solved it. I mean, you remember me a year from now, five years from now. However this situation resolves you know the outcome.'

Again the shake of his head. 'I've no memory of any of this. But that's not necessarily a disaster. It could just mean that at some point, for some good reason, you erase your memory of it.' He frowned. 'Even if that good reason is just so this timeline doesn't conflict with mine.'

'That sounds a bit . . . contrived.' I wanted the future that Demus offered, or at least I had thought I did. Guaranteed recovery from a particularly aggressive brand of leukaemia seemed like a bargain. The sacrificing myself for Mia part seemed less attractive, particularly as she was currently at a party with an irritating jerk, and probably snogging him right now. The longer I kept on this timeline the more secure my recovery was, and the rest of it might be up for debate years down the line; but the more this association between me and Demus became dependent on wiping this memory or that one, the more tenuous it became.

'It's not a very elegant solution,' I said. Telling someone their solution is inelegant is the mathematical equivalent of insulting someone's mother.

'I know.' Demus had yet to release the steering wheel and his grip turned from tense to throttling. 'There's more going on here than you think, though. Even back in 2011, something was off with the readings.

It's not the theory that's wrong. I swear it. It's that there's something else happening, something the equations don't consider.'

'What then?'

'Paradox.' He rolled the word across his tongue, then wrinkled his mouth at the taste. 'A paradox. Two timelines frozen into each other, when whatever allowed this conversation we're having right now happened.'

'Paradox?' I knew what it was. I had no idea how to fold the concept into the formal mathematics I was working on. Apparently Demus didn't have many better ideas himself. The mathematics of time travel was fiendishly complex without paradox in the mix. With paradox in there it became frankly scary.

'So what can we do about it?' I asked.

Demus shook his head. 'I don't know. My calculations suggested that the paradox had existed for decades in 2011. It should be both stronger and easier to unravel closer to the occurrence that should have split the timelines. But I've not figured out a way to track it down.'

'There are nearly five billion people alive right now and any one of them could be the source,' I said. 'It could be a shopkeeper in Japan, a railway worker in India . . .'

'It's you,' he said.

'The odds against it are astronomical . . . But I'm a statistical outlier!' I paused, thinking. 'If you weren't near the Winston Lab yesterday, then . . . it must be the girl.'

'What girl?'

'Helen.'

'Who?'

'Helen! You know.'

'I don't remember a Helen . . .'

'You must do. She saved me . . . us . . . when they were chasing me in that punt.'

A glimmer of recognition flickered across his face. 'Oh, right. She was called Helen? It's been a while. I don't think I ever saw her again though.'

'Really?' I felt a sharp and sudden disappointment. 'I kinda thought we . . .' I shook the feeling off. 'Well, you might not have seen her again but you certainly saw her before. I mean that first day with Halligan, just after that, walking to the station and she comes running along with all the ghosts of herself chasing her . . . and the tornado thing . . . And me collapsing. John thought I'd had a fit, remember?'

Demus's interest turned to a kind of frozen horror. 'No,' he said in a quiet voice. 'I don't remember any of that. But I do remember walking back with John from the lecture theatre. So I didn't wipe the memory.'

'Maybe you wiped . . . I will wipe . . . just that part of the walk back.'

Demus shook his head. 'You know the control isn't accurate enough to edit five minutes here, five minutes there. It can't really do much less than two or three hours. And are you telling me you are going to edit out the memory of every subsequent mention of that incident, the girl, your fit?'

'So does that mean . . . ?'

'That I'm not you after all?' He pursed his lips. I think his expression might have been the one I wore when they told me I had cancer. 'I think it does, yes.'

CHAPTER 8

'Hope,' said Demus, 'is an essential tool in any torturer's kit bag. Hope is the thing that we will torture ourselves with after he's knocked off and gone home for the night. That, sadly, is one of the lessons standing between you and me.'

'But there is still hope, though?' I repeated.

'Yes.' A sigh. 'There is still hope.'

'So what are we going to do?'

'*You* are going to do what I remember myself. And what I remember is spending an evening with my mum and catching the train to Cambridge the next day to continue my studies. Also some nastiness with the people following you. And *I* am going to—'

'Wait! There really are people following me?'

'Of course. Didn't you listen to anything Simon said?'

'Well, I did a bit. But he's . . . y'know . . . Simon.'

'Start listening to him! He's going to be prime minister in 2003.'

My jaw dropped. 'Simon? Prime minister?'

'No, you idiot. I'm fucking with you. But he's worth listening to. He keeps his eyes and ears open and he never forgets anything.'

'Nastiness?'

'What?'

'You said "nastiness with the people following you". What nastiness?'

Demus rubbed his chin. 'Best that I don't tell you. I lived through it, so I'm sure you will.' He raised a hand to forestall my objection. 'As I was saying, I am going to drive up to Cambridge and check on this Helen girl. What college is she at again?'

'Queens'.'

'And her surname?'

'I don't know. She's on the third floor in the hall of residence, room 307, I think.'

'That'll do. It sounds as if she is something to do with the paradox. Something major. It's possible we can do something about that and sort this mess out.'

'How possible?' I asked.

Demus held his hand up and squeezed his thumb and forefinger together until almost no space remained between them. He eyed me through the gap. 'There's always hope, Nick. Always hope.'

Demus left, both of us instinctively knowing that we should keep our interactions to a minimum. I thought that he might want to see Mother, maybe explain the whole thing to her, but he didn't. Maybe the reason why was something that takes twenty-five years to learn. In any case, he didn't want to talk about it, not even to himself.

I walked back to my house deep in thought. It was hard enough wrestling with time inside equations, forcing it to obey, calculating ways of twisting it with the minimum of effort. I could see that work consuming all the years I had between now and when it was needed. But encoding for paradox too? I had no idea where to even begin on that one. Demus had told me that when the loop with me and him was frozen into our timeline, a paradox had been frozen in, too. It could be something equivalent to going back and killing your own father before you were born. If he died . . . then how were you there to kill him? Or maybe it was a case of having a choice between two options, and instead of one option being chosen, both were, and the two resultant timelines failed to separate properly. To capture that in my equations, to find viable solutions and understand their impact on the universe . . . That was going to take some special kind of genius, and frankly the problem intimidated the hell out of me.

My mother failed to notice that I'd returned without my bike, which was good because I'd failed to hide the fact, or the large roll of tenners in my hand. I called out a lie about having already eaten and tromped upstairs to topple onto my bed without turning the light on. I lay there, miserable, staring at the dark ceiling. If I wasn't Demus, then my cancer had an open door to return in line with the doctors' poorly disguised expectations. If I wasn't Demus, then Mia's departure was probably exactly what it seemed: permanent. And, according to Demus, Helen with her impossibly giant, impossibly handsome boyfriend wasn't going to be part of my life either.

All in all it had been a pretty crappy day.

Eventually I levered myself up to clean my teeth and get ready for bed. I flicked my light switch to no effect. Enough illumination made it up the stairs for me to see my way into the hall and I flicked the switch there. Also nothing.

'Mother!' The Cambridge lot thought I was practically working class, but the truth is that while I referred to Mother as 'my mum' to friends, I could never actually bring myself to call her anything but 'Mother' to her face. To take the edge off it I always tried to do it ironically. It didn't really work though. 'Mother! Did the fuse blow again?'

'They all did!' she called upstairs, 'And the bulbs. Some kind of power surge, I think. I'm going to complain to the electricity board tomorrow.'

'Did you replace the fuses?' I hated doing that. It meant fiddling with bits of fuse wire in the cupboard under the stairs while spiders took the opportunity to drop on to your head.

'Yes, but we didn't have enough replacement bulbs so we've only got light downstairs. Also, the TV doesn't work any more.'

I paused. 'When did this happen?' I guessed that it could have been because of the paradox effects around me and Demus, even though we were two hundred yards away . . . But there surely hadn't been time for Mother to rewire eight fuses and replace half a dozen bulbs.

'A couple of hours ago. Around the time that girl came.' Her turn to pause. 'Oh, there was a girl here looking for you.'

I went down the stairs two at a time, seized by a cold fear. The people who were following me hadn't been chasing me on my bike. I'd been chasing myself while they were here in my house, letting me know they could reach me, reach my mother.

'Did she give a name? What did she look like?' I burst in on my mother, who had returned to the living room sofa with a book and a cup of tea. 'Wait . . . a girl? Like, a little girl?'

Mother put her book down and looked at me over the top of her reading glasses. 'A young woman.'

I tried to hold on to my anger. These people thought they could threaten me. And they could. I had no idea how to stop them. When they told me what they wanted they would be holding all the cards. 'What did she look like?'

Mother pursed her lips. 'Well, clearly I've grown too old to keep track of fashions because she didn't look like anyone I've seen. But,' she put aside her disapproval and played up to her self-imposed fuddy-duddy role, 'Eva was a very polite and very good-looking young lady.'

'Eva?'

'Eva Hayes.' Mother nodded, then laughed. 'No relation.'

'What did she want?'

'You know, she didn't say. I had a funny turn as I opened the door to her . . .' Mother frowned. 'Anyway she helped me to the sitting room, got me some water and waited with me to make sure I was alright. She was very chatty—'

'What sort of "funny turn"?' I asked, concerned.

'Oh, nothing to get worried about. I probably stood up too fast. Came over peculiar. Seeing lights and . . . shadows . . . like you do . . .' She didn't sound entirely convinced herself. 'Anyway. We just got chatting. I asked her if she wanted some tea. Somehow we ended up talking about family. Your father, my parents . . . All sorts. We went into the kitchen to make the tea and that's when I found the lights didn't work. Or the kettle. She said she was sorry to have missed you and would call you later.'

'Eva Hayes?' I didn't know any Evas.

'I guess I'll have to get used to pretty girls turning up and asking for Nick,' Mother teased.

'Ha, ha.' I turn and started back towards the stairs. It all seemed very strange, less threatening than I had first imagined, but still with an undercurrent of threat. Were they trying to find all my relatives? Was the interest in my grandparents just so they had other choices for who to tighten the screws on if I wouldn't play ball?

I took the torch from the cupboard under the stairs and trudged up to my room, tired but with too much buzzing around in my skull for sleep. The sweeping torch beam immediately revealed that there was something wrong with the small desk by the window. It was tidy! I was about to holler down to Mother when I realised two important things. Firstly that my mother was only marginally more given to neatness than I was and had never ordered my desk. Secondly that in the middle of all that clean desktop, which I hadn't had a clear view of in years, was a single book I didn't recognise. Something to intimidate me? Something the girl had left? At least it wasn't a horse's head in the bed. Demus had said 'nastiness' but I guessed these guys were working for a corporation rather than for the Mafia. I tried to reel my imagination in. The girl must have done something to blow the fuse box and come back to sneak up to my room while Mother was busy in the cupboard among the dust and spiders trying to fix the damage.

The hairs on the backs of my arms stood up as I approached. All of me tingled with electric anticipation. It seemed that even the torchlight itself began to pulse in time with my accelerating heartbeat. Without touching the intruding item I bent to read the title. *Curiosa Mathematica* by Charles Lutwidge Dodgson. Not someone I'd heard of. It looked ancient. Like the books Professor Halligan kept on the shelf behind his desk to help him play the role of serious mathematician. Of course, all work of real importance was in the tatty journals in his briefcase published monthly and with names like *Finite Fields and Their Applications*.

As if I were a detective in a movie trying to preserve fingerprint evidence, I turned the cover with a biro. It fell open on the publication page. The subtitle was *A New Theory of Parallels*, and it had been published in 1888. It meant nothing to me. With a sigh I reached to pick it up. The jolt that ran through my arm threw me back onto the bed. Yard-long sparks arced between my hand and the pages of the book as I fell. Time fractured around me but every path led to the same end. I hit the bed, it folded itself around me and darkness swallowed me whole.

CHAPTER 9

I woke, jolted by a gasp as if I'd been lying under water and had only now found the air. Casting about I discovered myself still in my room, still fully dressed. Sunlight lanced between the curtains to illuminate a bright band across my waist. The book lay on the desk, presumably where it fell.

'What the . . .' Raising both hands into my line of sight I expected to see flesh charred to the bone, scorch marks at the very least. But no, there was nothing.

'Jesus H.' I sat up. I had aches, but they were the kind of aches you get from sleeping ten hours with your legs dangling over the edge of the bed rather than from being electrocuted. I stood, shook my head, yawned and reached cautiously for the book.

My fingers refused to make contact. Sometimes when common sense fails to stop you repeating an action that pain has taught you is a very bad idea, it's your muscles that step in to prevent the foolishness. They're good at learning simple lessons. Fire hot. Knife sharp.

'Okaaaay . . .' I had a rethink and slid the thing into my D&D bag using a biro.

The train I needed to catch left for Cambridge at ten past eleven. And first I had to walk to Richmond tube station and then go halfway across London to Liverpool Street. I didn't need to look at the clock to tell I was unlikely to make it.

Mother had very new-fangled ideas about nutrition and refused to buy me Golden Nuggets, on the grounds that they were 96 per cent sugar. Which, oddly, was my main argument in favour of them. Instead she bought joyless boxes of Shredded Wheat, the contents of which I conducted mechanical stress tests on by loading them with as much sugar as they could bear.

'Do leave *some* milk in the bottle, dear!' Mother admonished as I attempted to drown the evidence.

I grunted and began devouring the contents of my bowl as swiftly as possible. I really did need to catch the 11:10 to Cambridge. Mia and the others had all finished their O-level exams, and although term wasn't officially over until the end of the month, the next few weeks were basically free time for them. As such they'd arranged D&D practically every other day, much to Simon's consternation. He wanted it every day.

Negotiating with Halligan over time spent on project was about as easy as negotiating with Simon over time spent on quest. Neither seemed able to imagine a world in which their particular interest wasn't up there with curing cancer and global peace when it came to worthy endeavours. I liked both pushing back the frontiers of knowledge and playing silly games where I got to roll polyhedral dice and be a mage, but I didn't want to be doing either 24/7. Eventually I'd wrangled a deal that saw me spending a small fortune on train fares and dividing the week between London and Cambridge. I even had a day off from both so I could mope about and listen to New Order while pretending I didn't care what Mia was up to.

'Mother . . .' I spooned up the last of the heavily sugared milk from my bowl.

'Hmmm?'

My mother taught science, and although she was well qualified she certainly wasn't a leading light in any particular field. What she was was as near to an expert on pretty much every subject as most people are ever going to need.

'Tell me about . . .' I struggled to remember the name even though I had seen it less than twenty minutes ago, '. . . Charles Lutwidge Dodgson.'

'What would you like to know?' She took another bite of her toast. Rye bread with a thin scraping of marmalade.

'Well, first I want to know how come you've heard of him and I haven't. I'm supposed to be the mathematician around here. If he's famous I find it impossible to believe you know about him and I don't.'

Mother arched an eyebrow at me and crunched. 'Sometimes I've believed as many as six impossible things before breakfast.'

'What?'

'I'm quoting the man,' she said.

'Uh.' I glanced at the clock and stood to go. 'Did he come up with anything famous?'

'He also said, "I can't go back to yesterday – because I was a different person then." If that helps?'

A cold finger ran down my spine at that. A time traveller? I grabbed my bags. 'Not really . . . I've got to go.'

'And he wrote an essay titled "What the tortoise said to Achilles".' Mother had a smile playing around the corners of her mouth, but was trying to hide it.

'I'm so late . . .' I started for the door.

'Better late than never or better never than late?' She sipped her tea. 'That was one of his too.'

I reached the front door.

'The essay title alludes to Zeno's paradox of motion,' she called after me.

'Paradox?' I stamped back. 'He's some big name in the mathematics of paradoxes? Is that why he's famous?'

'Well, no, I don't think so.' Mother frowned. 'He did some work on them. But he is famous because . . . he wrote *Alice in Wonderland*. Charles Lutwidge Dodgson is Lewis Carroll.'

'You could have just said that!' I ran for the door again.

'Where would the fun be?' Mother called. Her last words snuck out the front door with me. 'Don't go falling down any rabbit holes.'

Curiouser and curiouser.

I jolted along on the overcrowded tube train, my face practically jammed into the armpit of the next person hanging on the support straps. It wasn't even rush hour. Demus didn't have to put up with this sort of thing in 2011, I bet. Maybe it wasn't all hoverboards and jetpacks, but I could hardly imagine they were still packed like cattle into slow and noisy boxes.

The book lay in the kitbag wedged between my feet. Only the pressure of it between my ankles reassured me it was still there. Rattling along hundreds of yards beneath Earl's Court, the carriage grew too crowded even to look down, let alone see my feet.

By Sloane Square I became uncomfortably aware that the man pressed against my other shoulder was studying me with undisguised interest. There is an unwritten rule of tube travel, understood instinctively by every Londoner from young schoolboy to doddering ancient. You pretend it's not happening. You pretend that half a dozen strangers are not squeezing against you to a degree that is usually reserved for orgies. You pretend that your nose is not inches from the unwashed armpit of a beefy man, that a young woman's hair is not tickling your face, that you did not step on that person's foot. And yet here I had found someone who clearly had not read the unwritten rule. A madman. The sort statistical outliers attract.

Even the most seasoned tube traveller occasionally makes accidental eye contact, and when someone is staring at you from a distance of eight inches it's hard not to. As soon as I caught the slightly manic eyes of my new companion he began speaking.

'Most people think they're safe in a crowd,' he said without preamble. 'When it comes to intimidation it's important to let your subject know just how vulnerable they are.' He spoke in a gentle voice, just loud enough to be comprehensible above the tube train's chatter and roar, but made no effort to direct his words just at me. Half a dozen others crowding with me in front of the double doors could hear him at least as well as I could.

The man didn't look particularly intimidating. He was shorter than me, a little under six foot perhaps, wiry rather than broad, with a sharp, rather snake-like face and dark eyes that were as close to black as eyes get.

'A lot of people in this line of business like to introduce themselves to their targets in the target's bedroom or bathroom. Somewhere the target traditionally feels safe. They like to take that away from them. But what happens next is that the target makes an effort never to be alone. And by doing that they get back some of that lost feeling of security. Which is why we're meeting here for the first time, Nick. You're not safe anywhere. Not in company, not in a crowd, not at home on the toilet. I can reach out and touch you—' The train jolted us into even closer intimacy as if to make his point. 'Any time I want.'

Whether the man's monologue was washing over our neighbouring passengers without being noticed, an integral part of the background noise, or whether each of them had made a deliberate and sensible decision *not* to notice, I couldn't tell. The real test would be how many of them decided to leave at the next stop. Though some of them might actually consider the company of a dangerous lunatic preferable to having to wait for the next train and then having to fight their way onto that one.

'Don't look at them, Nick. Look at me. Look at this.' He jabbed me in the stomach with two fingers. 'Good lad.'

'What do you want?' The pressure of his fingers against my belly was rapidly becoming painful, though he could be holding a knife there for all the people packed around us seemed to care.

'I already told you that,' he said. 'I want to intimidate you.'

'But what do—'

He leaned in with the swaying of the carriage, our foreheads practically touching. 'It's best to leave a gap after the first meeting.' He kept to his conversational, almost friendly tone. 'That way you can get any of that kneejerk defiance out of your system. Let the fear soak in a bit. It works better that way.'

The train began to slow for the next station, then stutter to a halt in a series of violent lurches.

'I can tell you, though, that I live my life to a strict code. Rules are all we have to separate us from the animals, Nick. If you break my rules, then I'll break you. Stick by them, however, and I'll be your guardian angel. And you'll certainly need guarding. Before long it won't just be my employer who wants hold of your strings.' He offered a narrow smile. 'I'll be seeing you later, Nick.' He drew back his hand as the doors opened with a pneumatic sigh. 'I left you a present.' The rat-faced man glanced down, though we were still too cramped to see the floor.

Passengers began to spill out, some simply to make room for others to disembark. I saw a sturdy plastic shopping bag beside my feet with *Harrods* written across it in gold on green.

He pushed past me to leave. On gaining the platform he called back over the heads of the passengers cramming into the carriage. 'This whole thing is incremental. What's in the bag is step one. Be thinking about step two next time we—'

The doors closed on the rest of what he had to say and the train jerked into motion. I stood there, heart pounding, wedged vertical between strangers, with the unwanted bag resting against my leg. Unwillingly, I struggled to snag the handles and drew it level with my chest. Peering down into it, at first I could make little sense of the contents. They appeared to be a collection of everyday objects. A hairbrush, a bedside clock, a small plate, a toothbrush . . . It was the toothbrush that gave me pause. A cold fear started to prickle across my skin. I hadn't been able to find my toothbrush that morning. And suddenly I recognised all the stuff. Each object came from my house. An item from every room. My mother's hairbrush . . . Had she been in the house when he took it? Had the girl taken it for him? I found my hands trembling as I lowered the bag.

The programme of intimidation that the man subscribed to was clearly designed for people with less imagination than me. I already understood how vulnerable I was. My work was valuable. Someone powerful had seen that. They had seen that I was the source of it and decided to own me. The man left standing on Victoria platform might be just one of many, though he was probably all they would need. There'd been no compassion in those beady black eyes. He would do whatever his employer's goals required, and I really didn't see any way of stopping him.

CHAPTER 10

'So, how does this all work then?' Miles Guilder stood a little shy of six foot, broad-shouldered and tending to fat. The suit he wore had been expensively tailored to accommodate him and showed no signs of strain. He had one of those bullish faces full of barely repressed energy that might escape as a booming laugh or a murder threat, with even odds on either one. Eyes like grey stones watched me intensely above florid cheeks. 'Go easy, though. Pretend I know nothing.'

That last part wasn't hard. Guilder was a businessman, and although he specialised in high tech start-ups he wasn't in any way ready for the mathematics. What was hard was looking at him without snarling. A large part of me thought it was his money that had set the man on the train loose on me to protect his investment. The man who had been prowling through every room of my mother's house. I'd spent most of the journey from London alternately feeling furious then terrified about the whole thing.

'Nick?' Professor Halligan prompted at my shoulder.

We were standing in the Winston Laboratory. Workmen were already labouring to fix the lighting while others lugged away some of the burned-out equipment.

I drew a deep breath. 'On TV science shows when they try to explain about relativity they pretend space-time is a rubber sheet and demonstrate how a heavy object makes a dent. Other objects roll into that dent or orbit around inside it, and that's gravity for you. Right?'

Guilder nodded. I breathed a sigh. A lot of people didn't even have the kiddy version to hand, but given that he had seen the shows this would be a little easier.

'So Einstein showed mathematically that objects moving through space-time create ripples that spread rather like they would if you bounced on a big trampoline. Scientists have been hoping to detect these gravitational waves, but it may take them a while yet. They're tricky measurements to make.

'What the mathematics I've been working on shows is how to repeatedly hit that rubber sheet, space-time, so as to create a resonance. Like a kid on a swing moving their legs in the right rhythm so they swing higher each time. And also how to do that at multiple spots so that the effects combine at one focus where the oscillations become very large.

'Now, for this bit it helps if you think of that rubber sheet not as rubber, but the surface of a pond. I've shown that under the right conditions in the focus point where all the oscillations combine, we can throw up a spike of space-time, and if it goes high enough, then the tip of that spike breaks away and becomes a droplet; a localised sphere of space-time. That's our time machine.'

Guilder's slow smile became a grin. Perhaps relieved that it all sounded so simple. It sounded simple because I'd turned the creation of new mathematics for high dimensional topology into a baby story for him. 'How do you hit it? You know, to make the ripples.'

I shrugged. 'That's the hands-on side of things. I stick to pencil and paper.' I gestured to Dr Creed who stood at my other shoulder, barely reaching it.

Creed coughed and rustled the papers in his hands. He looked the part in his white lab coat, black beard bristling. 'We hit it with magnetic energy. It's the safest way to pack energy into a space you are ultimately going to want a person in. And I use "safest" comparatively. We need enormous currents to generate huge localised magnetic fields in very complex, very fast changing patterns. It's the details of those patterns that Bob and Nick's work provide us with.'

I blinked. If I'd ever been told Halligan's first name it hadn't stuck. I was almost surprised to discover he had one, though of course he must. Bob. Professor Robert Halligan. I had to stop thinking of him as if he'd been thirty-eight forever. He'd been my age once, and a mathematical prodigy in his own right. And currently he was perhaps the only person on the planet who could understand the progress I'd made over the last few months. His main role, though it would pain him to admit it, was to translate my work into something that Dr Creed, himself an extraordinarily gifted experimental physicist, could grapple with and try to put to work in a laboratory setting.

Dr Creed walked Guilder around some of the burned-out equipment and the first of the replacement capacitors that were being fork-lifted into place as part of the new, larger bank that would deliver the vast current we required. I noticed that for all his apparent robustness, Guilder walked with a limp, pausing whenever a chance presented itself.

If it weren't for my conviction that Guilder had set his man on me, I would have considered him the ideal benefactor. He had deep pockets, was eager to move things on swiftly, and seemed determined not to share. That last part was important to me. If I let the government get their hands on my work it would be very hard to approach actual time travel without an enormous amount of red tape, and once we got there it would immediately be world news with all manner of rules and regulation and oversight already waiting for us.

Dr Creed stopped next to one of the new capacitors. It towered above him.

'It's the efficiency of those resonances that mean we don't have to explode the sun into a supernova in order to get the energy we need. Each time Nick finds a new solution to the Hayes equations we're able to get more for less.'

Guilder nodded. 'We're going to need to press on with these experiments and delay some of the technical publication. Don't want the theory getting into the public domain before the patents are secured. I want to see a stage two cycle soon, then a three-stage attempt.' Clearly the man had read and absorbed more of the technical detail than I had credited him with. 'I'm going to need that stage two cycle run tomorrow.'

'Tomorrow?' Creed look startled. 'But I—'

'My contractors can have all the equipment in place by midnight,' Guilder said. 'It's vital that we steal a march on the competition before any of this gets out.'

While Creed chewed on the impossible timescale I raised my own objection. 'The aftershocks that nearly wrecked this place were unexpected. There wasn't anything in the calculations to suggest that would happen.' The reason being that there was nothing in the theory to cope with paradoxical timelines, but I didn't see the need to share that information.

'That's why it's called *experimentation* rather than implementation!' Guilder favoured me with a smile that showed his teeth. 'A stage two cycle tomorrow. Thank you, gentlemen.'

Creed and Halligan looked deeply troubled, but neither spoke.

'But the next time could be much worse,' I protested. I wasn't clear why health and safety was being left to the sixteen-year-old. 'What if—'

'Risk-taking is part of business, Nick.' Guilder advanced on me. 'Don't let a challenge like this intimidate you.' He set his hand on my shoulder and took an almost painful grip. He hadn't stressed the word *intimidate*, but something in the hold he took on me did that for him. He knew all about my encounter on the tube. I had no doubt of that now. None at all.

Miles Guilder left a quiet panic in his wake. Dr Creed worried that the next anomaly might take out most of Cambridge.

'Let's call it what it was.' He rubbed distractedly at his beard. 'That was an electromagnetic pulse. An EMP. A nuclear weapon without the blast.'

'Guilder has covered the insurance. It's very comprehensive.' Halligan didn't look as convinced as he sounded.

'But what if a hospital—'

'Enough, Ian.' Halligan shook his head. 'We're doing this.'

I stood quietly and watched them. They both had loved ones that Guilder's people could reach out and touch. I too worried that we might shut down a hospital mid-operation, kill the machines keeping people alive. But I also had a bigger concern. It seemed to me entirely possible that with a paradox frozen into our timeline, and without a sound theoretical understanding of what we were doing, it could well turn out that we were tugging at the zipper of creation. If that were true then sooner or later we would yank it hard enough to undo the universe.

'Well, you don't need me here. I can't even wire a plug.' I turned to go. 'I'll see what I can do with a pencil and a lot of paper. Maybe I can figure out our anomaly and stop us crashing any passing aircraft.' And on that happy note, I left.

Despite my parting claim, attacking the mathematics wasn't top of my to-do list. It had taken Demus a lifetime to solve the problem to the point where a working time machine could be constructed. And in all that time he hadn't figured out the paradox problem. Though to his . . . my . . . credit, there hadn't been any real reason to. He didn't remember the problems we were now encountering. That was part of the paradox!

Rather than tackling the sums, I decided to tackle the girl. I walked across the city centre and along the riverside towards Queens' College. Demus had said he was going to do his own investigations into Helen. I assumed that meant some kind of covert operation. If he started hanging around the girls' floors in the hall of residence he'd soon get himself arrested. I, on the other hand, knew Helen and had an excuse for visiting.

I thought about buying flowers. A thank you for saving my arse the other day. But it turned out that I lacked the flower-buying type of courage as well as the standing up to threatening men on the train type. I actually passed a florist on the way over. I'd even mentally picked the blooms and set my hand to the door. But standing there, I imagined carrying that bunch of roses to Helen's room under the idle scrutiny of whoever was loitering in the corridors. I imagined my knock on her door being answered by the handsome ogre from the Master's soirée. Whatever confidence I had left vanished entirely. I abandoned the idea of flowers and came to Helen's empty-handed. I found myself sweating unaccountably, shifting my weight from foot to foot. I knocked, dry-mouthed.

I waited. The blonde girl who had tried to kill me with her flowerpot came out from her room to watch. I felt very glad not to be standing there like an idiot with a bunch of roses. Standing there like an idiot *without* a bunch of roses was much better. Turning my back on my audience I knocked again. A muffled shout came from inside. Something about waiting, maybe. With a sinking feeling I realised that I might well be getting her out of bed and that having the handsome ogre open the door was still a distinct possibility.

Helen came to the door tousle-headed and sleepy-eyed. She opened it a hand's breadth, wearing a man's shirt. A large man's shirt. 'Oh, hey, Nick.'

'Er . . . hi.' Smooth. 'Bad time?'

'No.' A yawn covered by a hand whose nails were random colours, one black, two green. A yellow and a blue. 'Come in.' She turned and vanished bare-legged into the gloom.

I followed on, somewhat relieved. She went to the window and drew the curtains. The light of a sunny late afternoon illuminated the mess: clothes strewn with an abandon I couldn't quite manage even though I knew Mother would never know, coffee cups, and beer cans laid out as an obstacle course, cushions everywhere, a wine bottle, a stray cork, an overfull ashtray teetering on the windowsill.

'Are you allowed to smoke in here?' The words escaped before I realised how lame they were.

'No.'

I tried again. 'Late night?'

Helen nodded and pushed her hair out of her eyes, yawning again. 'Room party. I haven't been sleeping all day. Just ran out of go-juice and needed to crash for an hour or two.'

She sat on the bed cross-legged. I tried not to stare and instead found the armchair and cleared enough space to sit. The beige material was more stain than non-stain and the whole thing felt sticky. I wondered if the handsome ogre had been part of the room party. Weird if he wasn't. And if he was, then weird he'd left. If I were her boyfriend I'd have been there and stayed. Mess or no mess. Maybe they broke up . . .

'So . . . ?' She peered at me as if slightly short-sighted, inviting me to speak.

'So,' I said, eyeing her long brown hair. 'Unless that's a wig then I've kind of answered my own question.'

She took a handful and tugged. 'No, it's real.'

'I saw the girl who looks like you again. She was watching me down at the Winston Laboratory and some weird stuff happened. But she had . . . shorter hair. And I thought it was you with a haircut, which was odd, but possible. Growing it back again in a hurry, though . . . not so possible.'

'I had a doll like that.' Another yawn. 'You could pull her hair to make it long and then draw it all back into her head again with a slider on her back.'

I leaned, pretending to look at her spine. 'No slider.'

'No.' A smile. 'What kind of weird stuff?'

'A massive power surge.' I decided to leave out the time echoes.

'And I don't have that effect on you?' She feigned disappointment.

'I . . . uh.' I thought then that perhaps John's success with girls largely boiled down to not running out of words at key moments. The part of my brain that wasn't paralysed screamed at the other part to say something. Anything. 'I, uh, best let you catch up on that sleep.'

'That's it?' She blinked.

'Well, I thought she was you. I had questions. But now all I've got to say is that you have a twin running around.' Twin was probably putting it too strongly. I wasn't great with faces. They were definitely similar. But 'definitely similar' sounded too lame a reason for being there, even to me.

'Oh. OK then.' She watched my slow retreat towards the door as I attempted not to knock over any of the booby traps scattered in the way. I was closing the door when she added, 'I might see you at the ball then?'

I leaned back in. 'Ball?'

She rolled her eyes. 'The Trinity College May Ball.'

'Oh, right. That.' I'd known about it but had no intention of show-ing up. 'Professor Halligan gave me a bunch of tickets but—'

'That's settled, then. I'll see you there.' She smiled, and all of a sud-den I actually wanted to go. Even if it meant a return to Moss Bros to hire the appropriate evening wear. For that smile I would dress up as a penguin again. I just hoped the staff at the hire shop wouldn't remember me from last time.

I moved to close the door again, a foolish grin on my face, when a valid question occurred to me. 'How come you're going to Trinity's ball, not the Queens' one?'

'Piers is taking me. He's at Trinity. You met him at that last thing. The big guy. Piers Winthrop.'

'Oh yeah.' The big guy. I closed the door.

As I turned away, I almost walked into someone standing close by. 'Sorry, I . . .'

'No harm done,' said the man who had taken my mother's hair-brush from beside her bed and given it to me on a crowded tube train that morning.

CHAPTER 11

The man from the train finished making a note of Helen's door number on his pad.

'I thought you . . .'

'Got off the train?' A tight smile, no joy in it. 'Yes, I did. Got back in the next carriage. Easier to follow you that way.'

'What the hell are you doing here?' I didn't want any of this falling on Helen. I hardly knew her, anyway.

'Charles Rust.' He stuck out his hand. I didn't take it. I wouldn't have wanted to take it if I'd known nothing about him. Despite his grooming he had a feral look to him. Also, there was something unwholesome in the way he looked at me that would make me want to wash afterwards. He lowered his hand without seeming to take offence. 'I like to introduce myself. You give someone your name in circumstances like these and it shows you're not afraid of what they'll do with it. Shows them that they're the one who needs to do all the worrying.'

'What are you do—'

'I'm doing my job, Nick. You should stop bothering this young lady, go home and do yours.' He tapped his teeth with his pen. 'You'll be wanted at the demonstration tomorrow. Don't be late.'

The anger that rose through me died somewhere between stomach and chest. What could I do? If by some slim chance I could give him a good kicking rather than embarrassing myself and ending up in an arm lock, what good would it do? He would just come after me. I couldn't kill him or hurt him badly enough to stop him. And Guilder would have other people on the case. He could hire more. As many as he needed.

'Take care, Nick.' Mr Rust nodded down the corridor, encouraging me to leave. 'You're a valuable asset. My job is to let you know that, like any other asset, you have an owner. And like any valuable asset you're to be protected. I'm the blade that cuts two ways. If you're a good lad it's only the one edge I'll be cutting with, keeping you safe.'

'From?' Was this psychopath claiming to be my bodyguard now?

A slow smile. 'From anyone else who wants to own you. It's all about the rules, Nick. All about debt and obligation. Your experiments require finance. That's a debt. Now you have an obligation. I live and die by my rules, my debts and my obligations. And I intend to see that you honour yours, too.'

I stalked off, my mind a rolling boil. Even warning him away from Helen would just make her more of a target. I'd never imagined this was how things went in the world of scientific research, however valuable the end results might promise to be. Then again, maybe it wasn't always like this. I only had a sample of one to judge by; and I was, after all, a statistical outlier.

The late afternoon sun shone, in defiance of the rain that traditionally signalled the start of the British summer holidays. Birds sang their tiny hearts out in the trees. Tourists browsed the streets of Cambridge recording the old stonework on celluloid, buying postcards, amusing hats and guided tours. Students zipped to and fro on bicycles. And I wandered through it, devoid of ideas.

By the time I arrived at Trinity College and crossed the green expanse of lawns to reach my wing, I had almost decided that none of it really mattered. Guilder's desire to protect his investment was intrusive and outrageous, but it wasn't as if I didn't *want* to research the subject. He wasn't forcing me to work on something I didn't need to do. Also the practical side did need very expensive equipment that would require financial support, and it wasn't as if he were planning a third world war or to make himself emperor . . . hopefully. I just didn't like not being in control. That only left the small matter of whether allowing his financial greed to dictate the pacing and risk level of the experiments would end the world.

I climbed the stairs to the first floor to find Crispin Waugh and one of his cronies lounging in the corridor holding a loud conversation about skiing holidays and yachts. I wasn't sure how the two subjects fitted together, or if they were just broadcasting their family wealth to everyone within earshot. Neither were so engrossed in their conversation, though, that they didn't have time to pause and throw a few jibes at my back as I passed.

'Someone should tell Halligan his dog's off the leash again,' Waugh offered.

I slowed and looked back over my shoulder. 'It's sad to see what generations of inbreeding have done to our upper class.' Shaking my head in mock sorrow I added, 'I suspect that one of your distant ancestors might actually have made it to Cambridge on merit. In your place he might have found something witty to say.'

'Hey! Do you even know who I am?' The friend was broad-shouldered and tanned, though something weak about his mouth made it seem unlikely that anything kind ever came out of it.

'I really don't.' And I didn't. I did notice now, though, that he was carrying an unsheathed sword. Which was strange. It seemed unlikely that he was the D&D type who like to role play. I kinda wanted to ask about it, but instead I turned and walked away. He shot both barrels of his surname at my retreating back as if I should be impressed. I'd forgotten it before I reached my room.

I closed my door and fell backwards onto my bed, arms spread. 'Fuck.'

It seems that the richer you are, the louder you speak, and Waugh's resumed conversation boomed into my room while I eyed the ceiling. Apparently, the sword belonged to double-barrelled's brother who had graduated from naval college. He planned to use it to remove the corks from champagne bottles at the upcoming ball because . . . well, there didn't seem to be a 'because', but maybe it was fashionable among the old Etonians.

The conversation had ended by the time I'd gnawed my way moodily through a rather stale packet of digestives. I made a cup of black tea and sat by the window overlooking the lawns across which evening was making a stealthy approach.

All of a sudden I remembered. The book!

I approached my bag with trepidation. This morning seemed a million years ago, given all that had happened since. The split second, however, when I had touched that cover and received a massive shock that had thrown me unconscious back across the room . . . that seemed only moments ago. Pulling the zip revealed the old volume sitting there, innocuous, nestled among my other books. My hand did *not* want to touch it. I tried, but got the same sensation I once had several years before, when ambition exceeded bravery and I climbed boldly up to the highest diving board at the local swimming pool. Twelve feet doesn't sound very high, but peering over the drop with my toes curled around the edge, I knew with certainty that my legs would not take the next step. Enduring the mocking looks of a sea of bobbing faces and the jeers of those already climbing the ladder behind me, I had retreated without dignity.

'Just do it!' I shouted, grabbing the wrist of my right hand with my left and trying to force my fingers onto the book. But I couldn't, any more than I could wrap my fingers around a lump of red-hot iron, glowing from the forge.

A better idea occurred to me. I went to my doorway and listened. All quiet. Carrying my bag, I snuck out into the corridor and went along to the door bearing the elegantly scrolled name plate 'Crispin Waugh'. Gingerly I tipped the mystery book from the bag without ever touching it. The thing was carrying some kind of charge and I needed a way of defusing it, of using up energies stored inside. It reminded me of how Demus had to approach me and retreat several times before it was finally safe to meet face to face for the first time.

I left the book lying on the floor, just where a person would see it when they came out. Next I knocked twice, then legged it back to my own room three doors along.

'Come.' Waugh's muffled voice.

'Come!' Vaguely annoyed now.

I heard the door open. 'What the—'

I risked a quick glance from my doorway. My assumption was correct. He had spotted the book and was bending to retrieve it.

'Ow!' Waugh drew his hand back as if stung. 'God damn it!' Looking puzzled he tried again, more cautiously. 'Ah!' But this time he kept a grip, picking the book up and juggling it hand to hand as if it were hot.

I stepped smoothly out into the corridor, feeling distinctly pleased with myself. 'Sorry, that's mine.' A few strides later and I was reaching for the offending item. 'Must have dropped it when I went past—' As my fingers touched the covers an almighty shock ran through me, hurling me all the way back to my own doorway where I lay twitching. I didn't lose consciousness this time. Or at least I don't think I did. With my ears ringing and every muscle trying to wrench its way out from underneath my skin, I sat up. I was surprised to find that I wasn't smoking.

It was hard to hear what Waugh was yelling about but clearly a small fraction of the shock had run through him too. His neatly combed hair was in disarray, his V-neck jumper rucked up, shirt out at the side.

I got unsteadily to my feet as the double-barrelled friend emerged from behind Waugh, gesticulating at me with his brother's sword.

'—tried to kill me with a booby-trapped book!' Waugh was shouting. 'I'll burn the damn thing!'

'No!' I held a hand out. I needed the book. I wasn't sure why I needed it, but I was sure that I did. I stumbled forward intending to scoop the book up ahead of Waugh, but somehow tripped over my own feet just before I reached him.

In the same instant I realised that the idiot friend still had his sword pointing at me. Time fractured. I saw a dozen images of me skewered on the blade. Through the eye, through the neck, through the mouth, through the chest. I was still searching for a timeline where I didn't impale myself on the sword when it lanced through me.

It didn't really hurt. It just looked rather odd, sticking out of my side like that. I took a step back and the sword came with me, pulled from double-barrelled's numb fingers. All around me other Nicks staggered or fell, overlaid one across the other, each similarly injured, some stuck through the stomach, others with the sword wedged between their ribs.

I bumped against the wall and slid down it, my legs unaccountably weak. I held the steel blade in both hands now because it was starting to sting somewhat as it waved about. Blood was running out of the wound. Not gushing. Trickling would be accurate. Other Nicks slid down beside me, all of them wounded much the same, as if I were narrowing down to one particular future. I wanted to reach out towards a better outcome. I tried, but the pain had its teeth in me and everything seemed too hard to do.

My backside met the floor.

'Oh,' I said. And I don't remember much of what happened after that.

CHAPTER 12

I had wiped away the memory of how Demus died. It wasn't something I wanted to keep. If in twenty-five years' time I was still actually going to be Demus, I didn't want to be carrying those memories with me when I stepped into whatever room I was going to get killed in. It seemed very unlikely now that I would ever become Demus. Our timelines had been split and the recent events that didn't match his recollections were the proof of it. Besides, right now I found it hard to believe that I would be sacrificing my life to save Mia. I still had feelings for her, but that didn't change the fact that she now counted among her pastimes swapping saliva with an over-acting wannabe pop star.

I hoped that however Demus met his end five months earlier, it wasn't with a large blade stuck through him . . . or me, because I'd tried that now and didn't like it at all.

I opened my eyes to a stark white ceiling and fluorescent lighting, all rotating about some central point. Closing them again, I sank back into the slow churn of my thoughts, half-dream, half-delirium. Eva Hayes. Charles Rust. Those surnames seemed too coincidental. I knew Ian Rust had killed a drug dealer and died around the same time that Demus met his own end. The new Rust and the old shared some similarities beyond their delight in other people's suffering. They had the same eyes, and a snake-like quickness to them.

A slow blink and the white ceiling returned, and the lights. The spinning of the room was almost imperceptible now. The sound of distant clattering reached me. I retreated again to the darkness behind my eyelids.

Eva Hayes . . . Hayes . . . a relation of mine? Mother hadn't known her. A half-sister my father had secretly raised with another woman? It seemed unlikely, but then how well does a twelve-year-old know their father?

Another look at the world outside. White ceiling, check. Fluorescent lights, check. The clattering had got louder, closer. I turned my head in time to see a metal trolley laden with food trays approaching between two aisles of hospital beds. The large black lady pushing it handed a tray to the man in the bed beside mine, balding, with tufts of grey hair at the sides, and a leg in plaster raised on a frame.

'Beef stew and carrots,' she boomed. 'Puts hair on your chest, love.'

I tried to sit up and failed, collapsing with a groan, my side on fire.

'Hey now! Don't move!' A nurse came in from the other side. 'Lie back, Nick.' She reached for my wrist and looked at the watch pinned to the lapel of her uniform.

I lay back as instructed. The nurse, a matronly type, though not I thought a matron, took my pulse. She set her hand to my forehead. 'So you're feeling better.'

'The sword!' I remembered it lodged in my gut, its sharp edge held by the meat of my body, blood spilling out. Foolishly I tried to rise again so I could look at the wound. The pain made me cry out and slump against my pillows.

'Beef and carrots.' The orderly set my meal on the bedside table with a wide smile.

'That idiot ran me through—'

'All taken care of. Don't worry about it.' The nurse loomed over me to check my wound, dark haired, her broad face showing the muted no-nonsense compassion I remembered from the oncology ward.

'Do I get to keep the sword now?' I hadn't meant to say that. Maybe it was the anaesthetic talking.

Nurse Robson – according to her nametag – frowned. 'It was a sword, was it?'

My turn to frown. I thought everyone knew a sword when they saw one. 'How long was I in surgery?'

'You didn't go to surgery, dear. Dr Patel did your stitches in A&E, then you came up to the general ward for observation. We're wanting to understand why you were unconscious. Your friends thought you might have hit your head when you fell?'

'I . . . don't remember.' I reached down to my side to pat the dressings. 'I passed out because I had a sword sticking through me!'

'It went through your clothes, Nick, and gave you a nasty cut on your side—'

'It was stuck in me!' I remembered that more clearly than I wanted to.

Nurse Robson shook her head. 'You had twenty-six stitches and lost some blood. You should be good to go in a day or two. The doctor has prescribed some antibiotics as a precaution.'

She shone a penlight in my left eye, then my right. I saw the sword more clearly than I saw her little light. It had been a foot deep in me. Right through whatever organs you keep below your ribs . . . Liver? Kidneys? I hadn't paid close attention in biology class, but it was the sort of stuff you got in a good fry-up. The sort of stuff you needed to keep you alive.

'But the sword was stuck in me . . .'

'An inch to the left and it would have been.' She nodded. 'Do you have a headache? Blurred vision?'

I ignored her. I must have found another option at the last possible moment, a future where the blade just grazed me. 'Can you help me to sit?'

She bent and started to turn the handle that angled the top third of the bed. More of the ward came into view. Old men lying grey and disinterested, middle-aged men behind their newspapers, listening to hospital radio, chewing grapes, a couple of younger guys. The orderly dispensing the last of the meals. The windows were on the far side, running with rain as the sudden fury of a summer storm lashed them. It looked to be early morning out there. I'd been there all night!

'Visiting time soon.' The nurse wrote some of her findings on the chart at the end of the bed. 'The doctors will be around to see you later. The buzzer is that big orange button. Let someone know if you start feeling sick or your vision blurs. You may have a concussion. There's a bowl next to you if you need to vomit.'

With that she gave a final smile and left, bantering with a patient here and there as she passed.

I glanced around. I'd spent more time than I wanted to on hospital wards, and the main thing about them is that they are boring as hell. A good book helps, but all I'd brought in with me was a Royal Navy sword, and now even that turned out to have been in an alternative timeline. A tingle in the fingers of my left hand made me look down. Apparently I did have a book with me. *Curiosa Mathematica*. Whatever else had gone wrong, it seemed that at least I had successfully drawn the teeth of Lewis Carroll's little book on maths. Time to see how deep the rabbit hole went. I picked it up and opened it. Just inside the cover someone had written, 'To Eva, love from Dad.'

I set my fingers to the words. Something about the inscription nagged at me. Before I had a chance to figure out what it was I became aware of someone angling toward my bed.

'Dr Pritchard?'

She gave me a tight smile. When I moved to Cambridge I'd been assigned to Dr Pritchard's team for my ongoing monitoring. Leukaemia doesn't like to let go once it has its teeth in you. They talk about remission rather than cure, though sometimes that remission can last a lifetime. But everyone who goes through chemo is monitored and tested regularly for signs that the monster that took a bite of us has come back to finish the meal.

'Nicholas.' She was an old woman, older than my mother, withered and almost swallowed by her white coat, but with a certain fierce determination in unexpectedly bright blue eyes. Mother told me that Elise Pritchard must be quite a woman to have become a successful oncologist at a time when medical schools routinely forwarded applications from female students to the nursing college. She said I was lucky to have her.

Dr Pritchard began to pull the green curtains around my bed, wrapping us in a poor illusion of privacy. She drew up a seat in the narrow space between my bed and the curtain. Half a dozen comments and questions dried up on my tongue. Suddenly I really didn't want to know why she was here.

'I've got the results of your last test,' she said, meeting my eyes with her bright gaze before I could turn away.

'I got stabbed by a sword,' I said. 'Well, maybe a sabre, technically. Not sure. And . . . I guess it was more of a cut than a stab. But an inch to the left and—'

'I was going to call you today.' Dr Pritchard kept her voice low and calm, the eye contact constant, not allowing me to avoid the subject in hand. And when the top item on the conversational list is *not* the fact that you are lying in bed with a sword wound, then it can't be good. 'I wanted to set up a meeting with you and your mother.'

'I'm sixteen. I live alone. I'm legally old enough to get married, have sex, father a child and pay taxes. I don't need my mother present in order for you to tell me that my leukaemia is back.' I did want her there though. They say that soldiers horribly wounded in no-man's-land between the First World War trenches called for their mothers.

Dr Pritchard pressed her lips into a grim line, her face full of a weary but genuine compassion.

'So,' I asked. 'Is that what you've come to tell me?'

She gave a slow nod of her grey head. 'You'll need to start chemotherapy again. We should do it today, but I want to give it forty-eight hours to give your body a chance to heal after your accident.'

'Shit.'

There wasn't any fracturing of time on this occasion. Either this wasn't part of the bizarre series of attacks on me, or it was and there simply were no alternatives, no options, no way to dodge this bullet.

The doctor patted my hand. 'We've caught it early with regular monitoring. The prognosis following a sequence of chemotherapy is good. But you should call your mother, get her to take you home for a while. It's not good for you to be alone at a time like this.'

'I will.' I fought to keep my voice level. 'Thank you.'

Whatever she'd just said about not being alone, Dr Pritchard knew that right now I wanted some moments to myself. She stood and pulled the surrounding curtain to one side. 'Talk with your mother and decide if you want the sessions to be here or in London. I'll come and check on you tomorrow.'

She withdrew and I craned my head back into the pillow. I'd avoided nearly a dozen deadly events in the past few months, but for all their sudden shock and heart-pounding aftermath, none of them were a hundredth as scary as cancer. The gruelling prolonged torture that kindly Dr Pritchard had in store for me held far more terror than any sword thrust. It was dull, demoralising, depressing, nauseating. I'd seen it work and I'd seen it fail. I didn't want to end up like that. I had a life needing to be lived. Work to do. It wasn't right or fair.

A cold fist knotted my guts about it. I felt sick and sorry for myself, but I'd feel sick enough soon without making myself ill now. I struggled to sit, the pain in my side no less sharp but suddenly unimportant. I stared at my arm on the sheet before me, at the veins, blue beneath the skin, at the treacherous blood within, manufacturing poisons to kill me, spreading the cancer to the organs that it was supposed to serve.

I wiped some tears away. I didn't feel strong, or ready to fight, or any of those positive go-get-'em things that you're supposed to feel. Strangely it was social embarrassment that kept me from crying my eyes out, shouting at the injustice of it, kicking tables over: the idea that the strangers to either side might have heard my diagnosis and even now be listening and silently judging me. How terribly British.

A bell rang and at the far end of the ward I heard the doors open. The first of the visitors would be bustling through with their cards and chocolates and magazines. They began to pass by my bed, shadows on the curtains, greetings ringing out. 'Hello, Bob!', 'Stan, how you doing?' 'I brought you those nuts you like.'

A shadow darkened against my curtain. The material rustled, a hand seeking the join where someone could enter. A head pushed through. My eyes were still a bit blurry. I squeezed them, thumb and finger, to push the last of the tears out.

'Hello.'

'Hi.' I sniffed and looked up. It was the girl who wasn't Helen.

As one, every buzzer in the ward went off, while overhead the lights all flared then died.

CHAPTER 13

'The universe is trying to kill you.' The girl stepped fully into view. 'And we need to get out of here.'

'Who are you?' I picked up the book she had left for me and held it to my chest as if it were some kind of shield.

'Eva,' she said. She watched me with bright eyes and an unsettling intensity.

I wasn't sure how I had mistaken her for Helen. Close up they were quite different. Both brunette, brown eyed, pretty, but hardly twins. 'I know your name.' I had to raise my voice above the multitude of buzzers. 'I want to know who you are . . . Why . . . all this?' I gestured around at the scene we couldn't see because of the curtains. 'And why this?' I held up the Lewis Carroll book. 'The book that bites!'

Eva took a seat. Her hands trembled. I cancelled the call button while she gathered herself. All along the ward nurses clattered about, running hither and thither to silence the alarms.

'Well?' I raised my voice over the excited chatter of patients and their visitors.

The confidence the girl had worn when she came through the curtain seemed to have deserted her. She looked too pale, as if she were the one who should be lying in a hospital bed. 'A paradox builds up vast amounts of energy,' she said. 'Titanic, world-shattering amounts of energy.'

'As much as I didn't like being thrown across the room . . . twice . . . I'd hardly call it world shattering.' I frowned even as I joked. Why was she so familiar?

'The spare energy reduces exponentially the closer you are to the paradox event in time. And if it hasn't happened yet, it's even smaller.' She shook her head as if this were all incidental. 'Look, we need to leave.'

'I . . .' I had cancer again. The resurgent memory of Dr Pritchard's pronouncement closed my throat on the words. Suddenly none of this mattered. The mystery girl, the weird effects, Guilder and his paid goon, Charlie Rust. None of it. 'I don't care. You should talk to Demus about it. He's the one that knows all this stuff. He's running the show. I just do the sums.'

'Demus?' She frowned.

'Future me. He's around somewhere . . . Wait, you *are* from the future, right? Otherwise this has been the anaesthetic talking and you should ignore everything I said.'

'I'm from *a* future.' She stressed the 'a'. 'Anyway, I told you, we need to get you out of here.'

'That would be nice,' I agreed. 'But I'm hardly dressed for it.' I glanced down at my hospital gown, suddenly aware that I'd been undressed while I was unconscious. 'Also I can barely sit. I've got twenty-something stitches in my side.'

'I stole a wheelchair. It's just outside the curtain.'

I shook my head. 'If the universe is trying to kill me then surely a hospital is a good place to be. I'm not leaving this bed without an explanation of why I should.' I wanted to add that I also wasn't leaving it without a strong dose of painkillers, someone to carry me and something to wear that didn't hang open at the back. 'Start by explaining this!' I held up *Curiosa Mathematica*.

Eva glanced at the curtains, then sighed. 'The book was something I brought back with me. It allowed the paradox energy to be released more gently. A way of grounding ourselves before meeting, so no serious sparks fly.'

'They felt pretty serious to me.' I winced, remembering the shock that had thrown me unconscious onto my bed. 'Wait. You brought it back with you? But Demus said only living things could come back. He turned up naked, for Christ's sake!'

'I found a way around that,' she said.

'You?' I asked, incredulous. I hope I didn't sneer at the idea, but I admit there was a sneer inside. I'd spent too long being told I was a genius – by Halligan, by the newspapers, even by myself. Demus said that nobody but him really understood his work even years after it was published.

'When has Demus come back from?'

'2011.'

A muscle twitched in her cheek and her lips moved as if trying to begin a difficult word. She turned her head, then went to the curtain, but not quickly enough for me to miss that there were tears in her eyes.

'Who *are* you?' I asked.

'Let me tell you about what happens when two timelines are bound together.' She kept her face averted. 'They're paradoxical by definition, since the only reason that they are not the same timeline is that something happened in one that did not happen in the other. The difference could be tiny, trivial – a molecule in a fly's brain reacts this way, or it reacts that way, the fly lands here instead of there . . .' She touched two adjacent spots on the curtain. 'Everything else is aligned and in the two timelines all subsequent outcomes of every uncertain action continue to be the same, except where the ongoing effects of the paradox cause disagreement. Initially it's easy to move between the timelines—'

'Moving between timelines isn't possible,' I said. 'I can show mathematically . . .' But then I realised what I should have realised long ago, and would have if I hadn't been so focused on other problems. 'I've been doing it! That's why I'm lying here with stitches in my side rather than with a hole right through me.'

'You can do that?' It was Eva's turn to look surprised.

'Not well enough, apparently.' I touched my dressing and winced. 'Tell me what happens. With the paradox, I mean.'

'The divergence grows. It always grows. Slow or fast, but always more. The example with the fly – well, that might take a while for noticeable differences to accumulate, but they will. Wait long enough and cities will stand or fall on that small initial change. And if the time-lines remain bound then the energy associated with those differences grows too, bubbling under the fabric of both realities.'

'Until?'

'Space-time itself starts to boil.' She met my gaze with a level stare.

'What does that mean?'

'Local temporal distortions. In the year I've come from, some parts of the world can be microseconds ahead or behind others. London could be a microsecond ahead of Glasgow one month, a microsecond behind months later.'

'Honestly, it doesn't sound that apocalyptic. I was thinking you'd come back from the future to save us from an army of terminators hunting down the last dregs of humanity.' I offered her a smile.

'Think about it.'

I thought about it. 'Um . . .'

'The whole planet is—'

'Moving! OK. Got it.' Earth hurtles through space, orbiting the sun, which in turn orbits the centre of the galaxy at more than a hundred miles a second. Make different bits of the planet experience time at different rates and they would travel different distances. For microseconds' difference, that might be a metre or so – enough to cause earthquakes, perhaps. If microseconds became milliseconds then the world would tear itself apart. 'Pretty terminal then.'

'Not as immediately terminal as the gas explosion that wrecks this ward.' She stood and reached for my arm. 'So we *have* to leave. Now!'

The contact between her hand and my arm made an unpleasant tingling and a crackling that sounded as if my flesh were crisping under her fingers. She helped me to sit, or forced me to, depending on your point of view.

'You know this place is going to blow?' I bit down on the pain in my side and slid my bare feet to the ground.

'I know that it did. I've read the newspaper reports.' Eva helped me to the end of the bed, the curtain slithering over us as I hobbled along, gasping. 'You weren't one of the casualties, but it's different now. I'm here and everything is in flux.'

'Shouldn't— Ah! That hurt . . . Shouldn't we warn someone?' I limped out onto the ward, my whole side aching, the pain shooting through me with each step as my stitches pulled.

'It's you that the universe is trying to kill. If we get you out of here it probably won't happen.'

I sank into the wheelchair with a gasp, sure that my wound was bleeding again. 'But you said it had already happened.'

Eva looked at me as if I were an idiot. She dumped my clothes in my lap then went around the back to push the wheelchair. 'This is a new time-line. When someone comes back they start a new timeline.' She said it as if instructing a child, though she was a year or two older than me at most.

'Demus remembers himself coming back. His timeline has his time travel baked into it, and as long as he doesn't do anything incompatible with that experience he thinks he can change his own future by what he does in this here and now.' I got it all out in a hurry, not caring if it made sense. Now that Eva had told me about the impending explosion I could visualise the fireball consuming the ward, withering skin and melting the flesh beneath. 'You could push a little faster!'

'I'm trying not to be notice—'

'Hey! Hello? Where do you think you're off to?' A rather fierce nurse with short red hair and a thick Irish accent came up from behind to intercept us.

'I'm just taking him for a little walk.' Eva tried to steer around the nurse.

'He shouldn't even be out of bed!' The nurse's outrage grew. 'He's lost a lot of blood and been unconscious for a prolonged period. Let's just hope he hasn't ruptured any stitches with this foolishness!'

Eva pressed forward with determination until my toes were against the nurse's shins. I started to wonder if I could smell gas . . . or was smelling things that weren't there a symptom of concussion? I didn't know if I'd hit my head on the way down, but it certainly ached.

'Look, if it's dangerous moving him out of the bed, then it's dangerous moving him back in, and he clearly needs a rest before you do it.' Eva shoved the wheelchair, forcing the woman out of our path. 'We'll be back in twenty minutes.' And with the nurse's protests falling around us we banged through the doors at the end of the ward.

We found ourselves in one of those endless hospital corridors that vanish into the distance until the curvature of the Earth takes them from view. Eva sped us along it towards a distant exit.

'So, we escaped the gas explosion or prevented it. I'm safe. Well, safer . . . in less immediate danger . . .'

'Critical but stable.' Eva put it in medical terms since we were still in the hospital.

'But the world . . . two worlds . . . maybe more, are going to end because of the spreading effects of some paradox that is . . . going to happen soon?'

'Yes.' Eva kept up a steady pace, the exit less distant now. 'It happens on Thursday. It sounds as if I'm not the only one with an interest in it either. How many of us have you seen?'

'Just two. You and . . . uh . . . me.'

'Well, that's two more than most people meet.'

'Only future me didn't come back to avoid any paradox . . .'

'But . . . why else he would come back?' Eva sounded surprised. 'Unless he just wanted to split off a new timeline and live in it . . .'

'It's complicated,' I said. 'There's a girl and—'

'Helen?' Eva asked.

'You know Helen? I knew it! She's your sister, right? Right?'

Eva stopped just short of the main doors and came to stand before me. 'He's come back because of Helen?'

'No. He's come back for a girl called Mia. But something went wrong and he's here in June rather than back in January. But if he gets to January and if he sticks to what he remembers he reckons he can change what happens after he left, and save her life.' I raised a hand before she started lecturing me on how things worked. 'It's not how it's supposed to work but there's something special about his timeline. A kind of feedback loop got frozen in. Perhaps whatever caused that is the same thing that left your timeline tangled with another one. I'm guessing his timeline is the one that's got fused with yours.'

Eva returned to pushing me in silence. A thoughtful silence. Just the low rumble of hospital life and the clack clack clack of her shoes as she took me ever closer to the sun-bright exit.

'So, why is the universe trying to kill me?' I asked.

'Like any semi-stable system, the universe is a low-energy solution to an equation. Paradox is an unstable high-energy solution and the universe tries to configure itself to regain the low-energy solution. That means tearing up the affected timelines. Or making sure they never happen. There's nothing personal about it. It's just physics.'

A visitor held the doors wide as we passed through into the open air.

'You're saying I cause the paradox.'

'Bingo.'

I grabbed the wheels and brought the chair to a halt. I tried to swivel round but my side hurt too much, so I settled for craning my neck to look at her.

'Who *are* you?' I held up the book from my lap. I realised now that the handwriting in the dedication was what had been troubling me. It looked familiar. 'And who gave you this?'

Eva paled and her cheek twitched again. She tried to speak but her voice came out as a strangled whisper. 'You did . . . Dad.'

CHAPTER 14

In the space of one day I'd had a psychopath invade my home, an idiot stab me with a sword, had my leukaemia return and at sixteen years of age I'd met my eighteen-year-old daughter.

Eva wheeled me through the streets of Cambridge with no apparent destination in mind. It was an arrangement that saved us both from meeting each other's eyes and seeing the confusion of our own emotions mirrored there.

I had a lot of questions. The only difficulty was asking them. 'So . . .' The words dried up on my tongue for the fourth or fifth time. 'So, Helen is your mother?'

'Yes.'

It explained why they looked like sisters.

'And I'm . . .'

'My dad. Yes.'

As much as I liked the idea of making babies with Helen, it seemed rather unlikely given how things had been going so far. Plus where did that leave things with me and Mia? And were these the kind of things I wanted to discuss with my daughter . . . who was older than me. Had I been a good father to her? Why was it Eva standing in front of me . . . well, behind me . . . rather than the older me who had watched her grow? Why hadn't the me from her timeline returned instead?

We were heading into the old part of town towards the main colleges and the river, the streets growing more crowded, our going slower. Clearly returning me to the hospital was not on Eva's to-do list. I wondered how she was at changing dressings and taking stitches out.

I attracted a few stares as we went, my bare legs and feet emerging from the hospital gown, very pale in the sunlight. My head ached worse than the wound in my side, and thinking clearly was proving difficult.

I decided to start with something easy. 'What were those things you were running away from, and where did you go?'

'What things? When?'

'The first time we met. You called me by name. Asked for my help.'

'When?' she repeated.

'You know. When I came to see Halligan that first time, back in February.'

'Really?' She sounded surprised. 'I go back further?'

'I . . . uh . . . guess so?'

'Well, I haven't done it yet. That's your past, my future.'

I ran a palm over my forehead, trying to press the ache out of my brain. It was easier to get my head around it on paper in the form of an equation. Words made it more complicated. Living it made it even harder to understand. Especially with mild concussion. 'OK. I guess we'll understand that bit when the time comes . . . again . . . or something.'

Eva wheeled me on in silence for a while, not speaking again until we passed the Gothic glory of King's College and its chapel, towering to one side like an over-decorated stone cake. We came to a halt on the lawns leading down to the Cam.

'So,' Eva said. It seemed to be a family habit. She came and sat cross-legged on the grass in front of me. 'So.'

'Did I send you back?'

Eva shook her head, eyes on the grass.

Puzzled, I tried again. 'Did I tell you *not* to come?'

Eva shook her head again, biting her lip. 'I thought I would be better at this . . .' Her voice sounded choked.

'Better at what?'

'Until the hospital just now, I'd never spoken to you before.' She rubbed her shoulder while she spoke, as if offering herself comfort. 'You died, Dad. You died when I was a baby. And . . .' A sob, a gasp for air, then the words came quickly. 'And I've spent a lifetime in your shadow, looking back at where you stood. The great Nicholas Hayes. The Time Lord who gave humanity the key to the TARDIS. And I worked to find a way back to you. I worked so hard to use that damn key. I thought . . .'

'You thought it would be different. That I would recognise you. That somehow I would say the right thing, know what to do, make up for all those missing years.' She'd told me I was going to die young. That I would marry Helen and make a child who I would never see grow. It should have cut me too deeply to care about anything else, but right then and there I cared more about making this right for her than I did about how wrong it was for me. And it wasn't the selfless love of a father for his child. I already knew this scene we were acting out. I knew it from the other side, had imagined it a thousand times. Four years earlier my own father had left the house and never returned. There had been few days since that one when I hadn't wished for that morning back: for the twelve-year-old me to have noticed him at breakfast. To have unwrapped myself from whatever nonsense had been on my mind and to have seen my father, truly seen him, for the last time. Maybe I could have somehow stood myself between him and that train he thought he needed to catch. Maybe now, if I went back, I would know the right words to say, might be able to unveil enough new wonder in the world to make him want to stay, make him want to fight his cancer. So, yes, I knew the sort of thing she needed from me, just not how to give it to her. 'I'm sorry I wasn't there for you.'

Eva looked up, eyes bright above a forced smile. 'Well, you're here now.'

We probably should have hugged or something, but we were Hayeses and nobody in my family had been given to hugging for generations. Instead we talked mathematics.

'If I die when you're a baby – and I have to say that I'm really not on board with that at all – how do I manage to find time to solve time travel? Demus told me it would take twenty years to iron out all the wrinkles. Or . . . do Helen and I wait a long time before we . . . I mean . . . when were you born?'

'You're sure you want to know all this?'

'I know a future where I live for another twenty-five years. And I saw a whole bunch where I didn't survive past lunchtime and died skewered on a sword in a stupid accident. So sure, tell me about one where I get to be with Helen and have a daughter.'

'OK . . .' She spoke slowly, picking her words with care as if knowing that all of them came with sharp edges. 'I was born in 1989.'

'Woah! I was quick off the mark! Or will be . . .' A father at nineteen. Mother would not approve.

'You and Mum weren't sure you were still fertile after the chemo, and it looked as if you were likely to have more rounds of treatment. She said you both decided to try while there was still hope.'

'There's always hope, Eva.' I quoted Demus.

'Well . . .' She sniffed and wiped her nose. Her mascara had run. 'There was hope. You got me! And two years later you died.'

'Aged twenty-one?'

Eva nodded.

'The leukaemia?'

Another nod.

I took a while to chew that one over. 'But . . . you didn't come back just to meet me, or at least not only for that?' Time travel was a big deal.

It wasn't something you did for personal tourism, even if the sights and destinations included lost relatives. 'Did you?'

'No,' she admitted. 'I had a bigger reason too.'

'You came to escape the paradox breakdown?' Even that seemed wrong, to run away by herself, leaving behind everyone she'd ever known.

'I came to stop it happening. I'm not entirely sure it can be done yet, but if it can, this is the time and place to do it. I just need to take some more measurements, do some more calculations. I'm going to need help, though, and now it turns out I've got *two* dads right here in this city. Maybe that's enough to help me save two worlds.'

I couldn't help but grin at that. At the sheer craziness of it. I wondered what Demus would make of this daughter he'd never had. It might seem even stranger to him than it did to me. We sat for a while in the sunshine saying nothing, bees in the clover, white clouds dotting a blue sky.

'And when have you come back from?' I asked at last.

'2007.'

'How's that possible, though? I mean . . . you said I died aged twenty-one. I couldn't have worked out all the theory in five years, could I?'

Eva shrugged. 'You broke the back of it. You're famous as hell! And a bunch of other mathematicians carried on where you left off. Halligan led a team that did a lot of the remaining work. Uncle Bob, I call him. He died the year before I came back. Choked on a fishbone.'

'Uncle Bob? You knew him like twenty years in the future?'

'Sure. I worked with him. Here at Cambridge.'

The light slowly dawned. 'It was you. You finished off my work!'

Eva shook her head. 'Nope. I've been working on something else.'

'What, then?'

She tapped her chest and for the first time I noticed that written in white across her black T-shirt were a collection of closed integrals. The notation didn't make a lot of sense.

'Are those tensors?' I asked.

She nodded.

'And those look like terms you find in work on turbulence.' I frowned. 'And *that* looks suspiciously like the generator for the Mandlebrot set . . .'

Another nod.

'Tell me . . .'

So she did. At first she just talked, and later she took a pen and a pad of paper from her bag and began to write, page after page of tightly packed equations. Before long I started to see the forms rise from the notebook, the multidimensional shapes that cast their shadows on the paper below. Eva saw them too. I could tell it from the way she hardly glanced at the page as she wrote, but looked into space with a defocused gaze as though she were sketching what she saw.

'Slow down.' I'd never said that before. Not about mathematics. Even Halligan crawled compared to the speed I wanted him to go at when we discussed this stuff. With Halligan I would slowly reveal the inner workings of the mathematical universe, piece by glowing piece, while he steadfastly laboured through the dead ink on the page as if it were the secret itself rather than just being the grass rippling in the wake of some larger truth passing him by. With Eva I sat amazed while she spun and juggled structures of such grandeur and complexity that I strained to see the whole of them. 'These are the foundations, aren't they?'

'Yes.' A grin spread across her face. 'I'd hoped you would see it. Nobody else ever has, just the local implications. The small theories, minor proofs.'

'But this . . . this is big.' I tried to grasp the meaning. 'This is about paradox!'

'Yes. I've done a lot of work on it. It would take quite a while to explain. But it all rests on this. Which I wanted to show you. And leads here.' She tapped her heart again, and the four equations scrawled across her T-shirt. She was wearing the answer. The answer to the most complicated question ever asked.

'And you did all this . . . All this! By yourself?' I didn't understand it properly, but I understood enough to know that it was a work of genius. Something I might better comprehend given time, but could never have dragged out of the universe's protesting grasp to put on a page. 'By eighteen?'

'Yes.' She looked down, but I could tell that a smile was teasing the corners of her mouth. The first I'd seen.

'Wow!' Then I told her what I'd been wanting my father to say ever since the day he left us. 'Eva, this is incredible. I can hardly believe anyone could crack it.' A deep breath. 'Any father would be proud of you.'

She looked up, smiling properly now. 'I have good genes.'

CHAPTER 15

According to Eva's calculations, a direct meeting with Demus would likely destroy both of them, along with several city blocks. Since her analysis had allowed her to make a staged contact with me where neither of us died, it seemed that her equations had passed at least one experimental hurdle. Now that she knew Demus existed, she promised to run the numbers and devise a strategy that would allow them to meet.

In the meantime she wanted me to leave for London.

'I thought fathers were supposed to do the ordering around,' I grumbled.

'If you're nearby when I start approaching Demus for the first time, it's just going to be that much harder.' She was wheeling me along the street where we first met, or in her terms where we were going to meet.

'I can hang back, give you guys some space. I'm sixteen, not an idiot.'

'Well, you might say something insensitive, it's true, but I'm more concerned about you unbalancing an already highly unstable equilibrium and getting us all killed. Two-body problems are so much easier to solve than three-body ones.'

I allowed myself to be silenced by this piece of mathematical wisdom. While I wasn't looking forward to being jolted around for an hour on the train, I did quite want to go home. Hypothetical daughters and new theories aside, leukaemia felt like the most pressing and most real of my problems, and when any animal is sick or injured the most basic instinct is to return to its den.

'How will you even find Demus?' The station was in sight now, and it seemed as though time were running out for all those unasked questions.

'I've built a little device,' Eva said. 'A paradox detector, if you like. Not very accurate but it should lead me to him after a bit of wandering about.'

Eva took the Lewis Carroll book from me and pressed something smaller into my hands: a photograph of her sitting on a wall somewhere sunny. 'In case you forget what I look like.' She sounded embarrassed.

We left the wheelchair in the parking lot and I hobbled on to the London-bound platform with Eva hovering around me as if I might fall at any moment and need catching.

'You need to check into an A&E as soon as you get to King's Cross. Have them look the wound over.'

'Yes, Mother.'

She shook her head at my tone and that made me laugh, which made my stitches hurt, which made me resolve to do exactly what she'd just told me to.

I got onto the train unaided and turned in the doorway.

'Stay safe.' We both said it together, then grinned, then looked away awkwardly.

'Demus knows where to find me,' I said. 'I'll catch up with you guys when you have a plan.'

On the train journey to London I found myself exhausted, maybe from blood loss, and dozed on and off the whole way. I would have guessed that any one of the day's revelations was sufficient to make sleep an impossibility, but somehow all of them together seemed to cancel out, as if they were all battling for my headspace, and I nodded off while they were fighting among themselves. I did wake up somewhere around Letchworth, though, and for long enough to marvel at the simple fact – well, simplish fact – that I had a daughter. True, among the infinite timelines of the future I had an infinity of children, but we humans care about what *is*, about what's in front of us. Untouchable realities are too academic. If a man is starving to death on our street we empty the larder to feed him. Move him to a country a thousand miles away and our compassion shrinks a hundredfold. Move a child to another universe and we cease to care.

I got home late having spent most of the day in a crowded A&E department full of noisy drunks and noisy children in equal measure. The doctor spent two minutes inspecting the wound and ten more scolding me for the idiocy I'd displayed in opting to discharge myself in Cambridge.

I managed to get past Mother without admitting to either my sword wound or my new diagnosis.

'You look terrible,' she'd exclaimed as I leaned into the living room on my way to bed.

'The student life,' I said. 'Wall-to-wall parties at this time of year. It'll all be over by next week. I just need sleep now.'

'Take some vitamins, get an early night and have a lie in.' She sounded concerned. There would be hell to pay when she found out I had to go back on chemo, but right now it felt like a fair price. Oddly, I felt as if I'd somehow let her down, that I'd failed at getting better and that it was my fault. I nodded and retreated to the stairs. Let her have another night not knowing.

The sleep that had come easily on the train eluded me for most of the night, despite the fact that I still felt achingly tired. My wound stung and itched. The glorious structures that Eva's equations had hinted at drifted behind my eyes, illuminating a restless mind. And every so often a darkness would loom, swallowing new ideas and pains alike with the cold certainty that my returning cancer would take me down on this second try. In one of these darknesses I remembered the girl I'd met during my first round of chemo. The chatterbox who didn't fall silent until the day she died. The girl I had searched for in the hospital and sat with on her last day. Her name was Eva. I think I must have named my daughter after her – to remember her struggle, and maybe to remind me to be kinder, better, less focused on my own worries.

I guess I slept, because I recall waking and those few glorious seconds where I remembered none of it, where I was just stretching beneath the covers in my own bedroom, safe and warm. Then like the jaws of a steel trap the whole thing closed around me once again and all I wanted was to leave the curtains drawn and sleep the day away.

In the end, it was fear of Simon's disapproving phone call that got me out of bed and into clothes. There were very few things that would move Simon to use the phone, but not showing up for D&D was one of them. And when it came to awkward phone calls, well, let's just say that Simon had a weapons-grade long silence.

I changed the dressing on my cut, replacing it with a bandage that a nurse at the A&E had given me amid the scold-storm. The cut seemed to be healing, but it still hurt like hell if I moved in a way that pulled on it. I got dressed slowly, as if I were sixty rather than sixteen. Some dark voice inside me suggested that I would never make sixty, so I may as well get in a little experience of being old now. I told that voice to shut up and that a universe of infinite possibility lay ahead of me. Some of the timelines running right from this moment held Nick Hayeses that lived to be a hundred. It comforted me a little, so long as I didn't let myself think of the odds.

Getting to Simon's posed a problem, since I didn't feel up to cycling and then remembered that I'd left my bike outside Tony's Cabs anyhow, and it was sure to have been stolen in the first hour of its abandonment. If I asked Mother for a lift she would assume I was ill and would have me down the doctors, and if I told her it was because I lost my bike she would give me grief over that, too.

In the end I remembered the roll of ten-pound notes Demus had pressed on me. I called a taxi from the phone box down by the bus stop and travelled in style.

'You're late.' Simon had the door open before I could finish the second of an intended three swift raps.

'I came by cab and it takes longer than cycling.' I followed him up the stairs, wondering how he knew to wait by the door. He must have been upstairs with the others, surely, and his room didn't have a view of the front street . . .

Simon stomped to his chair and sat down heavily while I greeted the rest of them. 'Hey, Mia. John.' There was something about Sam's face that made me want to punch it. Mostly it was how close his mouth got to Mia's on a regular basis, so it wasn't a very grown-up urge. But even so. 'Sam . . .'

Sam beamed at me as if we were best buddies. 'Nick! Take the weight off. You're looking tired.'

'I got cut with a sword.' I lifted my shirt to show the dressing. It sounded way more sexy than *my leukaemia came back*.

'Shit, man!' He sounded genuinely concerned. All those acting classes had paid off.

All I got out of Simon was a frown. John and Mia both rose from their seats for a closer look.

'How the hell did you do that?' Mia asked.

'It's pretty hard to cut your side with a sword,' John observed. 'Even for you, Nick. Besides, you don't have a sword. And if you do, can I borrow it?'

'It was some other idiot. An accident. I kinda fell into him.'

'You fainted again?' Mia looked worried.

'No.' I waved the idea off as though it were silly, and tried to imagine how she would look when she found out the real bad news. Guilty is how she'd look. And I didn't want that. Not at all. I scattered my dice across the table. All ones. I guess if the universe wanted to kill me, then pushing me to the extremes of every probability distribution was a good way to do it. I mean the universe didn't *desire* to kill me, not in a sentient or malicious sense. I was like a clog in a pipe with the pressure building up behind me. Something had to give. Either I got blown away or the pipe cracked and everything burst out. 'Let's play, shall we?'

We settled to the game. Mia and I both failed saving throws, meaning that our characters remained bound in mutual chemically induced adoration, the love potion refusing to loosen its hold on us.

Our party of bold adventurers soldiered on into the labyrinthine workshops of the famed alchemist, Mercuron. Making progress required overcoming the natural hazards of experimental alchemy: explosions, toxic fumes, the wandering and dangerously mutated survivors of potion testing. In addition we had to defeat the guards and other defences set in place by the Guild of the Hidden Eye, Mercuron's paymasters and owners in all but name.

Many of the encounters began with a fierce argument between our thief, Fineous, returning with news of what lay ahead, and our paladin, Sir Algernon, vehemently disagreeing with Fineous's cunning plan for dealing with the problem. Meanwhile my magic-user and Mia's cleric would canoodle at the back, the irony dripping off us like sweat, and John's fighter would roll his eyes while dropping heavy hints that maybe she could save some of her energies for healing his wounds.

The next stage of the process was typically Fineous and Algernon's argument growing loud enough to draw the attention of the opposition, rendering all planning moot as the enemy charged down the corridor towards us.

In Dungeons & Dragons, the alignment of your character plays an important role. Characters are temperamentally lawful, neutral or chaotic. They are also morally good, neutral or evil. It's a very crude assignment when projected on real life. I tend to think, for example, that everyone I like is in many senses 'good', and that few people are so shallow that they can be well categorised by so simple a system. *However*, if you forced my hand I would have said . . . Simon is lawful neutral, Mia is chaotic neutral, and John is chaotic good. Simon's own fascination with and respect for laws, be they technical, mathematical or legal, was the reason it took so long before Fineous came back to report with blood on his hands. His understanding of how lying worked was more theoretical than practical.

Sam, on the other hand, appeared to be lawful good through and through. Either that or just so dedicated to playing the saintly role of paladin that he was happy to see our mission crash and burn around us rather than bend the smallest rule or stray but a little from the path of righteousness.

We'd penetrated deep into the laboratory complex and left chaos in our wake. So many guards were searching the wreckage behind us that retreat had long since ceased to be an option. And we'd been waiting a worryingly long time for Simon's thief to return from scouting ahead.

'What's awaiting us, Sir Fineous?' Sir Algernon asked. He liked to call everyone 'sir', regardless of knighthoods earned or not.

'Well, I snuck along, quieter than a mouse in socks,' Fineous answered, 'keeping to the shadows, and came to a small guard chamber by a large blast-door. And there were two guards in there, big men in chain-mail armour, with swords that burned with a kind of black fire—'

'And your suggestion for dealing with the situation?' Sir Algernon queried dubiously.

'None,' Fineous said. 'We can all go forward and—'

'I am pleased to see that my moral instruction has had an effect upon you, Sir Fineous. I expected you to insist on some unworthy and underhand strategy. I misjudged you, brother. Forgive me.' Sir Algernon rubbed his chin. 'Hmmm.' He turned to John's fighter. 'A stern challenge awaits us, Sir Hacknslay.'

John shook his head. 'My warrior's barely standing. A goblin with a sharp stick could probably finish him off. Your paladin isn't doing much better. And the cleric's used all her healing . . .'

John was right. Our fighting force needed hospitalisation, not another battle. Sir Algernon's insistence on the fair fight had brought us to the edge of ruin.

Sam thumped the table in defiance. 'We must return to the fray once more. In the name of all that is good and honourable let us gird our loins and—'

'I wasn't finished,' Fineous interrupted. 'These two guards I told you about . . . they seemed to have had some kind of argument just before I arrived. One of them had stabbed the other in the back and then, overcome with remorse, poisoned himself. A tragedy.'

'Nice one!' Nicodemus the Mage swirled his robes. 'Well done, Si . . . I mean Fineous!'

'I knew it!' Sam got to his feet. 'All that dice rolling when Mia took you into the other room! I knew it! You murdered them!'

'Hold your horses, Sherlock.' John leaned back in his chair with an easy grin. 'You can't go accusing people without evidence. I find Fineous's report . . . entirely plausible.'

Sam scowled, rapping the table in irritation. 'He's lying! Hasn't your cleric got a *detect lie* spell, Mia?'

'No,' Mia lied.

'Anyway,' Simon continued. 'I noticed that the blast-door was unlocked—'

'Unlocked?' Sam snorted. 'You mean you picked the lock.'

'Unlocked.' Simon was getting good at this lying stuff. 'So I crept in and found a laboratory with an alchemist at work. He had some assistants stirring cauldrons and some kind of mechanical soldiers by the far door. I really think this could be Mercuron. I think we're this close to getting out of here at last.' Thumb and forefinger demonstrated how close. 'Anyway, I didn't want to tackle him myself, but I did find this on the floor close to where he was working. I think he may have dropped it.' He held up an imaginary something.

'Dropped? You stole it off him you . . . you . . . kleptomaniac!'

'What is it?' John asked.

Mia stepped in with the explanation. 'It looks a bit like a flattened gravy boat that has been cut in half and sealed closed. Fineous is holding the handle end. If it ever had a spout end then it is missing. The whole thing is made out of copper and has seen plenty of life. It's tarnished and dented.'

'Why would you even bring that back?' John asked.

'It fell out of a very hard-to-get-at pocket and was next to a pouch of gold,' Simon said. 'It has to be important.'

'Gold?' John sat up. 'I grab Fineous by the ankles and shake him until the gold falls out of him.'

'I draw my knife and dodge away!' Simon pulled his character figure away from John's warrior.

'You hear a distant clang like the sound of a door being thrown open,' Mia said. 'And the tramp of very heavy feet.'

'Shit, Mercuron's noticed you robbed him!' John shook his head. 'He's sent the mechanicals after us.'

'Si, throw me the thing!' I said.

'Fineous tosses Nicodemus the thing,' Simon said.

And while John and Simon rolled dice to determine the outcome of their chase, Mia drew me a picture of the thing. She came around the table and leaned over me to sketch it. Her proximity pricked against my cheek. The familiar scent of her made me want to reach out, take hold, press my face against her. Instead I kept rock still.

'What is it?' Sam asked, also leaning in and far less welcome.

'Is it heavy? Does it rattle or slosh?' I asked.

'It's heavier than you expect it to be, but doesn't rattle or slosh,' Mia said, standing back to admire her handiwork.

Simon and John paused their chase to look, both looking as confused as I felt.

'Is that a lid?' I pointed to something at the top.

'It's half a lid,' Mia said.

'I pull it off.' Sam tapped the drawing before anyone could stop him.

'No!' A protest from all the other players.

'The lid won't come off. Sir Algernon nearly jerks the object out of Nicodemus's hands while trying,' Mia said.

'What the hell is it?' John picked up the page and pored over it. 'To me it looks exactly . . . like . . . a . . . thing.' He slapped it down.

'Those footsteps are getting close,' Mia noted.

'Barricade that door!' I ordered.

We barely had it closed and barred before the first blow landed from the other side, shaking all the timbers in their frame.

'Come on, guys,' John said. 'What is this thing? Simon never forgets anything and Nick's got the biggest brain in Britain. The two of you must know the answer between you.'

We didn't.

While Sir Hacknslay and Mia's cleric held the splintering door closed, we argued back and forth about the weird object for ten minutes before, with the most annoyingly over-the-top laugh ever, Sam solved the puzzle.

'It's half of an oil lamp. It's a bit like the one we used in Aladdin.'

'I give it a rub,' I said recklessly, irritated at being out-thought by a trainee actor.

'There's a puff of smoke and a half-genie appears,' Mia said.

'Which half?' asked John.

'A half-genie, not half a genie.'

'So what does that look like?' I asked.

'Well . . .' Mia scanned her notes. 'You know how the books show them as a turbaned man with the lower half of his body a wisp of smoke?'

We nodded.

'This one is a turbaned woman and the lower three-quarters of her body are a wisp of smoke. She looks right at Nicodemus.' Mia placed a figure for the half-genie and moved her own character, the cleric, possessively in between Nicodemus and the new arrival. 'She looks right at Nicodemus as if she has been waiting forever to see him and she says, "Master, your limited wish is my command."'

'Limited wish?'

'She's only a half-genie.' Mia rolled a die. 'Also, the other door to the room you're in starts shaking as multiple blows rain down on it from outside.'

'A limited wish?' Across the table John slumped. 'What good is that then? They're coming at us from all sides and when Mercuron gets here . . .'

Simon nodded. 'It would be better if she granted full wishes. Three would be nice.'

Sam shook his head. 'You're all seeing the half-empty glass, guys. Let's have some positivity. This glass is half full. A limited wish could come in very handy.'

And as much as I hated to do it, I had to nod. Half a wish was much better than none. Life had been coming at me from all sides for some days now, and frankly any help, no matter how limited, would be welcome. Some situations are beyond fixing, but still there can be something to salvage. As Demus put it: *there's always hope*. It put me in mind of a song my father used to love, 'You Can't Always Get What You Want' by the Rolling Stones. In it Mick Jagger sang a lot of sense about compromise.

Simon's mum came in, opened a window, offered tea and observed that it would be much healthier for all of us to be out in the sunshine on a beautiful day like this instead of closeted in the twilight of a bedroom. Sam agreed a little too eagerly for my liking. He went downstairs with her, offering to help and clutching a teabag of his preferred brew, which seemed to be flavoured mainly with ill-smelling smoke.

Mia laid her Dungeon Master's screen over her books and maps, then made for the door. 'Be right back. No peeking.'

We grunted our agreement. Dungeons & Dragons was a game where cheating really made no sense at all.

'What even is a limited wish?' John asked, still seemingly unconvinced that our genie was even half useful.

'A seventh-level magic-user spell,' Simon said. 'It works like a wish spell but . . . less so. You don't get everything you want, or you do but it's only temporary, or you get what you ask for but there's a twist in the tail of it.'

John pursed his lips, then perked up as he remembered something. 'Tell us about this sword fight you lost then, Nick!'

I touched my side without thinking, and winced. 'Oddly, almost getting impaled on a navy officer's sword was only the third or fourth strangest thing to happen to me yesterday.' I remembered something myself, and frowned. 'You don't recall if Ian Rust had any brothers, do you?' John and Simon had both been at Maylerts from preparatory school days and had a longer association with the place than I did. 'An older brother, to be specific.'

John and Simon's faces changed as they always did at any mention of Ian Rust. We had all known instinctively that he was capable of murder during our shared time at school, known it long before he actually beheaded a man. John's cheeks stiffened, his lips narrowed, his eyes became guarded. 'He did have a brother in the sixth form, the upper sixth, just when we joined the school. Charlie. A high flier academically, I heard, but a bit of a nutter. Had all sorts of rules, and woe betide anyone who broke one. He hated little Ian though. Wasn't scared of him, but never raised a hand to him either. Got expelled over some run-in with the form teacher.'

'He went to the teacher's house, I heard.' Simon shuddered. 'Broke in when she was asleep.'

'Crap. Well, now he's one of the goons I've got on my case to make sure I do what the big boss says. They want me not to publish my work and they want to drive on with the experimental side of things before we really know what we're doing.'

'Sounds like the guild has its claws in you.' Simon tipped his dice from one fat-fingered hand to the other. 'Should we start calling you Mercuron now?'

I snorted but it wasn't really funny. 'Oh, and I found the anomaly. The real one. And she is *much* stranger than we imagined.' I reached into the pocket of the coat hanging off the back of my chair and pulled out Eva's photo. 'There she is.'

'Hot!' John leaned in, leering. 'That's the girl who you fainted over.' He nodded sagely before adding, 'I'd do her.'

I pulled my daughter's photo back before John could snatch it off me and dig himself a deeper hole. He was all mouth and no trousers, as Mrs B would say, but his casual declarations of lust seemed more shallow and less funny when the target was someone I cared about. Which in turn showed how shallow I was, I guess.

'What've you got there?' Mia returned from the loo just as I was pressing Eva's photo to my chest to keep it from John.

Like a guilty schoolboy caught by his teacher doing something he shouldn't, I showed her the picture.

'Pretty.' Mia arched an eyebrow. 'What's her name?'

'Eva.'

'Well.' Mia narrowed her eyes. 'I hope you're both very happy together.'

'It's not like—' I was going to say that it wasn't like that. But more questions would lead to the truth, and the truth would make one of them ask who Eva's mother was. And right now the last thing I wanted to tell Mia was that I had doomed two Earths to be torn apart, and had done so by having sex with Helen. Especially as I hadn't done it yet. 'She's just a friend.'

Sam chose that moment to return carrying a tray laden with mugs of tea, glasses of squash and Hobnob biscuits.

'Cute girl!' he said as I tried to hide the photo. 'I like what she's done with her hair.'

Mia's lips pressed into a hard line. I hoped Sam was going to pay for the comment, because I already knew I was going to.

CHAPTER 16

The morning after D&D I had to confess about the leukaemia. I call it a confession, as if I were guilty of something, because that's how it felt. The sun shone in through the kitchen windows, Mother was pottering about, getting her first of many cups of tea; it was peaceful, normal. And here I came with my big black bundle of bad news. Your son is sick. Probably going to die this time. How could I not feel guilty telling any mother that? And this was *my* mother that I was having to hurt on a sunny morning over tea and toast. But as much as I knew about time, and that was a lot, I knew of no good time to tell her.

I went to stand beside her as she reached for her cup. Closer than I normally would. She paused and looked up, questioning. I looked away, towards the back garden, the bright rooftops. I'm not good with strong emotion. For most people, if you plot how their emotion grows in response to increasingly stressful situations you have some kind of a ramp – make things twice as bad and they get twice as anxious, tearful, sad etc. With me it's more like a step function. You get nothing, nothing, nothing, and then suddenly all of it, too much. We had a tap like that in the bathroom. Broken washer. So I try to steer my life away from situations where I might suddenly break down. It can be embarrassing watching movies, too. One minute everyone thinks I'm a heartless bastard for not even sniffing when something sad happens . . . then it gets just that bit worse and I'm hitching in my breath, trying to stifle sobs, and the people who thought I was heartless now think I'm too soft.

'I saw Dr Pritchard in Cambridge. I have to go back on chemo.' I managed to say it all without my voice breaking, though it trembled at the end. I was close to that step function, right on the edge. A single kind word from my mother and I would fall apart.

Thankfully, whatever she had going on inside, she managed to respond in a bright, albeit somewhat brittle, businesslike voice. 'Right then. When's the first session? I'll call in to work and drive you.'

She phoned Dr Parsons, the doctor who first broke the news to me back in January. I was booked in for a session that evening, an overnight stay the first time. The same ward where I met the other Eva, on day one of my treatment.

I had been scheduled to return to Cambridge on the midday train, but instead I retreated to my room and lay with pen and paper, alternating between doodling in the margins and recreating some of the theory my daughter had sketched out for me two days before. I'll admit that I played my Sisters of Mercy tape too loudly, daring Mother to complain, and wallowed in the darkness of the lyrics. But frankly I felt by that stage that I deserved some self-indulgence and self-pity.

Eventually, after the third run through my mixtape of concentrated nihilistic angst, Mother's voice made it up the stairs. I spun the volume knob and Sisters of Mercy's 'Temple of Love' dwindled to a whisper.

'What?' I yelled back, full of unfocused anger and ready for a fight. She surprised me. 'There's someone at the door for you.'

I came down with a mixture of reluctance and curiosity. I didn't want to see anyone and nobody had said they were coming over. The thought that it might be Mia or Eva got me down the stairs. My best guess was that it would be John, though. Whatever his faults, he seemed to have a sixth sense for when his friends were hurting.

'Hello, Nick.' Charles Rust stood framed by the front doorway, his sharp black eyes finding me on the stairs before I could retreat. He beckoned me forward as though I were a reluctant child, his smile narrow and malicious.

With mounting anger I descended the remaining steps. The bastard was here, an inch shy of actually being in my house, again, talking to my mother. The cancer news had burned through me now, leaving behind it a reckless sense of being beyond other threats. This grinning monster on my doorstep had picked the wrong day to fuck with me.

As I set foot on the tiled hall floor I noticed the Harrods bag in his left hand, bulging with its own threats and promises. It gave me pause, but still my anger lent me the momentum to reach him with harsh words on my lips, albeit delivered in a strained whisper so Mother wouldn't be dragged into this. 'What the hell are you doing here? Is this because Guilder wanted me at that experiment? You can tell him I'll quit entirely if I see you here again.' I found myself poking my finger accusingly at his chest to help make my point.

Rust reached up, snake-quick, and caught my finger in his hand, twisting it. The pain was so excruciating it paralysed my chest and escaped as a hiss.

'Nick and I are going for a short walk, Mrs Hayes,' Rust called out to my mother, who had retired to the front room. 'I'll bring him back in a minute.' He lowered his voice. 'Tell her.'

'Back in a minute,' I called out in as normal a voice as I could manage.

'We have bigger fish to fry than your failure to keep appointments.' He led me off, prisoner to my trapped finger, all my dark thoughts and pondering on bleak futures blown away by the agony of the here and now. A lesson of sorts. Things are never so bad that they can't get worse.

We halted in the shade of a tree just beyond the garden gate. Rust eased his hold but didn't release my finger. It was an oddly intimate sensation, deeply unpleasant and underwritten with the imminent threat of sudden pain. 'You want to remember your place in the food chain, young Nick. You have a debt to my employer, and thus to me. I have no debt to you.'

I glared at him, but didn't dare contradict him. If he broke my finger they would probably have to delay the chemotherapy. And besides, I really didn't want to find out what someone breaking my finger felt like.

'Now, in my capacity as investigator of all things "you" on my employer's behalf, I've had occasion to sit down with the collated information gathered so far.

'It seems that a friend of yours, one Elton Arnot, lost his father recently. The gentleman in question met a violent end in a factory. This may seem a matter of no great importance. Fathers die all the time, don't they, Nick?' Another twist. 'But by strange chance, I happen to have a particular interest in this factory. Mr Arnot was not the only person to be found dead when the cleaner arrived the next morning. One of the corpses was my own rather dim little brother, and the third was what the Americans like to call a John Doe – an unknown person. He was then, and still is now, a mystery. This despite fingerprints and photographs.'

A car drove slowly by and Rust levered me around the tree to shield us from unwanted attention. Even in my suffering I found it amazing how much control he was able to exert over me by taking possession of just one finger. I made a mental note never to poke anyone again. It would be a fist to the face or nothing.

'Anyway, I must let you get back to your mother.' He offered that narrow, predatory smile of his, very reminiscent of his brother's. 'Only, although I never liked young Ian, it's not really something I can let stand, if you see what I mean. It's something in the debit column, and that always has to be accounted for.'

'Could you—' I wanted to ask for my finger back but Rust just bent it further, and gazed down the street without seeming to see it.

'Actually the little shit nearly killed me with a kitchen knife on my twelfth birthday. If the blade had been an inch longer it would have taken my eye . . . Even so, he was my blood, so it's as if somebody took something from me, and when somebody takes from me they have to pay. Rules have to be obeyed. You can see that, can't you, Nick? Otherwise it would be chaos out there.' He pressed his fingertips along his cheekbone just below the eye he nearly lost. 'On the other hand, if he had managed to stab me in the face I would probably be thanking whoever killed him for making an end of him. That's how the world works, see? Debts and obligations.'

'Uh.' I tried to distract him if only to lessen the pressure and the pain. 'You'd have killed him yourself if he'd done that. Stabbed you in the face, I mean.'

Rust eased up a little. 'You've not met our father.' He shook his head, eyes narrowing, perhaps with a touch of fear at the corners. 'Debts and obligation. I would never have laid a finger on that boy. No sir. Not even then.' He paused. 'Speaking of fingers . . . Tell me about this John Doe that died in the same room as my brother.'

I fought the need to kneel as he increased the twist, sending white-hot pain streaking through my whole hand. 'I don't know anything—'

'I think maybe you do, though,' Rust said. 'You see, the file I got to study had police photos of the corpses. Poor Mr Arnot. Dim little Ian. And a bald man. And there was something about baldy that made my brain itch. Itched for a long time. You know how that is. Then finally you can scratch it. See, he looked a bit like you, Nick. About the age your dad would be if he wasn't dead. Your look around the eyes . . . the nose . . . the mouth. I have the photos here if you'd like to see . . .' He patted at his pockets. 'So, what do you know about our John Doe, Nick?'

'Nothing.' It was a one-word lie, but I managed to make it sound unconvincing, even to me.

'Do you know what DNA is, Nick?'

I grunted my yes.

'Of course you do, you went to a fine school. I happen to know it well. I'm sure you got a solid education. But what you are less likely to know about unless you pay close attention to the news is that earlier this year, for the first time ever, police were able to secure a conviction on the basis of what's called a DNA fingerprint. Linked two murders together just like that.' He twisted my finger, only a fraction, but enough to make me gasp. 'Stop me if I go too fast for you, Nick.'

I gritted my teeth against the pain. I couldn't believe he was getting away with this in a residential street, in front of my own house, with my neighbours going about their lives on the other side of a few dozen windows.

He relented, reducing the pressure. 'So, this DNA, it always tells the truth. Reliable science instead of unreliable witnesses. My employer owes me some favours. All I need is a little of your blood and to lean on the right people and we can soon find out if this John Doe is related to you. But that would be slow, and boring and costly. More fun to just hurt you until you tell me yourself.'

He twisted and I cried out. 'S-stop!' I hated to beg, but the pain was past bearing.

'Who's the John Doe, Nick?'

'I don't know!'

'Did he kill my brother?' A savage twist that would have wrung the truth from me if I still remembered it.

'I don't know!'

'No? Perhaps we should stand here breaking fingers until you *do* know. You can do your work with one hand – you don't strictly need two for mathematics.' He bent my finger, forcing me to cry out again and drop to my knees. 'You're going to tell me all you know now, aren't you?'

'Yes!' I shouted. 'Stop it! Stop it!'

There was a loud crack and suddenly he did stop. His grip slipped, nails tearing at my hand as it fell away.

I thought for a moment that my finger bone had snapped, but as Rust gracefully folded on to the dog-soiled earth around the base of the tree, I realised I wasn't hurt. Demus stood there with a broken branch in hand.

'It was lying in number 15's drive.' He shrugged apologetically.

I stood, still shaky, and looked down at Rust. He was clutching his head and cursing softly, dazed but already trying to get to his feet.

'Come on!' Demus made off towards his car.

I followed, bundling into the passenger seat. Looking back, I saw that Rust had managed to stand, though was still bent double, one hand on his thigh, the other pressed to his head wound; and that Mother had come to the door, still in shadow so I couldn't see her face to read her expression.

Demus drove off swiftly, but managing to avoid a squeal of tyres. 'What the hell was that about?'

Twisting in my seat, I saw that Rust was staggering across the road, presumably aiming for his own car. That was good, as it meant he wasn't going to turn on Mother, but bad for us. 'Drive faster!'

Demus slung his BMW around the corner into the next street. 'So? Who did I hit?'

I looked down at my aching finger, still bleeding from where Rust's nails had torn the skin. 'That was Ian Rust's older brother, Charles. He works for Guilder and—'

'Yes, I know all about Guilder. My memories of me coming back didn't include me telling you, though. So I didn't. But now we've gone totally off script, I don't suppose it matters any more. I know Charles Rust. Just didn't recognise him from behind.'

'He's the shit who broke in and went through the house.'

'He's done a lot worse than that.' Demus sounded nervous. 'I'm glad I hit him. Wish I'd done it harder and knocked his eye out.'

'Eye?' I asked, puzzled. 'You mean eyes?'

It was Demus's turn to look confused. He covered one eye with his hand. 'Charles Rust wears an eye patch. Always has.'

I shook my head. 'Nope, he has a full set.'

A frown. 'Things must have started to diverge when Eva came back.'

'Eva! So you've met her now.'

'I have.' Demus turned into a residential street close to Richmond Park and pulled over. There was no sign of pursuit. 'I met her in

Cambridge. She's a remarkable young woman.' He sounded proud of her. 'Cleverer than us, but let's keep that one quiet.'

I nodded. If I was going to be upstaged mathematically, then having the person to do it be my daughter was the best option. That still didn't mean I had to like it, though.

'So,' I asked. 'How did it go?'

'Well, I think they're going to have to repair a few electricity substations and replace an awful lot of burned-out wiring. Let's just say that the meeting wasn't gentle on the timeline. We actually managed to call down lightning!' He shuddered. 'Not fun.'

'I mean, how did it go? You know . . .' I didn't think I should have to explain what I meant to myself.

'Ah, right.' He grinned. 'Well . . . she's something. It's pretty weird to discover you have a fully grown daughter. I mean, weirder for you, being as she's your age.'

'Older than me, in fact.'

'Right. A year or two either way doesn't seem like such a big deal in your forties. You're both kids. Anyway, I guess for me it was no stranger than those sperm donors who suddenly have an unknown young man or woman showing up on their doorstep saying, "Hi, Dad." But that's not to say it wasn't strange.'

I wanted to ask Demus if he had kids with Mia, but I knew it was better not to know, even if his past was no longer my future. Instead I asked about Eva's work. 'Can her paradox stuff help us sort this out? I mean, even if you do save your Mia by going back to January, the whole timeline she exists in is going to get ripped to shreds along with Eva's . . . according to Eva.'

Demus pursed his lips and gazed over the steering wheel. 'She certainly has a better grip on it than I do. I knew something was missing from my equations. All those strange effects when we first met, for example. None of that was in my calculations. But I never understood that it was down to paradox, or that my timeline was bound to a second one.'

'Can you explain the ghosts?' I asked.

'Ghosts?' He frowned. 'You mean the time echoes we see when we meet?'

'No – like poltergeists, book-throwing, writing on windows, honest-to-God ghosts! You don't remember being haunted?'

Demus shook his head. 'I'm out of my time, out of my timeline, caught in paradox. I've edited my memories. I barely know what's real any more, Nick. I see the world but it doesn't stick. All I am is this scrapbook of memory, fading, twisting as if it were written in smoke. I guess that's all any of us are, but for me it seems more tenuous each day.'

I think that might have been the first time I really understood, at the core of me, that Demus and I were the same man. He talked to me as if he were talking to himself, maybe even as if he were running the lines in his head without any intention to speak them aloud.

'I guess they're like stronger versions of the time echoes,' I volunteered.

'Could be. Leakage from timelines very close to ours. Frustrated possibilities given reality by the stray energy of the paradox. Let's leave the proof to Eva.' Demus grinned again, recovering his humour. 'Anyway, she and I were able to pinpoint the moment of paradox and, unsurprisingly, you're at the heart of it, Nick.'

'Should you be telling me this?'

'I don't think it matters. It might even help. It all boils down to the upcoming May Ball at Trinity.'

'I'm not even going to that.' I had already decided to pass on the chance to watch Helen twirl around the ballroom with Piers Winthrop. He looked like a male model who also happened to captain the rugby team. Even his name sounded as if it was shaken out of *Debrett's* having formerly belonged to Biggles's wingman.

'You're going. You do it in both timelines.'

'I don't even have anyone to go with.'

'You invite your friends, duh.'

'Well, I guess John would come, and then while Helen slow-dances with Piers, I can also watch John get off with the second prettiest girl at the ball. Whoop.'

'The big picture here is slightly larger than your . . . our . . . unrequited love and sulky teen attitude. Besides, you're a rock star, albeit of mathematics. And this is Cambridge. You'll have to take a stick along to beat off the nerd girls.'

'Now I *know* you deleted your entire memory of going to university . . .'

'Anyway, you're inviting Mia and Simon too.'

'Mia who hates me and Simon who would rather die than socialise?'

'She doesn't hate you. They both just need the right motivation to go.'

'Like a gun to the head for Simon?'

'Like knowing you need his help. You have Charlie Rust on your case, after all. Though I'm not sure why.'

'It's all to do with . . . actually, best you don't know. Though I'm not sure why you would go ahead with your plan any more. You could just go back to your time now. Everything's messed up.'

'Ah!' He quirked his mouth in that way I sometimes do, a strange mixture of sad and excited. 'Well, the thing is that we might just be able to put everything back on track.'

I guess I made that same quirk of the mouth. I was due for chemotherapy that evening and if I had to go through that shit again, a guaranteed twenty-five years seemed the very least I wanted to accept as pay-off, rather than dying by degrees and finally checking out aged twenty-one or even earlier. On the other hand, some part of me had relished being free of Demus's life, especially having to know when and roughly where my life would end. 'How could everything be fixed?'

'Eva calls it a phase shift, but you and I are going to call it a time hammer.'

'That does sound . . . more impressive. What is it?'

'Well, you take this big hammer and hit time with it just at the right moment and bingo, two paradoxical timelines untangle. And the shake-up sets both back to how they would have been.'

'What's the hammer?'

'It's the difficult part.'

'How difficult?'

From Demus's frown, my guess was 'very'. 'I'm going to have to break into a nuclear power station.'

'Fuck that! The guards there have guns!' I didn't know if that were true, but they probably did, and if they didn't then they should.

Demus shrugged. 'I was going to have to use a power station anyway, just to jump me onwards . . . or backwards . . . to our first meeting in January.'

'So . . . you break into a nuclear power station and . . . do what?'

'I'll need to reconfigure the reactor. I have to put it into overdrive to generate a pulse of current big enough to power the electromagnets that I'll have ready.'

'Sounds like you're planning a meltdown. Jesus, this isn't going to be another Chernobyl, is it?' It had been eight weeks since the explosion and the papers were still full of the fallout drifting from the Soviet Union. Apparently we had radioactive sheep in Wales now.

'Let's just say that the needles will be heading into the red. Should be fine, though.'

'This gets worse and worse . . .'

'Well, I remember myself turning up in January, so it must work,' said Demus. 'At least the part of it that throws me back another six months must work. I've been planning that bit for quite a while now. And I do have loads of money. Which helps.'

'So that's the hammer. Where does it have to hit, and when?' I asked.

'Bradwell is where.' Demus set a finger to the dashboard as though there were an invisible map there. I'd never heard of the place. 'It's going to be the first nuclear power station in the UK to be decommissioned.

By 2010 it's just a collection of highly dangerous nuclear waste in a bunch of holding pools and glorified warehouses. But right now its main benefit is that it's close. On the coast halfway between Cambridge and London. We need to strike as close to the event as possible.'

'And the when?'

'That's tricky.'

'I thought the breaking into a nuclear power station and reconfiguring the reactor would be the tricky part.'

'Well, the thing is that in one timeline you leave the Trinity May Ball with Helen, marry her at nineteen and five months later become the proud father of young Eva Hayes. Which is all fine and dandy, except for the part where you die two years later. And in the other timeline you leave the ball with Mia and twenty-five years later she has a terrible accident that sends me back here to make sure she recovers her mind.' Demus checked the mirror and put the car back into gear. 'So the tricky part is determining the crucial moment where that choice exists and hangs in the balance. Plus you have to remember that it may not be your choice that causes the paradox. And having determined the exact moment, we need to get it to coincide with the hammer blow that I'm striking against the universe down in Bradwell. On the scale of the universe, that blow is almost nothing, so it only has a chance of untangling two things as vast as timelines if it is struck close, both in time and space, to the event that tangles them. So yes, the whole thing is . . . tricky.' He drove off smoothly. 'I guess we'd better get you back to Mother now.'

'Yeah,' I said unenthusiastically. 'I've got to get to my chemo session.'

Demus turned the corner and winced. 'Sorry about that, mate, but I had to do it, too. It's shitty but you endure it, not because you're a hero, just because there's no better choice.' Demus set a hand briefly to my shoulder. I guess it was a form of self-pity, but actually it did make me feel a bit better.

'Anyway, chemo isn't the only thing on the to-do list,' he said. 'You've also got to arrange the most important double date in the history, and future, of mankind.'

CHAPTER 17

Demus dropped me off at the end of my street and watched for any signs of Charlie Rust as I walked back to the house.

'What on earth was that all about?' Mother didn't let me get as far as the stairs.

'Academics,' I half-lied. 'My work is getting quite well known now. I think we might be getting a lot more of these sorts of visits. Those two I don't want to speak to again. I've answered their questions and have nothing more to say to them. Best to just not open the door to anyone you don't know.'

'I didn't get a good look at the man who drove you away, but something about him seemed very familiar. I rather feel I *do* know him.' Mother frowned. 'Anyway, it all seemed very odd.' She was anything but stupid, but who knows what fame entails until it actually happens to them or to someone close to them?

I left her puzzling in the hall and went up to my bedroom. I no longer had an appetite for the self-indulgence of angst-laden new wave bands. The mood had not survived the harsh-edged reality of Rust's threats or Demus's can-do refusal to quit. Instead I returned to my work.

Trying to figure out how to get Simon and Mia to the Trinity May Ball was beyond me, but on the subject of high-dimensional topological manipulation of space-time manifolds I felt much more confident. Eva had filled my head with new ideas and I was eager to chase them across the landscape of my imagination.

'Nick!' Mother's voice reached me from downstairs to drag me from my thoughts. I looked up. A plate with an untouched apple, sandwiches, milk and crisps sat to one side of me. I didn't even remember Mother bringing it in. 'Nick!'

'Coming!' I stood, my legs aching from sitting too long. The clock said four. Hours had flown past.

'Someone's here for you.' Mother met me on the stairs. She lowered her voice. 'I don't think he's an academic. More musical theatre, if you ask me.' A smile.

I followed her to the front room where a dark-haired someone was sitting in the comfy chair that had its back to the door. My visitor got to his feet.

'Sam?' I blinked. Sam came a very long way down the list of people I might have guessed would turn up at my house. Though in truth it wasn't that long a list. 'What are you doing here?' It was a pretty blunt question, but in my defence I was taken by surprise.

'I'll leave you boys alone,' Mother said, heading off to the kitchen.

Sam's grin was a touch less confident than usual. He was dressed with his usual flamboyance – a mauve shirt with a slight sheen, tight jeans whose label probably would have impressed someone who knew about brands of jeans, boots with heels and toes sharp enough to get a whelk out of its shell, an earring glittering in one earlobe. His hairsprayed quiff bounced slightly as he nodded to the other comfy chairs, inviting me to sit.

I took the hint and forced a smile. 'So, what brings you to this neck of the woods?' I sounded like my father.

Sam waited until the chair had swallowed as much of me as it was going to take. 'It's a bit awkward.' He hesitated and then, seeing that

I wasn't going to throw him a rope, ploughed on. 'I wanted to talk to you about Mia.'

I started to bristle, almost rising from my seat. 'You want advice from me? About Mia?' I thought that, all things considered, I'd gone above and beyond in my efforts to accommodate Sam. He was in our D&D game, for Christ's sake, but I was damned if I was going to give him tips on keeping hold of my girlfriend. 'I really don't—'

'I met Mia a couple of years ago through my friend Elton,' Sam pressed on.

'I know Elton.' I used to know him, at least. Hadn't seen him for months now. He didn't trust me to keep his surviving family safe from all the crazy in my life. 'I'm still not sure what you want.'

Sam leaned towards me in his chair in that slightly over-intimate way of his. 'Do you believe in love? I mean, in finding the love of your life?'

'Uh . . .' He was speaking in song lyrics as far as I was concerned. I didn't believe in love, not the instant infatuation, the Disney fiction. But I could hardly deny it was powerful stuff. The adult me died for it. And according to my daughter, love had put the whole of Sam's existence and that of the timeline he lived in at risk. Worlds hung in the balance simply because of the fact that a moment existed where I could turn one way and spend my life with Helen, or the other and spend it with Mia. 'I'm not sure what—'

'I mean, you should know, shouldn't you?' Sam said. 'When you first see the person that you're going to spend your life with. There should be a kind of electric shock. A thrill that runs through you.'

'I guess. I mean . . . most of us are just wondering if we have a chance and how far we'll get.' Though even as I said it, I realised that I was channelling John. There *had* been something with both Helen and Mia. A cynic might say it was just because I met so few girls. But there had been *something*. Not a literal shock. Not calling the lightning down, like when Demus met Eva. But something, a spark, a moment of recognition . . . 'Maybe you're right, though. I really don't know. I'm not exactly Mr Experienced here.'

'Mia asked me out, you know?'

'Uh, that must be nice.' I still couldn't quite get my head around the idea that Sam could be so self-absorbed as to come here seeking advice on his relationship from me.

'But it's you she's always talking about.'

'Oh.'

'I mean me and Mia, we're not really . . . I mean, we're good friends, but we don't really do anything . . .'

'You don't?' I wasn't entirely sure what he was saying, and couldn't quite bring myself to ask.

'What I think,' Sam said, 'is that you two should talk more. Some would be a start.'

'What sort of things does she say about me?'

'Well . . .' Sam frowned and shrugged. 'You know, with Mia it can all be a bit chaotic. Sometimes I'm not sure when she's talking about real life or some space-age D&D game you lot must have played before I knew you. I mean, I try to be open to all the new ideas . . . you know, like crystals and meditation and stuff. But there's a lot of weird things she says about fate and who you're going to turn into, and who she's going to become, and time and destiny. . . Goes over my head, if I'm honest.'

'So you think I should talk to her?' It didn't sound like something I would be good at.

Sam nodded. 'Definitely. She didn't say much, but I could tell she was upset about your new girlfriend.'

'My new . . . ?'

'You know. The girl in the photo?' He smiled a faint smile. 'Did you get that electricity when you first saw her?'

'Like you wouldn't believe!' The entire laboratory had short-cir-cuited. 'I mean no, not like that!'

Sam looked confused. I was rather glad there hadn't been any spark of the sort he meant. Finding myself attracted to my daughter, whatever the circumstances, would have been very hard to swallow. I never wanted to be that person.

'Well . . .' Sam leaned in even closer across the coffee table. 'I really think you two should talk. I just don't know how to arrange it.'

'I appreciate the thought, dude.' I almost never said 'dude'. It was just a sign of how awkward the conversation was. 'But Mia and I did a lot of talking. Too much, maybe. And this is where it got us.'

'Time heals all wounds.' Sam offered the old cliché.

'Time causes a lot of them, too.'

'If you just took her somewhere new . . . broke out of the old cycle . . . maybe you two could fix things up?'

I was about to opine that Sam was the worst boyfriend ever when my brain shook off the amazement that had clogged it thus far and kicked in with an idea. 'Sam, how would you like to take Mia to a ball in Cambridge? A posh honest-to-God dress-up-to-the-nines ball? Evening gowns and dinner jackets?'

His eyes lit up, and I knew I had him.

By the time I'd sent Sam on his way, Mother was waiting with the car keys, ready to take me to hospital. Technically I was old enough to go to the adult wards at Ealing General, but since I had started my treatment at the Chelsea and Westminster Children's Hospital and was only just over sixteen, I was allowed to do my second round in the same ward that I did my first in.

I led the way in. The place was full of kids. I guessed it would stop me feeling too sorry for myself – some of them couldn't have been ten yet. They kept the really little ones on a ward down the hall. Some of those were barely old enough to walk. It would have broken my heart to have to work there every day, but I felt unutterably glad that people existed who could shoulder that heavy burden.

Mother saw me settled in, my books and snacks arranged on the bedside table. Not that I felt like eating. My stomach had clenched itself into a sick knot, like it already knew what was coming.

The familiar antiseptic reek of the hospital began to infect my sinuses. The clean white efficient lie, the illusion of control as left and right children slipped through the grasp of nurse and doctor alike, falling into their sickness.

'I'll pick you up at noon tomorrow, dear,' Mother said, checking her watch. 'Dr Ellard said you'll be able to come back for the remaining sessions during the day, and leave within the hour if there are no adverse reactions.'

I grunted. The medical profession's view of what was 'adverse' differed considerably from mine. Going bald I considered adverse. I didn't believe the words 'mild' and 'vomiting' were ever meant to be put next to each other, unless by 'mild' you meant the type of beer, and you set the word after 'vomiting' rather than before. I also didn't feel that veins itching on the inside was a tolerable side effect.

'I'll see you tomorrow then.' Mother's eyes shone and her brittle tone reminded me that she needed me to be strong. Otherwise I'd just end up pushing her over her own emotional step-function into an embarrassing breakdown.

'I'll be fine.' I reached out and squeezed her hand.

She nodded, squeezed back and left.

That was fine. I could handle this. I could do it alone. Alone was good. Me versus my disease. I'd always faced my challenges alone. There wasn't anyone alive but me who could wrestle the truth from the mathematics that stood between me and breaking time. At least not until Eva arrived. I was used to tackling invisible enemies alone and coming out on top.

'Medicine time.' At the far end of the ward a thickset nurse wheeled in the steel trolley laden with the bags containing the chemo drip, the same lambent yellow that haunted my dreams. She and a colleague set to hooking up the first two children. And suddenly I felt far more alone than I ever wanted to be.

I'd set maths aside and was elbow-deep in my ultimate comfort read, *The Lord of the Rings*, when someone called my name. I looked up to see John and Mia closing on my bed. Behind them came Simon, and bringing up the rear, Elton, looking uncharacteristically self-conscious, darting looks at the bald kids to either side.

'Nick!' John grabbed one of the two plastic and tubular steel chairs, both of which looked to have been swiped from our old classroom, and sat down heavily. 'What is this shit?' He waved a hand at me, at the drip stand beside the bed, the line feeding it into the veins of my arm.

Mia came to the bed before I could answer. 'Leave him alone.' She took my hand. 'Seriously, though, you should have told us.'

Simon took the opportunity to take the remaining chair and stared at me accusingly as if leukaemia were my secret plan to inconvenience him. It was just how he was. At the core, though, I knew I could rely on him.

'You got through this before, man. You'll do it again.' Elton slapped my shoulder and backed off.

'I thought—' The words dried in my mouth. Elton's dad had died and although I didn't remember the details, at least some of it was on my hands.

'Just 'cos I can't hang out with you don't mean I don't care what happens to your skinny arse.' Elton shook his head, half a smile showing.

Embarrassed by how grateful that made me, I asked Mia a question instead. 'Maybe I should have told you. But I didn't. So who *did* tell you?'

'Your mother, of course.'

An excess of emotion huffed out of me as my chest contracted. The others tactfully gave me a moment. 'Thanks for coming, guys. It means a lot to me.' I looked around. 'Sorry about the chairs. Maybe you could ask—'

'I could stand all day.' Elton smacked his legs and grinned. 'Body of a Greek god! You didn't forget that, surely?'

I laughed out loud at that. Mia laughed too. She went and scrounged two more chairs and soon all four of them were huddled around my bed, me the focus of their attention. The thing about hospitals is that they eat conversation. There's something about being there under the bright lights with beds crowding to either side that makes every attempt to spark a new line of discussion peter out into an awkward silence.

'So . . .' John said, as his D&D anecdote about what a dick Sam was died an uncomfortable death under Mia's hard stare.

I let the silence stretch. I shouldn't have left a mate hanging, but I kinda did. I could have pitched in to help make fun of Sam, but since his visit earlier that day I'd begun to see all of Sam's actions in a much more positive light. I didn't really feel like trashing him just because he was a more committed role-player than the rest of us.

'So . . .' I echoed John, and lacking any other conversational gambit I began to tell them all the truth about Eva.

CHAPTER 18

'That's crazy! You've got a daughter!' Elton shook his head.

'A hot daughter,' John added.

'That explains the anomaly.' Simon seemed unimpressed with the whole 'daughter' bit and instead focused his interest on the temporal implications.

'You marry some Cambridge student?' Mia frowned, obviously piecing together what that meant for us. 'So all that stuff Demus said . . . ?'

'Well, it seems unlikely now. I mean he's still trying to "fix" things, but I've no idea if it will work. Most likely is that although both things will happen, it won't be me they happen to, just another version of me. I am infinite, you know.' I grinned sardonically. 'Just like you.'

Mia pressed her lips together into a thin line, crooked at the side, like her mouth went when she was puzzling through something she wasn't sure she approved of. 'And what happens to you in this . . . Helen timeline? Do you . . . are you OK?'

'It doesn't matter what happens to me if I do this or if I do that. That's no way to live. When I roll the dice I don't want me or anyone else to already know what the result will be—'

'It'll be ones.' Simon held out a twenty-sided die to prove his point.

'That's just a side-effect of the universe trying to kill me.' I waved his hand away. 'I'll make my choices based on how I feel, on gut instinct and past evidence, like everyone else does. I can't be responsible for a billion billion future versions of me, or for particular versions of me that happen to come back for a chat. I'm done with it. I—'

'Wait. What?' Mia, whose smile had been growing throughout my declaration of independence, now frowned. 'The universe is trying to kill you?'

'A little bit,' I admitted. 'It's the statistical anomaly thing. I keep getting into fatal situations.'

'Like what?'

'Uh, falling plant pots, exploding chip shops, that sort of thing.'

'That. Sort. Of. Thing?' Mia repeated.

'Don't forget the sword thrust,' Simon added helpfully. 'And the car crashes.'

'Car crashes. Plural?' Mia scowled at Simon, then returned her glare to me.

'Hey.' I held up both hands. 'I wasn't in any of the cars. They just kinda . . . swerved at me.'

'Why is the universe trying to kill you?' Elton's usually open, friendly face had become guarded.

'Well. If I don't die before the Trinity May Ball tomorrow, then I cause a paradox that will destroy Eva's timeline and Demus's timeline about thirty-two years from now.'

Elton stood and set a hand to my shoulder. 'You know I love you, man, but I gotta go. I can't be part of this. I got my mum—'

'I know.' I patted his hand before he withdrew it. 'Thanks for coming. It meant a lot.'

Elton nodded, eyes bright, and left, his stride that of a man unsure whether he should run or turn back.

'So just don't go to the ball, Cinderella.' John took Elton's seat and moved in closer. 'No paradox, no worlds ending. Everyone's happy.'

'I wish it worked like that.' I sat up straighter and began to draw lines in the air with my finger. 'Demus and Eva came back to this timeline thinking that it's their own. Demus thinks so because he remembers coming back, and Eva thinks so because her timeline is bound to Demus's and she's done the sums to prove it. But, like Cinderella, if I don't go to the ball I ruin everything. If I don't go it means that Demus is deluded, his memories are false, and Eva got her sums wrong. It means that this isn't either of their timelines, let alone the root of both of them, and that nothing they do here can save the existence of the worlds they came from.'

'But if you don't go it means that the universe no longer has an imbalance to correct,' Simon said. 'It'll stop trying to kill you.'

'That sounds good to me.' John nodded.

'Me too,' Mia said.

It didn't sound too bad to me, either, but I shook my head. 'I can't do that to them. Or to their Earths. That's billions of people.' Even as I said it I knew that it wasn't the billions of people I cared about. It wasn't a baby in Argentina, it wasn't the Amazon rainforest or a giant turtle, baby seal, pristine wilderness or whatever that I wanted to save. I was as shallow as anyone else. What mattered to me were the people I knew, had met, had touched. Two possible Earths out of an infinity were an academic concept. Future Earths pour out of every decision every one of us takes. Every roll of every die, real or imagined, creates a bunch of them. What mattered to me were Eva and Demus. They were *now*. They were real, concrete, touchable. 'I have to go to this damn ball and I need you guys to come with me. I've got enough tickets and—'

'No way.' Simon shook his head.

'So, Si's in,' I said. 'How about you, John?'

'You bet. I can borrow my dad's DJ.'

'I still don't think you should go,' Mia said.

'But I *am* going. So are you going to come and keep an eye on me, or leave that duty to Simon—?'

'I'm not going,' he repeated.

'To Simon, John and . . . Helen?'

Mia harrumphed and folded her arms. 'I don't even have a dress.'

I lifted my pillow to reveal Demus's roll of notes. 'There are some benefits to having time-travelling friends,' I said.

'I'll think about it,' she said.

'Can we play now?' Simon asked.

'Play?' I frowned.

'Of course,' John said. 'You didn't think Simon came all the way to this miserable hospital just to see you, did you?'

With an audience of sick children, my bed as the playing area, and a kidney dish for rolling dice in, we set to a quick spot of D&D. There is of course no such thing as a quick D&D session, but ours lasted a mere hour, which is the blink of an eye compared to the usual.

With Sam absent, the control of Sir Algernon fell to Mia along with her cleric and of course the running of the whole game. Having so much on her plate, it wasn't surprising that she needed a little prompting.

'Saving throws first,' said Simon.

Both my mage, Nicodemus, and Mia's cleric, Sharia, needed to roll to see if they could shake off the effects of this seemingly everlasting love potion. I threw my D20 into the kidney dish before anyone could mention the statistical curse I was labouring under.

'Saved!' Simon blinked in surprise. I'd rolled a seventeen.

Mia rolled. An eighteen. She too had saved, after failing the throw six times in a row previously.

'You're free!' John grinned. 'Free! Fly, my pretties!'

'Well. That's good then?' It felt a bit odd.

'Good.' Mia nodded, a tiny frown wrinkling her brow.

Simon clapped his hands and rubbed them together. 'So now all we need to do is deal with these mechanical guards advancing down the corridor towards us, then go and free Mercuron from his laboratory, hand him over to the Guild of Golden Truths, spend our reward to buy degrees and graduate from this damned university so we can get on with our lives.'

'Simple!' John said, moving his warrior to defend the doorway. 'How many of these guards are there?'

I moved Nicodemus to the far side of the room. The 's' on the end of 'guards' already told me that there were too many of them. We had fought one similar guard earlier on, while penetrating the laboratory complex, and had survived only by using all our reserve magics. Even so, both our fighters had been badly injured, hardly able to swing a sword until the cleric had exhausted her healing spells patching them up.

The door burst open, flying across the room in splintered sections, one of which brought Sir Algernon to the ground. Arrayed in the corridor beyond the doorway stood four of the mechanical soldiers. Each stood studded with crude pieces of armour plate alchemically welded to their metal skeletons. Behind their ribcages sat large black coil-springs, wound tight by unknowable forces, a reservoir of energy to power their attacks.

I used Nicodemus's last spell and sent a lightning bolt ricocheting down the corridor. The electricity grounded through all four of the enemy, leaving them sparking and immobile as the lightning rattled around inside whatever enchantments supported the mechanisms.

'Quick.' Nicodemus waved the others ahead. 'Don't touch them!'

Fineous and Hacknslay took off up the corridor, the nimble thief weaving a path between the paralysed mechanicals. Hacknslay brushed against the last one and hopped on, yelping, patting at the burned patch on his arm where a small electric discharge arced out to reach the ground through his body.

Sharia was more hesitant. 'What about Sir Algernon?'

'Well . . . I guess we could drag him,' Nicodemus suggested in a slightly grudging tone, eyeing the unconscious paladin.

'What?' Hacknslay stared back, incredulous.

'We found him here, we leave him here,' offered Fineous from the far end of the corridor. 'Hurry up!'

John was making furious eyes at me over the bed when he thought Mia wasn't looking, but I felt kind of guilty abandoning Sam's character after his visit earlier. 'Can we drag him?'

'What's your strength again?' Mia asked.

'Uh, six . . .' It meant that the average thirteen-year-old could beat me in an arm wrestle.

'Sir Algernon is six foot four, well muscled and wearing full plate armour . . .' She shook her head. 'Even with two of us we could never manoeuvre him past the guards, and it looks as if they're starting to recover.'

'We take his armour off then,' I said.

Another shake of the head and a grateful smile. 'It would work, but there isn't time. It takes an age to get armour off even if you cut the straps rather than undoing them all.'

'So let's drag him.'

Mia bit her lip. 'Leave him. It's us they want. He'll be OK.'

I met her eyes. 'Are you sure?'

She looked down into her lap and nodded.

So Nicodemus and Sharia ran after Fineous and Hacknslay, dodging the jerky, ill-coordinated lunges of the recovering mechanicals.

At last, after all this time searching, we burst into Mercuron's laboratory and there before us stood the man himself, tall and angular, his white robe stained in most shades of the rainbow, eaten away in patches. He stood before a huge fireplace beside a bubbling cauldron large enough for three very close friends to bathe in at once. One gnarled hand clutched a steaming ladle, the other a long-necked flask in which

163

a glowing liquid swirled as though it were a snake coiling continuously around and about itself. His assistants appeared to have fled the scene.

'Who the hell are you?' he demanded.

'We've come to rescue you, Mercuron.' Hacknslay advanced on the man, sword in hand, while Fineous worked to lock the heavy door behind us.

'Rescue me?' Mercuron's tufty white eyebrows rose. 'You mean I can go home to Malda?'

'Well . . .' Hacknslay drew the word out. 'That's the retirement plan, but first you'll be doing a little work for the Guild of Golden Truth.'

'So, you're kidnapping me and selling me to new owners?' Mercuron gestured with his ladle, and the black drips that fell from it ate through the workbench before him, vanishing into deep smoking holes.

'Well . . . yes,' Nicodemus admitted, since the truth was hard to deny.

'To get yourselves out of here after . . . how long?'

'Months!' Fineous stood with a long-suffering sigh, having finished relocking the door.

'I've been working for the guilds for nineteen years!' Mercuron shouted, his face reddening. More drops of the black liquid fell and hit the flagstones, sizzling into the stone. 'Nineteen years! You've been here months and you want to trade me into a new prison?'

'Well . . .' Nicodemus didn't need to go back and ask Sir Algernon the rights and wrongs of the situation. He knew exactly what the paladin would say.

BOOM

The great door behind us shuddered beneath a massive blow. One of the iron bolts securing the long black hinges pinged across the laboratory, missing Sharia by inches before demolishing a row of test tubes. The mechanical guards had recovered and wanted back in.

BOOM

Long splinters of wood broke free this time, and the hinges sagged on screws already half out of the doorframe.

'We need to go!' Hacknslay advanced on Mercuron, but the old man tossed his flask into the warrior's path. A great cloud of misty fumes billowed up and from it came a serpent of glowing smoke. In two heartbeats it wound itself about the warrior. Thick as a man and longer than a tree is tall, the serpent took him to the ground. Their struggles became lost in the mist, which in turn took up the serpent's glow, releasing it as a diffuse light of fluctuating colour.

From the two far exits Mercuron's assistants returned mob-handed, boiling through the doorways in their thickest aprons and furnace masks, all of them armed with bottles and flasks, no doubt containing the most noxious of all their alchemical workings.

BOOM

The door Fineous had locked surrendered to the pummelling of metal fists. The thief leapt clear but by remarkably bad luck, the very lock he had been working on shot out from the cloud of debris to hit him in the back of the head.

'One!' Simon exclaimed. 'I rolled a beeping one. A beeping two or more would have saved me!' Simon never swore. He very rarely got worked up enough to need to, and when he did he used 'beeping'. His mother swore like she was practising for the Olympics when she thought none of us were listening, but Simon had not inherited the talent.

'Fineous collapses to the floor not far from the edge of the cloud that Hacknslay is in. He lies there, limp, blood pouring down both sides of his head.' Mia looked up from her notes at me. 'What now?'

'I pull out the lamp.'

'Half-lamp.'

'Rub it quickly and—'

'Poof!' Mia used her hands to mimic the half-genie's smoke. 'Your limited wish is my command, oh master.'

'I wish . . .'

Mia edged the figures on the map closer, closing from all directions.

'I wish . . .' What should I wish for? I wanted it all. I wanted John's character free of the serpent, I wanted Simon's character whole again. I wanted Sam's character back with us and on his feet. I wanted the attackers turned to dust. I wanted some way to free Mercuron from his contract, not because I suddenly cared about him but because that was me right there, in the grip of Guilder's money. And in the game we were acting out, the role filled by Rust and the other goons on Guilder's payroll. I wanted a way to get our characters through this, graduated and out of that endless university, back following our own star. I wanted it all and I knew that whatever I got, it wasn't going to be all of it.

CHAPTER 19

It occurred to me that since Dr Pritchard had announced that my cancer was back I hadn't had any near-death experiences. Even Rust's manhandling, painful as it was, didn't trigger any of the effects I associated with the universe trying to rid itself of me before the moment of paradox. Of all the incidents so far, it had been the sword thrust that had come the closest to successfully ending me. Then came the diagnosis. And now . . . nothing. The dice had even stopped rolling ones. Almost as if the universe knew the cancer would do its job and had stopped trying.

If the leukaemia was going to kill me before the ball arrived, then things would have to go downhill for me pretty damn quickly. But I honestly felt more than half dead already, so it seemed to be on track.

I lay in my hospital bed waiting for Mother. Rain pelted the windows and the morning sun refused to show its face. I felt like crap. The chemical sludge they'd filled me with was clawing at the insides of my veins. The sour stink of vomit hung around me. I'd grown used to it, but I saw the nurses wrinkle their noses each time they came to take the sick bowls away. I'd been there two days and for most of that time it seemed that doctors had been hovering grim-faced around the end of my bed, discussing my chart in quiet voices. And, given that doctors are actually quite a rare sight in hospitals, to have two or three of them on my trail like vultures following a lame mule . . . well, it wasn't a good thing.

For the first time since this whole leukaemia business began, I had actually seen worry behind those brisk professional smiles. Doubt behind usually calm eyes. As if the doctors saw something new when they looked at my charts, when they took my pulse, when they peered into my eyes. As if for the first time they saw their enemy staring right back at them. Cancer. No longer lurking but laughing, its teeth deep in me, daring them to do their worst, or their best – it didn't matter. There had even been talk of moving me 'upstairs'. Upstairs was where they had taken that girl, Eva, just a few days before she died. All prospects of making it to the Trinity ball that evening had vanished, along with Eva and Demus, neither of whom I'd seen in the two days since being admitted. Something had gone seriously wrong inside me. My body had started to close down.

'How are you feeling, Nicky?' It was Lisa, the gorgeous redheaded nurse I knew from my previous stay. Don't believe the TV shows; nurses in general are no more attractive than any other random group of women, but Lisa could have walked into a spot in any episode of *General Hospital*. That didn't stop her 'Nicky' grating on me, though.

'Not too bad,' I lied. It surprised me to find that I wasn't quite far gone enough not to sit up and pay attention whenever she came by. The day I gave up on that, I guessed it would mean that either puberty was truly finished with me, or they should start measuring me for my coffin, or both.

'How are you feeling, really?' she asked.

The kindness in her voice made my cheek twitch, and ridiculously I found myself on the edge of tears. I felt hollowed out, weak, sick, burning up, ready to curl in about myself and die. 'Been better.'

'Well enough for visitors?'

'My mother's here already?'

'No.' Nurse Lisa pointed to the end of the ward where a familiar face was peering in through the small window in the door. 'Shall I tell her to come in?'

'Yes, thanks.' But Eva had already pushed through and was advancing on my bed. I leaned back into my pillows and spotted Helen behind her. 'Oh, nurse, could you . . .' Suddenly self-conscious, I waved towards the sick bowls.

'Of course, Romeo.' Lisa grinned and hurriedly picked up the worst of it, along with my untouched breakfast, taking them with her as she left.

'Helen!' I looked past Eva as she took her seat. 'What on earth are you doing here?' Suddenly I felt stronger. Not strong, but at least on the right side of half dead.

Helen reached my bedside and exchanged amused glances with Eva. A tension ran beneath the smiles though – I must have looked like shit. 'He's a charmer, isn't he?' She set a box of chocolate brazils in my lap. 'Eva says you like them.'

'I do.' Though right then the idea of eating one made me want to hurl. 'How—' I was going to ask how Eva knew, but Helen herself must have told her when she was growing up. It was so strange to see mother and daughter sitting beside each other. Instead I asked, 'You two know each other?'

'We met on the early train,' Helen said. 'Piers had a football match in London today. A university thing—'

'Football? I thought he'd play rugby!'

'Oh, he does. He's on the uni first team for that, too. But it's football season.'

Of course he did . . . I looked at my thin white arms and tried to imagine how long I'd last on a rugby field even at my best.

'So,' Eva took over, 'we met on the train and it turned out that we both knew you. And when Helen heard you were in hospital she wanted to come with me to visit.'

'Won't Piers—'

'Oh, he won't care if I don't watch him.' Helen shook her head. 'He always has an entourage whenever he travels. He just sort of attracts followers, I guess.'

Piers definitely had that whole maximum charisma thing going on, but I manfully resisted saying so in order to conceal the true extent of my nerd credentials. 'So, you can see why I mistook Eva for you at a distance.'

Helen frowned and looked at her daughter. 'Well, I mean, we have the same colour hair . . .'

That coaxed a laugh from me. 'I guess you're right. Completely different apart from the hair. Don't know what I was thinking.'

Eva's bag started beeping in a most unusual manner. She reached in and pulled out what looked like an oversized, rather clunky pocket calculator. She pressed one button and held the thing to her ear. 'Right,' she said. 'Yes. Yes. Not yet. Uh huh. Meet you there then.'

'That's a phone?' I asked, amazed.

'It's one of those new cell phones,' Helen said, eyes widening. 'Piers's dad has one. Very expensive.'

'I have to go and help another of your visitors find their way in, Nick.' Eva always hesitated for a fraction before saying my name, as if she were having to push the word 'Dad' from her tongue. 'I'll be back in a minute.' She stood quickly and strode away.

That left me and Helen rather surprised at finding ourselves alone, or at least as alone as you can be in a room full of sick kids lacking entertainment.

'So . . .' I found myself smiling despite the awkwardness of not knowing what to say. I met Helen's eyes and, although it wasn't that electric thrill that Sam had been describing, there was definitely something there. The way she looked back, unguarded, knowing, echoing my smile. I didn't feel like an invalid any more. I no longer noticed that I was lying in a bed propped up on pillows. My body's complaints dwindled to whispers and then to nothing. 'Not a fan of football then?'

A slight frown wrinkled the smoothness of her brow. The wrong thing to say. Piers was already casting a long enough shadow over both of us. 'Not so much,' she said. 'Eva tells me you're coming to the ball?' Her eyes travelled doubtfully along the shape of me beneath the thin green hospital blanket.

'She did?' I looked around as if there might already be a doctor bearing down on me, ready to forbid it. 'I don't think they're going to let me.'

'Eva said she already busted you out of one hospital . . .'

'Yeah, but this is a bit more serious.'

'Being hacked with a sword isn't serious?' Helen gave me a stern look and somehow in that moment I really wanted to go. But with her. 'You should have told me.'

'Well . . . I mean . . . I only just met you. I don't even know how to call you.'

'There's phones in the hall of residence! The closest to my room is in the corridor one floor down. Just ring and ask for Helen in three-oh-seven.' She rummaged in her bag and produced a biro to write down the number. 'You arrived mid-term, younger than all the rest – it's hard to get to know people. Especially in a place like Cambridge, full of landed gentry and other posh bastards.' A grin.

'So, how did you meet Piers?' I couldn't stop picking at that particular scab, but I did manage to avoid starting with 'speaking of posh bastards', and to be fair nothing I'd seen had suggested he was a bastard.

She gave me a look that said, 'Really? You really want to talk about this?'

I stared her down. I was the one the doctors were shaking their heads at. The one they wanted to move upstairs. I didn't really have time for beating around bushes, even though in my natural state I would have waited an age before straying onto such ground. And by an age I mean forever.

Helen gave in first. She looked away. 'He just loomed out of the crowd at a party last month. I don't even know why he chose me. We didn't have any friends in common. I just got swept along, I guess. He's like that. It's a kind of gravity.'

'Chose you? You make it sound like all the choice was on his side.'

A sigh. 'I don't want to sound like an empty-headed Disney princess . . . but the guy is perfect. You know? He's kind, caring, compassionate, funny . . . The only thing to complain about is not having something to complain about. How stupid is that?'

I shrugged. 'My dad used to say that he didn't love my mum because she was perfect, he loved her because her imperfections were a good match for his. Like a lock and a key, he said. I guess I'm not exactly an expert, but it seems to me that perfection is hard to live with. I'd definitely need someone who could forgive my failings, and I'd feel a lot better about that if they had some I could forgive back.'

Helen gave me a crooked smile. 'I get that. Piers is great and everything, but everyone wants a piece of him. He's always busy. Sometimes I think he only has a girlfriend to point at so he can keep all the other girls at arm's length. People are always trying to fix him up with someone.' A frown. 'Anyway, I refuse to talk about him another second. How did you meet your last girlfriend?'

'My last and only girlfriend,' I said, and, seeing her look of surprise, added, 'I went to a boys' school! Also, yeah, I'm a slow starter.'

'How did you meet your first girlfriend then?' she asked.

'My friend John. He's our D&D group's speaker-to-girls. Without him I literally need to be running for my life, maybe from a punt full of drunken toffs, before I even come close to a pretty girl.'

'Ha,' she said. 'Even then I had to make the first move.'

We chatted for a while then. I'm not sure about what. I just remember the warm rush beneath my skin every time her dark eyes met mine.

The time slid by easily and other visitors came and went. It was the sudden shuddering of the light that made me aware of Eva returning, Demus in her wake.

'Hey,' Eva said. 'We've come to bust you out of here.' The lights dimmed, then steadied.

Demus held up a dinner jacket and black trousers. He had a pair of black shoes in the other hand. 'Something tells me these will fit you.' He tossed them on the bed. 'I've called Mother as you and told her I feel great and I'm going to the ball.'

'I . . .' I wanted to tell them that I *really* wasn't well. That I couldn't make it.

'Shit! Is that the time?' Helen jumped to her feet. 'I have to run.' She paused, looking at me. 'See you at the ball tonight, yeah?'

'Yeah,' I said. 'See you there.'

She smiled and turned to go, hesitating as she saw Demus, glancing between him and me. Another look at her watch and she shook off her confusion, then headed off down the ward swearing colourfully all the way.

Demus tossed the clothes onto my bed and helped himself to a handful of chocolate brazils. 'Love these things.'

'You guys just set me up, didn't you? You've been waiting in the foyer the whole time so I could talk to Helen.'

'Maybe . . .' Eva said.

'It's what you'd do if you were me,' Demus said.

'Let's get you out of here.' Eva came to help me up.

I fended her off. 'I need to get dressed.'

'OK.'

'Alone.' I waved them both off, though what I thought I had to hide from Demus I don't know. I drew the curtain around my bed and got dressed, moving like an old man, or a young one who has been badly beaten. Eventually I emerged clutching my bag. 'I don't think—'

'Nonsense.' Demus grabbed my arm. 'It's the chemo making you ill. You'll feel better for getting out.' My skin buzzed where he touched me, an uncomfortable resonance. Right there between his fingertips and my arm was the strangeness that had somehow been woven into our timeline. Stars had died to make it real.

'What, no wheelchair?' I looked hopefully towards Eva.

'You need to be tripping the light fantastic tonight, so let's get those legs working.' She moved to take my other arm. As she made contact it was as if a circuit had been completed, linking the three of us. The world seemed to flex around me, time fragmented and fragmented again, a dozen images overlaid, each becoming a dozen more, almost but not quite the same. The three of us seemed the only constant thing, like a nail hammered through scores of paper-thin realities, anchoring them one to the next.

All of us felt it, and the other two let go of me as if I were scalding hot.

'Let's not do that again,' Demus said.

I nodded and stood trembling, my body still echoing with whatever that had been. The world blurred around me again, but differently this time. Just two overlaid versions of it, seemingly the same image but seen from slightly different angles. 'Weirdness . . .'

Both of them looked at me and I saw myself from the outside, too thin, too white, hunched around my poisoned blood. I tried to shut their minds from mine and my own singular vision returned, the product of my eyes and mine alone.

'You OK?' Eva made to reach for me, then pulled back, remembering.

'All good,' I lied. 'Let's get out of here.'

CHAPTER 20

'So you're just going to casually break into a nuclear power station and take over operations?' I asked Demus as he pushed me along.

'They're not that complicated.' Eva was walking beside my wheelchair. Demus had bought this one rather than stolen it, like she had.

'Any time traveller wanting to get back to when they came from is going to require a very large amount of controlled energy. A nuclear power station is the best option as it can generate the required current, and they're so automated you can achieve most of what's necessary from the control room,' Demus said. 'So, yes, we've both done our homework. And I've got a dozen what you might call "hired goons" on the case. We're taking half of them up with us, and I'm meeting the rest in Bradwell.'

'You can trust them?' It seemed to me that anyone you picked up for a job of this kind would be as likely to turn you in as to turn up, and this was the sort of case that government undercover operatives lived for. 'I mean, how long have you known these guys?'

'A few weeks.' Demus grunted as he tilted my wheelchair back to take a curb, then hefted the big rear wheels up. 'And also most of their lives.'

'Uh?'

'I checked their credentials before I left. I know they're who they say they are and that they all have a reputation for loyalty. Also none of them were recorded as being involved in breaking into a nuclear site. So that tends to indicate that it worked in my past and should work in this one. Be prepared, Nick, be prepared! Things in this game may not always be what they seem. It pays to have people you can call on in case of unexpected spanners in the works.'

'Even so . . .' I shook my head. 'It just can't be that easy to break into a nuclear power station, surely?'

Demus shrugged. 'The only people who the government think might target power stations are terrorists. And they aim to stop those in the planning stage by infiltration and intelligence, not at the doorstep. Onsite security isn't that tight at this time. There's no record of an incident at Bradwell, so I think the government are going to hush it up and put extra measures in place afterwards.'

We crossed a few more streets, the busy London traffic showing no special consideration for the invalid in a wheelchair, and came to the backstreet where Demus had parked.

'This is us.' He stopped beside a white panel van.

'What happened to the BMW?'

'There's going to be nine of us, that's what happened.' Demus looked around. Half the street lay in shadow, the other half still dazzlingly bright. 'They should have been here already.'

'Reputations for loyalty,' I said. 'Not for good timekeeping.'

Demus helped me into the front while Eva manhandled my wheelchair into the back of the van. The plastic seat cover felt searingly hot, even through my trousers. The van smelled of feet, and the footwell was littered with Fruit Pastilles wrappers. I loved those. Twenty-five years hadn't lessened Demus's sweet tooth any.

The back doors shut with a bang.

'Hey!' Eva called out, surprising me by still being inside the van. She rattled the doors and both Demus and I looked over the back of our seats to see what the problem was. 'I'm locked in!'

'I'll go round and let you out.' Demus turned and tried his door. 'What the—'

My yelp of fear cut him off. Standing at my door and favouring me with a narrow smile while he did something to the lock was Charlie Rust.

I started to wind the window down, then thought better of it. Even so, before I'd got it completely closed Rust slipped a small rubber wedge between the glass and the doorframe, holding it in place.

'I thought you'd like to know the results of that DNA test I was telling you about the other day.' Rust's voice came through the half-inch window gap. 'The good doctor assures me that the John Doe found dead with my brother is a perfect match for you, Nick.'

'You're lying,' I called back. 'You don't even have any of my DNA.'

Rust pursed his lips. He had to shout to make himself heard over Eva's attempts to force the back doors. 'I had enough of your skin under my fingernails to make a new you, Nick.' He shielded his eyes and pretended to peer at Demus. 'And this gentleman looks remarkably like our John Doe, only with hair.'

I noticed that in his other hand, Rust held a red plastic container with a yellow spout like the ones people use to carry petrol to cars. He swung his arm, splashing the stuff across the bonnet.

'We need to get out of here!' I told Demus, my blood running cold.

'Find something to break the windscreen,' Demus told me. He had a cell phone to his ear, rather like Eva's.

I dug into the compartments in front of me, finding only an A-to-Z map book, cloths and a plastic ice scraper. 'Eva, I need something metal, fast!'

Rust continued sloshing petrol liberally over the bonnet and windscreen. The chemical stench of it filled the van and immediately started me heaving.

'They don't tell me much, Nick, but I make it my business to find stuff out. And it seems to me that the fellow next to you must be you, just like the one who killed my brother was you, too.' He vanished around the car, still sloshing petrol. 'Don't suffer a witch to live, they used to say.' He was still shouting, though Eva had stopped banging. 'And it seems to me that time travellers are much more dangerous than witches.'

'Use your shoe!' Eva said.

'I'm wearing socks . . .' Next to me were the black shoes that Demus had brought for me. I grabbed one off the seat. Demus kept talking into his phone, one finger in the other ear.

'But,' said Rust, reappearing, 'this is really about my little brother.' He took out a cigarette lighter.

I started hitting the windscreen with the heel of my shoe. Desperation lent me a strength I hadn't thought the drugs and disease had left in me. Even so, the damn thing refused to shatter.

'Never liked him, but the thing is,' Rust said, trying to get a flame, 'the thing is that we can't have chaos in the world. There are debts and obligations. A man's not a man unless he keeps to his own set of rules.'

In panic I started to pound at the windscreen with both fists but found no give in it. Demus was now hammering at his side window, also wedged by Rust and also resisting his strength.

A dark shape hit Rust from the side, moving fast. Somehow he managed to twist and throw the man, not only keeping his feet but also managing to keep his cigarette lighter in hand. And now it sported a flame.

'I—' Rust's triumph proved short-lived as two more men jumped him. He sprawled across the bonnet, the lighter flying from his grip and arcing across my field of vision. For one heart-stopping moment it seemed impossible that it wouldn't hit the windscreen and send us all up in the same fireball, but it flashed by and was gone.

'Use this!' Eva pressed a short screwdriver into Demus's grasp. He stabbed the windscreen, once, twice, three times and in the next instant it was through, the whole sheet of glass now a milky assembly of tiny cubes held together beneath laminate.

Eva vaulted through from the back and struck the shattered windscreen with both heels, throwing it out of its frame. Rust rolled clear just in time to avoid being hit, taking one man down with him and leaving blood smears all across the white petrol-blistered paint.

'Come on!' Demus led the way, reaching back for Eva's legs.

I scrambled out. Even with the adrenaline pounding through my veins it felt like climbing a mountain.

Demus caught hold of me as I rolled out. He began to lead me away down the street, Eva helping to support me.

'Are those your men?' I asked.

'Yes.'

'All six?'

'Yes.'

'Why are we running?'

Demus glanced back. 'They seem to be losing.'

'More importantly, where are we going?' Eva asked.

'Right here.' Demus held out his car key in his free hand and seemed to be trying to squeeze the plastic part between finger and thumb. 'Damn, keep forgetting that . . .'

'What?'

He released me and went forward to the black BMW parked a few yards ahead. 'No remote unlocking back here in the Stone Age.' He unlocked the door. 'Get in, quick!'

I fell in on to the passenger seat, stinking of petrol. Eva got into the back. 'Who was that madman? I saw him stab a man in the neck just now!'

Demus's only answer was a squeal of tyres as we shot out into the road.

'Jesus, that was close. He almost burned us all up.' I found my hands shaking.

'We're going to have to deal with him somehow, if we survive this evening,' Eva said.

'Survive this evening?' I asked. 'Balls don't traditionally have a high mortality rate.'

'Well, there's the small matter of the time hammer.'

Demus turned a hard left and joined the traffic heading out of London. 'Our calculations do indicate a modest chance of disaster.'

'Disaster?' I strapped my seatbelt on, somewhat belatedly.

'Well, centring a severe blow to the space-time continuum inside a nuclear power plant does carry some inherent risks,' Demus said.

'And there may be unforeseen consequences for both the timelines we're trying to untangle,' Eva added.

'Like?'

'Like instabilities or . . .'

'Or?' I turned to look back at her.

'Well, there's a non-trivial chance of changes to the strong and weak nuclear force, leading to the destruction of matter.'

'Matter as in, all matter everywhere? Like all the atoms in the universe unzipping?'

'Yup. But as far as I can tell, that's quite unlikely.'

'Well, that's all good then.'

For a moment I saw myself through Eva's eyes again, sick and worried. I shook her vision out of my head, wondering what she thought of this father she had come back to see.

Half an hour passed in silence.

'Has it occurred to you, Demus, that here we are running from Rust again, a Rust at least, ready to break into a technical facility again, there's a party to go to where I'm hoping to kiss the girl, again, and oh yes, I'm in chemo again?'

Demus glanced away from the road for a second. 'Well, you do have the whole statistical outlier thing going on.'

'Temporal cross-resonance,' Eva said.

'What?' Demus beat me to it.

'It could be an echo between the two fused timelines,' she said. 'Yours and mine, fuelled by the building paradox energy. The same issues still trying to resolve themselves. Echoing back and forth between the timelines until we separate them or they overload.'

'Ah.'

'Or just chance!' She laughed. 'It's easy to come up with conspiracy theories if you only look at the evidence that supports your idea.'

On the drive north, Eva continued to check her calculations, spreading papers across the back seat. I would have offered to help but I felt too ill. Besides, she was probably too old to need her dad to help with her homework. Instead I asked Demus how he planned to deal with Rust, who would without doubt be coming after all of us. And while Demus could escape into last January and Eva could hurl herself back into 2007, I was left time travelling into the future at the same steady sixty minutes an hour that Rust and everyone else on the planet could match.

'Well. I could give you a lot of money and you could pay someone to—'

'Because that went so well just now, with those half-dozen heavies of yours,' I said. 'And besides, *you* might know where and how to rent thugs, but that's a skill I've yet to acquire. Plus I think it might take a contract killer to do for Rust. Maybe three.'

'We need to play to our strengths,' Eva spoke up from behind us.

'We calculate him to death?'

'We go back in time and sort the problem out,' she said.

Neither Demus or I said anything for a long moment, puzzled both by the fact we knew you couldn't change things in this timeline by going back into the past, and by the fact we knew Eva wasn't stupid. When we did speak, it was both at the same time to say the same thing. A weird feeling. 'You'd just start a new timeline. Nothing would change.'

'Normally, yes,' Eva explained. 'But this particular timeline is lousy with paradox, and it will have just been hit with a time hammer, putting everything into flux. In addition, if the individual going back is an integral part of the paradox, then I calculate that a small change could propagate through.'

'How small?' Demus beat me to it.

'Well, if I just went back twenty years and killed him as a baby – and I've no intention of killing anyone, baby or otherwise – or if, for example, I interrupted his parents having sex, then the change would probably be too big. However, for a smaller change then the conditions we're engineering, combined with the paradox issues, will be able to allow bundles of closely related timelines to mix. By which I mean reality will become unstable.'

'And you don't think destabilising reality is taking a sledgehammer to crack a nut in this case?' I asked.

'He was about two seconds away from burning all three of us alive,' Eva said.

'Point taken. I'll do it.'

'You'll do nothing but stay here and play your part. It has to be me that goes back. Demus has an appointment in January to keep. I can go back and then sort out my own return. As long as I don't go further back than the Manhattan Project, I'll still have access to nuclear energy and should be able to build something to send myself home.'

'Should?' I asked.

'The whole plan is built on a solid foundation of shoulds, maybes and probablys. I've only just come to the end of my time jump – I'm relatively easy to return to my original time. It's the sending me and

Demus further back in time that's difficult, but doable given the equipment Demus will have on site. Demus's jump is only six months. He can do that in one go. For me to go back decades it will have to be a non-conventional solution. The best we can do is drive a spike back through time, fracturing it. I have equipment that will let me track the fractures, but I'll have to race through time and space to the various splinters and let each carry me on. Also, because I'll be aiming to cause a low-grade paradox, I'll have some of the same sorts of problems you've been having. The universe will do its best to stop me.

'Anyway, if I do get stuck in the 70s, I'll just start a new timeline and make myself Queen of the World! Shouldn't be too hard with all the stuff I know.

'When Demus provides the juice, I was already going to return to 2007. The only change here is that I'll head in the other direction, into the 70s instead, and see what I can get done on the Rust front before going home. Between us we must have some information that I can use to pull his fangs. So tell me everything you know about him.'

So we did. It turned out Demus had been researching the man for years, having had other issues with him. He knew a lot more than I did, and pretty much all of it was scary.

CHAPTER 21

It took the best part of two hours to reach Bradwell, and that was with Demus driving like a maniac the whole way. Occasionally my perception would hop into his head, an effect lingering from when the three of us had first touched back in the hospital. Experiencing his driving first hand didn't make it any less scary. With a little effort, though, I could drag my focus back into my own head.

We had to skirt London and reach the coast. There wasn't enough time for them to take me to Cambridge and then get back to the power station, so Demus dropped me off in the town closest to it, Bradwell-on-Sea. He left me with another fat roll of tenners and the assurance that there was no place that any taxi driver shown a sufficient number of the notes would not agree to take me.

We pulled into a carpark behind the marina and abandoned the BMW. I stood there, sweating and shivering in my dinner jacket, nauseous and barely able to stand. I watched as Demus and Eva unloaded electronic equipment from the trunk of his car. Behind them the masts of several dozen yachts wagged gently against a paling sky.

'That's them.' Demus hailed a lone man smoking with his back to a panel van identical to the one we'd left behind in London. He turned to me. 'This is it, Nick. Nothing we do here matters unless you play your part in Cambridge.'

'You know this is all crazy, right?' I lowered my voice as Eva busied herself digging more stuff from the boot. 'I mean, you're me . . . how good are we at picking up girls? And I'm supposed to be able to leave this ball with either Mia or Helen, both of whom are way out of my league . . . and I'm supposed to do that while smelling of petrol, trying not to puke and seriously feeling like death . . . with both their boyfriends there?'

'Yup.' He offered me what I knew from my mirror to be my best attempt at an encouraging smile. 'Anyway, better go. Coming, Eva?'

'Ready.' Eva struggled around the car with a heavy-looking holdall in each hand.

'I guess this is it, then. We won't see each other again.' I felt slightly peeved that neither of them were taking this as hard as I was.

'Well, I'll be seeing you in January,' Demus said.

'Yes, but I've already done that, *and* forgotten most of it, on your instructions!'

Demus shook his head. 'I don't know what to say, Nick. You're me. It would be weird for me to worry too much about your feelings. And we both know hugging's out.'

'Not for me.' Eva moved in while my attention was on Demus and gave me a quick tight hug. 'Stay safe. Dad. Thanks for everything. And say hi to Mum for me.' She picked up her bags and set off for the van.

Demus shrugged and followed her, hefting two bags of his own.

I watched them go. I guess from Eva's perspective, Demus was a much more relatable father figure than some kid younger than her – even if he definitely wasn't her father, whereas I kind of was.

I felt a strange sort of separation as they left. Not emotional, or not just emotional, but as if the world were shifting out of phase again, rather like it had when all three of us were in contact back in the hospital. For a moment my vision went sideways and I started to see the van across the carpark as if I were approaching it. I shook my head to clear my eyes, took a deep breath and began to stagger off towards the town centre, hoping that the place was bigger than it looked and might actually have a taxi rank.

Demus's intuition about taxi drivers proved correct, once I finally found one. The money meant nothing to me, so I offered a ridiculous sum in cash just to cut through any haggling. And for an additional five hundred pounds up front, my driver, sporting the unlikely name Maximillian, agreed to ignore as many speed limits as I liked.

For my part, I lay on the back seat and did my best not to die. A fever had me, a reaction to the chemo maybe, or my organs shutting down, or just opportunistic flu. Whatever the cause, my breath came in short fast gasps, all strength left my limbs and my skin looked deathly pale, save for a mottling of bruises starting to form where I'd banged myself escaping the van and on the sides of my hands from trying to break the windscreen.

Somewhere around Saffron Walden the delirium took me and I began to hallucinate. I saw scenes sliding one way across the curve of the taxi's upholstery while the lights of the cars we passed slid in the opposite direction. If I closed my eyes I saw the images projected on the back of my eyelids, as if I were looking out from someone else's face. I began to hear voices. Eva's voice. The voices of men I didn't know. My limbs twitched with sensations I didn't own.

And suddenly I was there, free of pain and sickness, looking down at Eva, a long white corridor stretching off in both directions. I'd slid into Demus's head again, but this time I decided to stay. The view was more interesting that the one offered from the taxi, and leaving my sick body behind was a definite benefit too.

'Reyas and Arnold should have secured the control room by now,' I said. Or rather Demus said, but it felt like me doing it. 'They won't stay past the half-hour mark. I paid them a lot of money and they plan on getting away to spend it. Smith-one and Smith-two should have set the equipment up in the testing lab. Remember, they're techies and apt to panic if there's a problem. Check their work, if you have time, after you've arranged things in the control room.'

'Got it. We've been through this.'

'And going through it again makes it less likely it'll slip your mind when the pressure's on.' Demus sounded like my father, with the same voice and mannerisms my father had used when instructing me on taking the Maylerts entrance exam the year before he died.

'Yessir!' Eva saluted.

A moment's silence hung between them.

'Well, this is it then, I guess.' Demus rubbed his neck. 'If this works, I don't know if either of us will even remember the other existed.'

'Well, the quantum spin effects in memory storage are—'

Demus stopped Eva with a raised hand. 'I hope we do, Eva. Meeting you has been a privilege. The me that married Helen would have been very proud of you indeed.'

They hugged then, and I could tell from the way Eva shook that she was sobbing, though no sound escaped her. Demus let her go and walked away while he could still hold on to his own feelings. Once through the door at the end of the corridor he leaned back against it and with finger and thumb squeezed the wetness from his own eyes. I understood his emotion, but didn't share the depth of it. Another lesson I guessed that twenty-five more years had in store for me.

Demus hurried on down a staircase, across some office space, along another corridor, down another staircase. He appeared to be wearing some kind of white overalls and to have a radiation badge and official identification card pinned to his chest. A white hardhat bounced from the tie at his hip. Twice he passed other workers and once a young woman in a business suit. None of them gave him a second glance.

The place began to look more industrial as Demus progressed. The stairways changed from concrete to steel, the corridors became wider and crowded with thick pipes, some swaddled in silvered insulation. The distant thrum of turbines made itself known through the soles of his feet. A door marked 'Reactor Chamber, No Unauthorised Admittance' yielded to his touch, though surely it should have been guarded and locked. Cameras watched his progress now, a red light blinking above each of their dark and singular eyes. He clattered down a metal staircase into a brightly lit room full of computer monitors and control machinery. Two large men in white surgical masks were waiting for him. Three other men sat sullenly in the far corner, their wrists, ankles and mouths bound with black tape.

Demus nodded to the two heavies and glanced through the wall of windows to their left. The view was of a large chamber where a mix of steel walkways and gantries surrounded a deep concrete pool whose waters glowed with a curious blue light. The glow was the tell-tale signature of Cherenkov radiation, indicating that the nuclear reactor beneath the pool was busy spitting out its normal deadly mixture of charged particles and overexcited photons.

'OK, let's crank this thing up into high gear.' Demus picked up a telephone set into the central control panels and dialled double one. It rang twice.

'Hello?' Eva's voice.

'Ready to start?'

'We are.'

I watched from Demus's eyes as he moved around the control room changing settings, tapping dials, and throwing levers. The look on the faces of the taped men turned from a mixture of terror and resignation to astonishment. The two heavies checked their watches periodically.

After about ten minutes Demus returned to the phone. 'How's it looking?'

'At fifty per cent of max. I've killed the alarms.'

'It should be ninety by now at least.' Demus sounded concerned. 'You've withdrawn the control rods?'

'As far as they'll go. The reactor core should be buzzing away like mad.'

I was no expert, but I knew Bradwell was a Magnox reactor, its graphite control rods cooled by carbon dioxide gas, fuel rods clad in a magnesium-aluminium alloy that would start to melt if those control rods were withdrawn too far. And when the cladding melted the uranium-235 inside them would start to melt too, and if it all ran together that would be a meltdown. A critical mass would form, an explosion would rip the chamber apart and radioactive debris would decorate the countryside. If this went wrong, Chernobyl would be forgotten and Bradwell would live in infamy in its place.

'Someone has instigated undocumented safety protocols,' Demus said. 'It's the only explanation. I'll have to go into the reactor chamber and manually override so we can withdraw those control rods further and really get some juice out of this baby.'

For the first time since Demus had entered the room, the three captives began to struggle. Behind their tape all of them were trying to shout out.

'It doesn't sound exactly safe . . .' Eva said, her voice tinny and distant through the red phone.

'It should be fine. Besides, we don't exactly have a choice. Timing is pretty critical on this. Just see if you can disable any subroutines that are going to try to kick in and stop me.' Demus set the phone back down. He turned to his two men. 'When it gets to quarter past, leave the way you came. Change clothes in warehouse six. The balance of your payment will be in your accounts come morning.'

Without waiting for an answer, Demus took an odd triangular key from the small heap on the control panel beside the phone and left the room through the door opposite the one we'd entered by. He made his way down a short corridor ending in the kind of door you expect to see on a submarine. It had something of a bank vault door about it as well.

'We're nearly there.'

'Uh . . . What?'

'Trinity College. We're nearly there.'

It was Maximillian. I was still lying on the back seat of his taxi. All of me hurt. I tried to sit up, wheezing. I almost didn't manage it. Outside, the light had faded and the sky was shading through the deeper blues towards purple. I wiped my mouth and my hand came away bloody. The next corner nearly slung me into the footwell.

'There's another three hundred in it if you ram the college main door and drive me across the lawn to the far corner.'

Maximillian laughed. 'Twenty thousand and you're talking.'

'OK, the front door will do, but three hundred more if you help me to my room. And by help I might mean carry.' It was only money.

'Done.'

Getting to my room was agony. I guess Maximillian was trying to help, but he seemed to be all sharp angles and pincer hands, and the cigarette and Brylcreem stink of him set me retching. Thankfully he didn't have to haul me up the stairs because John and the others had seen me approach from the window of my room, and came hurrying down. I'd given John the key back in the hospital and now here they were, three penguins and a bird of paradise.

John and Sam took over supporting me.

'Easy now.' Sam seemed a little unsteady himself and smelled of Bacardi.

Together they got me to a bench while Simon, also in dinner jacket and bow tie, dug the roll of tenners from my pocket and, on my instruction, gave the whole lot to the cabbie. That last bit was more to save time than any great act of generosity.

'You're not well enough for this,' Mia said. She looked gorgeous in an evening dress of deepest blues, purples and black, all in crushed velvet, and her hair pushed up, coiled in dark rings, short at the sides in a punkish style. I half-expected her to be wearing DM boots under all the folds of her skirts, but didn't check. She looked around at the others. 'We need to get him to a hospital.'

'I'm *not* well enough for this,' I agreed. 'But I'm damned well doing it. Eva and Demus are risking their lives as we speak, and none of it will mean anything unless I'm at the ball.'

'Can you at least tell us why we're here?' John asked. 'How does someone undo a paradox? We can't help if we don't know what we're supposed to be doing.'

'I can't.' I shook my head and the world spun. 'Events have to unfold naturally. We can't just act this out to a script. Just do whatever you would normally do.' The truth was that I had no idea what would happen when the time hammer hit, and I didn't think that even Eva really knew. I couldn't even imagine a sequence of events that would lead to the critical moment, especially with me better suited to intensive care than to partying, but sometimes you just have to have faith. Against the odds I had them all here, and myself. The dice were rolling. We just had to wait and see how they fell.

We arrived late, missing the champagne on the lawns, the barber-shop quartets and the fine dining in the vast tent set out in the quad like a MASH station made of clear plastic. Still, we had the fireworks, circus rides, midnight punting, open air disco and bands to look forward to. Most ball-goers would last until dawn showed its face. I wasn't sure I'd last another hour but I was very pleased to have missed the meal.

I found myself a seat down on the lawns leading to the river and collapsed into it. Hundreds of students crowded the green acres, milling gently in the warmth of a summer night, the hubbub of their voices underwritten by the base thud from the disco pavilion further down the bank.

'Go on,' I said to the others. 'Mingle!'

'You're not fit to be left,' Mia said, brow wrinkling in concern.

'Whatever needs to happen here tonight isn't going to happen if you guys hang round me like a unit of bodyguards,' I said. 'Go on. Have some fun. It's a once-in-a-lifetime experience.'

'It happens every year,' Simon said.

'Trust me.' I fixed him with a stern stare. 'This year's going to be a one-off.'

John put an arm across Simon's rounded shoulders. 'Come on. I'll show you how it's done.'

Mia watched them go. 'I think Sam and I should stay.'

'I think Sam and you should go.' I waved them off. 'Quit cramping my style.'

Sam downed his champagne then quirked his mouth into a half-smile. His hair rivalled Mia's, pushed up into a high quiff of oiled curls. He had almost as much eyeliner on, too. He set his glass beside me, made a formal bow to Mia and offered her his arm. 'If I may have the pleasure, miss?'

Mia sighed, manufactured a bright smile, and took the offered arm. 'We'll be back to check on you soon.'

I watched them go, soon lost among the swirl of ball gowns and black-clad men. They looked good together. I tried and failed to make myself comfortable in my chair and wondered if I were doing what I was supposed to be doing. The crowd flowed around me and I sat apart, observing. Young faces – animated, happy, beautiful girls, handsome young men, privileged simply by virtue of being here even if you discounted their family wealth; full of potential, dreams, and ambition. I'd seen myself carrying another quarter century. I wondered what the next twenty-five years held for this class of '86. A quarter century on, would that girl with the long red hair be on benefits, a divorced mother of three, owner of her own business, reading the news at ten? Would that boy with the wild laugh be decades dead – killed in a car crash two years from now, CEO of a major bank, drinking Special Brew under a bridge to quiet the voices in his head?

'Nick! You made it!' Helen spun into my view in a swirl of gold and scarlet. A forest fire of a dress. Like Mia, she looked gorgeous. Too perfect, too alive to be in the same world as me, let alone to be in my arms. She settled into the chair beside me. 'Jesus Christ, Nick, you look fucking terrible.'

'Been better.' I got the words past gritted teeth.

'She's right, old chap.' Piers Winthrop, aka Adonis, leaned down from his imposing height to inspect. 'Can I get something for you?' He looked big enough to pick me up in one hand and cart me off to hospital by himself.

'Some paracetamol would be good,' I said. 'About twenty.'

'Ha ha!' Piers straightened and scanned the crowd. 'Give me a minute. I know just the man.' And off he went.

'He could at least have the decency to be a dick and make it easy for me to hate him,' I said.

Helen smiled and leaned in. 'Why would you want to hate him?'

'I'm jealous, of course.'

'Of his money, looks, charm and athletic prowess?' she asked.

'Well, those things as well.' I met her eyes.

She laughed. 'Well, don't be. Sometimes he's too perfect for his own good.' She sipped at her champagne flute. 'We're saving ourselves. You know, for marriage.' She rolled her eyes.

'Marriage?' I was shocked. 'Has he asked you?'

'Well, no. I mean . . . he's very Christian about all this stuff, though . . . you know . . .'

'Uh . . .' I wasn't sure I did know, but I found Helen's directness refreshing. She had that northern openness. Just told you what she thought, no messing. 'He wants a church marriage?'

'I mean as in "no sex before".' She laughed. 'I told him it's a lot too late for all that. At least on my side . . . But no, he wants to play it by the good book. It's driving me crazy, if I'm honest.'

'Ah.' I felt myself colouring. Very open and perhaps somewhat drunk, too. I wasn't sure what to do with the rather too much information she'd just dropped in my lap. 'So . . . did you find anything about magnetism and memory for me?'

Helen put back her head and laughed from the chest. 'See, that's something else I miss. Nerd conversation. Piers is reading English. Probably going to get a double first, but he doesn't know the first thing about anything technical. He thought if you boil water for longer it stays hot longer . . .'

We sat for a while, chatting easily. Piers returned with four tiny white tablets that were almost lost in the broad expanse of his palm. 'Codeine. Great painkillers. Doc prescribed them for Gideon's knee after the game.'

'Thanks. Thanks a lot.' I took them and swallowed all four with the last of Helen's champagne. 'You guys go have fun. I'll catch up later when these have had a chance to kick in.'

'You're sure?' Helen took my hands in hers, warm and full of some kind of magic that sent tingles down my arms.

'I'm sure.'

They left, and I slumped back in my chair as if she'd taken the last dregs of my strength with her. I knew myself to be retreating into the shell of my being, no more able to stand than to fly. I knew how bad I looked. I looked like the girl I watched die back in January. Little Eva, eaten by her cancer, death rattling in her chest with every slow breath in and slow breath out.

My mind drifted, and in the next moment I was with Demus again, watching the world through his eyes. I welcomed the escape. Perhaps I'd even been looking for it.

'Move, damn you!' Demus hauled on a large iron wheel set into the wall. The heavy engineering and requirement for physical strength seemed more nineteenth-century steel mill than late twentieth-century nuclear facility. The wheel lurched around a few degrees and Demus stumbled to an array of red buttons on a nearby control panel, cursing. He was in the reactor chamber directly below the window to the room where the engineers lay bound and watched over by his hirelings, if they were still at their posts. The blue glow from the pool beside the reactor had intensified into a glare, and a high-pitched whine tormented the air.

'Now work!' Demus jabbed one button, then the one next to it.

Somewhere deep in the bedrock of the place a mechanism began to grind away. Behind us a gantry groaned and the chain beneath it began to move. Unseen in the reactor core an array of hot graphite control rods were being withdrawn millimetre by millimetre, slowly relinquishing their role in calming down the nuclear chain reaction.

'That's all I can do!' Demus barked into his phone. 'What you got?'

The voice came faint and crackly, almost inaudible above the shudder and hum of the reactor. 'A hundred and twenty per cent. It's not enough.'

'Shit.' Demus punched the wall. 'Shit. Shit. Shit.'

He took up the sort of wrench you use for killing zombies and went to a bolted steel plate close to a bundle of power cables thicker than a man. One by one the bolts surrendered to him and at last the whole plate fell away with a deafening clang. A thick chain assembly lay exposed in the recess behind. Demus took the winding handle from its hook and fixed it in place. A red plastic sign read, 'Manual Rod Withdrawal. Reactor must be shut down prior to use.'

'Shit.' Demus began winding. Almost immediately a loud alarm began to sound, a bell rather like the one for school assembly. The blue glare from the waste pool intensified, overthrowing the fluorescent lights above to cast Demus's shadow black on the wall before him.

After sixty seconds of winding, a second alarm began to sound. This one sounded serious. A cross between an air raid warning and a police siren. Every now and then it fell silent to allow a calm recorded voice to interject, 'Radiation levels at critical. Evacuate the reactor chamber immediately.'

Demus glanced down at his radiation badge. The dosimeter had shaded through yellow, orange and red into a purple so dark as to almost be black. 'Shit.'

He gave three more turns of the wheel, then scrambled up the metal ladder to the walkway above. A moment later he stumbled through the submarine-style hatch and heaved it shut behind him. He tried his phone. 'Eva? Eva? Got you the juice. I just have to reconfigure the distribution . . . Eva?' Silence. No line noise. The phone was dead. Killed by the radiation, no doubt. I now had my explanation for bald Demus in January. Radiation sickness will do that for you even quicker than chemotherapy. The Demus I met back then couldn't have had long to live, even if Ian Rust weren't waiting for him.

Demus swallowed some pills and went back to the engineering room where his men had been. Afterimages from the glare plagued his vision and the room seemed darker. Shutters had lowered themselves across the windows, sealing off the reactor room below. I hoped they were lead shutters. Thick ones.

'Davis? Jenks?' Demus couldn't be using their real names, not with witnesses, but either way there was no reply. He blinked and rubbed his eyes. Someone was standing in the opposite doorway. Demus patted his pocket. His hand curled around something metallic and heavy. A gun? I guessed that we were saving two worlds, so unavoidable casualties were an acceptable price to pay. But despite that I couldn't imagine shooting someone. I couldn't imagine a me who would do it, either, no matter what twenty-five more years had laid on their shoulders. Even so, he took the gun from his pocket. 'Who's there?'

'A gun. I didn't think you had it in you, Dr Hayes.' Charles Rust stepped into the room. He advanced at an even, unhurried pace. 'And given that you do seem to have it in you . . . why not a ray gun? I've watched Space 1999. They have ray guns, no?'

'Stop right there.' Demus levelled the pistol at Rust, no nonsense in his voice. Mine would have been trembling.

'If you were going to shoot me you'd have done it by now, Nick.' Rust had closed half the distance. 'I would have started shooting the moment I saw me. I did try to burn you up.'

'I mean it!' His voice shook now and so did his hand.

'It's a cliché, but most amateurs like you forget to take the safety off in moments like this.'

Demus glanced at his weapon. Rust moved faster than thinking. Somehow he had a knife in his hand. Before I knew what had happened, the blade was in Demus's guts. He collapsed under Rust, squeezing the trigger to no effect. He *had* forgotten the safety, and in any event Rust had that hand under control, pointing it towards the wall.

'I could have stabbed you in the head, of course.' Rust pinned Demus with one hand and his legs while the other twisted the blade. 'But that would be too quick. I mean you avoided the burning. Fair play. But I still have to make it hurt. Nothing personal, but a debt has to be paid.'

Demus screamed. The initial stab hadn't hurt, but as Rust twisted the blade I felt it as though it were white hot. Demus's free hand might have done something useful, but instead it struggled to push back Rust's knife hand. There's no choice under that sort of hurt.

'Where next?' Rust pulled the blade free and moved it up Demus's body, the strength in his scrawny arm such that even Demus's desperation failed to resist the advance of his knife hand.

Demus glanced at his gun. We both saw the fire extinguisher at the same time, a red cylinder of compressed CO_2 strapped to its wall-stand just over a yard from his swaying hand. The knife drove home again as Demus struggled to flick the safety catch off. He screamed and convulsed but managed to fire off a shot, then two more in quick succession. One of these hit the target and a blast of icy gas boomed across the room, instantly fogging the air. The force combined with the surprise of it proved sufficient to roll both men over, putting space between them. Demus fired blind into the fog, swinging his arm and shouting incoherent curses.

'Nick? Nick! Are you alright, Nick?' For a moment I thought it was Eva come to save me . . . or Demus, but I opened my eyes to see Sam's worried face inches from mine. He had me by the lapels of my dinner jacket as if he were planning to shake an answer from me.

'Y-yes.' I was very much not alright. Demus had been stabbed. I could still feel the knife in my guts. And Rust was still there, waiting for the fog to clear.

'You sure? You don't look alright.' Sam sounded drunk. I thought perhaps the grip he had on me was to hold him up. I swung my head. The crowd had thinned, and overhead the brighter stars had begun to poke their way through the light pollution. A string quartet had struck up beneath a nearby gazebo and were holding their own against the distant disco thud. A romance of strings swelling into the night. Somewhere far away Demus was bleeding to death. I wasn't going to last much longer either. But there wasn't a damn thing I could do about any of it. I surrendered. If this was to be my last night outside the walls of a hospital, I might as well spend it in good company. 'Where's Mia?'

But Sam was no longer looking at me, no longer gripping my jacket. 'Who is *that*?' He exhaled the question.

The violins swelled again, caressing the darkness. Scattered couples began to waltz, and winding through their number came a huge square-shouldered figure.

'That is Piers Winthrop. Don't hate him because he's beautiful.'

'Oh dear God, yes he is!' Sam looked down at me excitedly, both hands gripping each other at his breastbone. 'Electricity! Electricity!'

I glanced confusedly between him and Piers, who was now looking our way. 'You mean?' Was he talking about knowing the love of his life when he saw them? That instant attraction he'd spoken about back at my house . . . ? And somewhat belatedly, the penny dropped. 'You're Elton's friend. One of Elton's *special* friends. You're g—'

'Going in! Yes, I am.' Sam grinned. 'Wish me luck.'

And I did.

I slumped back into my chair and watched Sam zero in. I found myself feeling slightly more human. The codeine must be kicking in. I even felt sorry for his inevitable disappointment. Unless . . . unless, of course, Pier's refusal to consummate with Helen had more to do with taste than Christianity. Twenty years ago, being gay could put you in prison. Attitudes might have softened somewhat since then, but you were still breaking the law if you did much about it before the age of twenty-one . . .

I watched Sam and Piers talking for a few moments. The painkillers were helping, but I felt so damn tired. A yawn cracked my jaw. What I really needed was forty-eight hours of sleep. Maybe seventy-two hours. I closed my eyes, just for a moment. Just for a moment.

I had maybe three seconds of sleep before the nightmare reclaimed me.

Demus crawled through the clearing fog towards the nearest control desk. He held the gun in one bloody hand and red drool hung from his mouth as his breath rasped in, then out. I wanted him to watch for Rust, to hold the gun up, ready for that monster to come hurtling towards him. Instead the whole of his effort was laser-focused on the desk, as though it were a distant mountain peak towards which all his will was bent.

He hauled himself up it, blood flooding down his legs. With a groan he made it into the chair. The extinguisher lay like an unfurled metal flower, its fog now just traces around the edge of the room. Crimson footprints tracked towards the exit to the rest of the plant. At least one of the bullets must have caught Rust. I hoped the bastard was bleeding out in a stairwell somewhere.

Demus manipulated a set of levers and buttons on the desk, laboriously typing a long code into a fixed keyboard. Finally he threw a switch and reached for the red phone.

'Eva?'

'We're running out of time. Tell me something good.'

'Rust may be heading your way. Wounded. Don't know how bad.'

'Oh God.' Real fear in her voice. 'How did you get away?'

'I didn't.' A laboured breath followed by choking. 'Got you the current though. Check it. Then hit it. Be quick.'

'Nick, I—'

'Quick!' Demus managed a shout. 'Get out of there straight after!' He hung up and slumped over the desk. The contact that had been established between us began to dim and fade.

'This is what death's like, then.' Just a whisper. He knew I was listening. 'Hurts a bit. Not so . . . not so bad. Nothing. Nothing to be . . . scared . . . of.' A long silence, then, 'We're all infinities.'

And he was gone.

The blow of the time hammer hurled me from my chair. I opened my eyes, expecting to see scores of students thrown down in their finery like hay before the reaper's scythe. Everyone but me seemed unaffected. Although the fabric of the universe flexed and warped before my eyes, it seemed that my fellow ball-goers flexed and warped with it, noticing nothing.

Painfully and with almost as much effort as it had taken Demus to haul himself up to that last control desk, I regained my chair. I had no idea how long I had to reach the moment of paradox before the echoes of the time hammer died away and the chance of untangling the two timelines was lost. I also had no real idea how long I'd been asleep or where any of my friends were.

'Simon?' I hadn't noticed him when I was on the ground, or when I crawled back to my seat. It wasn't until he started to snore that I realised one of the chairs close by was occupied. 'Si!'

He stirred and grumbled.

'Simon!'

Simon cracked an eye open. 'Oh, hi.' He sat up, yawning. His dinner jacket really didn't fit him and he had what looked like chocolate cake smeared at the corner of his mouth. 'Can we go yet?'

'Where's Mia? Have you seen Helen?'

'Uh?' Simon rubbed his eyes.

'It's urgent. I need to find them!'

Simon looked over his shoulder, yawned again, and waved an arm vaguely. Following the line of his gesture I saw that, miraculously, it led to a distant table and set of lawn chairs where both girls sat alone. A moment later the view was blocked with the to and fro of scattered ball-goers but my glimpse had shown the girls facing away from each other, hunched and staring at their hands.

'I think Sam and Mia argued. And Helen was shouting at the big guy.' Simon couldn't seem to stop yawning.

'Get me over there. I need to talk to them.'

Simon gave me a look that said, 'Really? But I'm comfortable here . . .' To his credit, what he actually said however was, 'OK.' He got to his feet and reached for my arm. I let him haul me up, and leaning on each other we made slowly for the distant girls. This was it. I was going to make it, and the universe's best efforts to stop me had failed. Even cancer couldn't bring me down before I crossed the necessary hundred yards.

'Why, if it isn't Halligan's little doggy.' Crispin Waugh strode into our path. Thankfully his sword-wielding chum wasn't at his side.

'Ignore him,' I told Simon in a quiet voice. Waugh wasn't a brawler and he could call me all the names under the sun. That wasn't going to stop me. I limped towards him, leaning heavily on Simon.

'It turns out we have some friends in common, Hayes.' Waugh grinned and nodded behind me.

A large hand closed around my upper arm and spun me about. I found myself staring into a broad chest straining a wing collar shirt. Raising my gaze past the bow tie, I met the glaring eyes of the ginger giant who had so nearly caught me in the punt chase. To either side of him crowded the rest of that crew of drunken toffs, seemingly just as inebriated as they had been a week earlier.

'Time for some payback.' He grinned and drove a meaty fist into my stomach. I doubled up around the blow, all the air leaving my lungs in an agonised 'wuff'. A moment later I was on the grass with a big foot descending towards my face to blot out the sky.

The blackness turned to a dark corridor along which I seemed to be running for all I was worth. It was hard to care. Whatever was happening at the power station it couldn't change the fact that I'd failed. The universe had steered Waugh and his cronies into my path, and even if their drunken rage didn't kill me in my weakened state, there was no way I would reach the girls, let alone have that moment of paradox. The game was well and truly over. Only it wasn't a game. It was my life and the lives of people I cared about. And all our plans had come to nothing and despair.

The thud of the runner's feet might have been the thud of blows raining on me as I lay helpless on the lawn . . . I couldn't tell the difference. My mind sought escape and found what was perhaps the last time I'd been happy.

'*Poof!*' *Mia had used her hands to mimic the half-genie's smoke.* '*Your limited wish is my command, oh master.*'

'*I wish . . .*'

Mia had edged the figures on the map closer, closing from all directions.

What had I wished? Sam had wanted to know the answer while they were helping me out to the ball's riverside entertainments. The others wouldn't tell him. They said it had been me that wished and it was up to me to describe it.

John's warrior had been down in the smoke, entangled by the huge glowing serpent that Mercuron had let out of his flask. Simon's thief had been knocked unconscious when the mechanical soldiers battered down the door. Sam's paladin had been laid low earlier by another flying chunk of a different broken door and left for dead. Meaning that only Mia's cleric and my mage were still on their feet, no longer bound by the enchantments of a love potion but with enemies closing from all directions, far more of them than they could possibly handle.

'Well,' I told Sam. 'You have to remember that we were in an impossible situation. There was no way that all of us were getting out of there alive.'

'But you had a wish!'

'A limited wish. You can't get an awful lot done with one of those. Maybe I could have got out of there scot-free on my own. Possibly I could have got Mercuron out with me and completed the mission. But then you would all have died. Maybe I could have blasted half our enemies. But then the other half would have killed us all. Maybe I—'

'So what *did* you do? Is Sir Algernon still alive?'

'I don't know for a fact that he's dead,' I offered with a wan smile. 'What I did was convert an enemy into a friend.'

'Mercuron!' Sam declared.

I shook my head. 'Mercuron was a prisoner there. If he couldn't escape by himself, he was hardly going to be able to get us *and* him out. So I wished . . .'

'Yes?'

'That the snake was our friend.'

'That's it?' Sam looked disgusted. 'You thought that serpent from the flask could defeat four mechanical soldiers, Mercuron, and a horde of his assistants armed with God knows what?'

'No. But I thought it could escape up the chimney and take us with it!'

'But . . .'

'I shouted for it to get us out of there and for Hacknslay to hang onto it if he still could. Then I ran over and grabbed hold. It was semi-solid, which made it easy to dig in for a grip. Sharia froze Mercuron with a "hold person" spell.'

'She grabbed him? At least that was a success!'

'No, she grabbed Fineous and managed to catch hold of the snake's tail as it slithered towards the fireplace. It knocked the cauldron over, dousing the fire, and the place filled up with toxic steam. Then up it went, bashing through a dozen sets of bars. A few seconds later we were several hundred feet higher and on the outside of the university.'

'There's an outside? But they said . . .'

'They lied.'

'So you failed the mission, but you all survived. Except for poor Sir Algernon.'

'Actually, we succeeded if you think about it, because we were only trying to steal Mercuron to get money to graduate so we could leave the university. And we ended up leaving the university without having to do any of that.'

'The lying bastards! I—'

'There's no reason to assume Sir Algernon is dead, but we didn't all survive. Somehow Sharia didn't manage to hang on.'

'So you lost Sharia and Fineous?'

'Just Sharia. Fineous did manage to hang on.'

'He was unconscious, though!'

'Pretending to be. You know Simon. Once he saw how things were going he thought he'd play dead and see if he couldn't escape later, in the confusion.'

Sam had frowned. 'Not sure I like this game any more.'

I shrugged. 'I think results like the one we had are the reason why I like it. It's not an all-or-nothing game like those board games our parents made us play. Win or lose. It's more like life. Mixed. You can't have it all, but sometimes you can have what you need.'

'But you lost Mia.'

I winced at that. 'Won't happen again.'

The thudding stopped suddenly. That's what brought me back to it, back to the power station. Sometimes you only notice something when it's gone.

The running feet were silent, but there was still sound. A panting, gasping, almost sobbing. Hands rattling a door. 'Open! Open!' Eva's voice. I was back to seeing the world through her eyes. Our connection had survived Demus's death. It had been weakened, though. I couldn't feel her exhaustion.

A flash of torchlight back along the corridor. A man's voice ringing out sing-song through the darkness between them. 'Eva! Eva!' Rust, drawing closer. 'I won't hurt you. I just want to know where the boy is.'

Suddenly I was invested in the situation – not for myself; I doubted I'd live long enough for him to find me – but for my daughter. I'd like to think I'd care for anyone being pursued by a monster, but the fact that it was Eva pulled me out of the hole of my own defeat. If she could escape him she could stay here, decades away from the consequences of my failure. Live a life. Travel, love, party, do all the things I wanted for her, for both of us.

'Eeeeeeva!' Rust made a slow advance, either to terrorise her or because Demus's bullets had slowed him down. He must have got Demus's destination from the men who attacked him in London. Probably got the station floorplans from them, too. Knew the areas they would be taking control of.

Claxons were ringing out. There would be police and security guards flooding the buildings. The army was probably on its way, too. But I doubted any of them would reach Eva quickly enough to save her from Rust.

'I just want to know where our boy Nicky's at.' He was lying, though. He did want to hurt her. He couldn't leave an angry time traveller on the loose. Those are hard to deal with, even for someone like Charles Rust. 'Eva . . .' Closer now. Too close.

'Come on! Come on!' Eva managed to work the door bar and stumbled through into a long laboratory lined with workbenches. Acrid smoke hung in the air, thick enough to obscure the far end of the room. The time hammer appeared to have knocked out the power station's lights, but the laboratory lay illuminated by an unworldly blue glow hazing through the smoke. The quality of the light wasn't unlike that from the Cherenkov radiation bathing the reactor room.

Eva covered her nose and mouth with her arm and hurried towards the source of the glow. Demus's two techs had been busy before they ran. A ring of eight large electromagnets had been constructed on the floor at the far end of the room. Each one must have required a strong man and a lifting trolley to move. The main power line was thicker than my leg. The insulation had burned away from the metal. Here and there the copper had melted into gleaming puddles. A forest of cables snaked from each magnet, linking them to a bank of computer terminals, some still smoking slightly, that lined the nearest bench. During the power surge needed to strike the time hammer's blow, the equipment before us had siphoned some of the current to drive an energy spike back through the past. The net result shimmered in the space between the magnets. A dancing blue fracture in time. Whatever Eva had done was very different to the solutions I envisioned for time travel, but there are many ways to crack a nut, and doubtless hers was cleverer than mine.

'Got you!' Rust lunged out of the dark doorway, catching Eva's shoulder in a pincer grip.

Somehow she twisted away to leave him holding just her jacket.

'Run!' I shouted voicelessly.

Eva ran.

Rust roared in fury and limped after her at a frightening speed. 'You're mine now, bitch! And I'm going to—'

But she was through. Gone. Leaving only blackness behind her.

I saw daylight, a grey sky. Eva stood up, checked herself. Under the jacket she'd sacrificed to escape she had on a T-shirt emblazoned with 'Red Hot Chilli Peppers' . . . a favourite food in the new millennium? Quite how she had managed to bring clothes through the time fracture when Demus had to arrive naked after each jump I wasn't sure, but I was glad she'd cracked it.

'Quickly . . .' she muttered, pressing fingers along her cheekbone as if she were typing something. I saw goosebumps on her arm. Wherever we were, it was cold. A near-deserted city street . . . It looked a little familiar. Without warning, a glowing map overwrote her vision, a green dot pulsing at its centre. She had implanted technology! I was very impressed both by the tech and by how she hadn't boasted about it before. 'Come on . . .' A red dot began to appear on the map close to the blue one. A legend flashed: 'Warning: temporal anomalies.'

'Crap, that was fast.' Up and down the street the wind swirled in curious eddies, raising litter into dirty miniature tornados. The nearest one collapsed, and suddenly a glassy replica Eva was running at her. My Eva turned and fled.

All along the street, replica Evas started to give chase. Some kind of defence mechanism the universe employed against paradox, maybe . . .

Like antibodies created against an invading virus. Natural consequences of the energy gradient she would create when she did whatever it was she was going to do back in the past.

Eva rounded the corner, and on the display overlaying her vision we both saw a blue dot begin to pulse just a few blocks away. A helpful line joined Eva's green dot to the blue one, mapping a path through the streets ahead.

Eva sprinted, gaining a lead, but as the yards went by in their dozens, then scores, then hundreds, her breath started to grow ragged, her stride uneven. Glancing back at the next corner she saw that her pursuers seemed untroubled by issues of stamina and were closing the gap rapidly. And at the rear of the ten or so giving chase came a large tornado. Like the replicas, it was glassy and hard to see, merely rattling the trees as if in premonition instead of ripping them from the ground. But even as she watched, it spat out yet another replica.

On the overlay, the blue dot had begun to blink as if it might not stay for long. With a sob of frustration, Eva lurched around the corner into the next road. Whatever the blue dot was, it lay halfway down this residential street lined with tall townhouses. I could see nothing unusual ahead of us, though.

Eva broke into a sprint that she wouldn't be able to maintain for very long at all. The green and blue dots practically touched and still nothing . . .

Then suddenly there I was. Me and John, strolling down the street without a care in the world, both of us in school uniform. This was Cambridge. This was that February day we both skived off and came to see Halligan!

On wobbling legs, Eva practically crashed into me. I gave her a gormless stare as she grabbed my arms.

Streetlights flared and died all around us. The headlights of cars, the lighting inside the houses to either side, too. I'd noticed none of it the first time. Somehow my daughter had filled my vision.

'Nick, help me.'

'How?' I asked.

'Keep them off me,' Eva panted. She hauled a large and peculiar key from her trouser pocket, then stumbled up the steps to the door of the townhouse just beyond John and me. Already I was moving forward to intercept the things chasing her. I hadn't known why I did that. But of course I would. She was my daughter. Helen's baby. I would lie down in traffic if she needed me to.

Eva struggled with the key in the door, some kind of lock pick, though where and why she had learned to use it I had no idea. Within fifteen seconds she was through while I lay convulsing in the street behind her. She didn't spare me a glance, but I guessed she already knew I'd be fine afterwards. Well, fine-ish. Actually, truth be told, my acting as a lightning rod for what was following her was probably the reason for all the subsequent freak accidents and weird coincidences. A second Rust brother on my case, for instance. Or Waugh and his friends busy kicking me to death. Still, I didn't hold it against her. I just wanted her to escape and be safe and happy. I guess that's what any father wants for their child.

'Thank you!' Eva burst through the front door into a tiled hall. Blue light flooded from a doorway at the end of the hallway and an old man in a dressing gown stood bewildered, staring at the source. Eva barged past him and through into what turned out to be the kitchen. And there it was, a fierce blue fracture in time, barely wide enough to admit her and standing ragged-edged before a shuddering washing machine. The washing machine seemed to have been driven into such overdrive by the power surge that it was actively vibrating itself out from under the counter and across the floor. If Eva didn't win the race to the fracture, then a nearby spot some unknown number of months or years in the past would be receiving a brand new Zanussi washer!

Eva fell through the fracture a heartbeat before the runaway appliance reached the spot, and was gone, sinking through a sea of yesterdays.

After that I caught only flashes. One chase after another. A desperate race to reach the cracks that the time spike had driven back through the world's history before they healed over and left her stranded in the wrong year.

In between Eva's pursuits, I caught fragmentary images of a night sky emblazoned with exploding stars. I thought at first I might be seeing some grand cosmic event: the universe consuming itself at the end of time, perhaps. But no, a gleaming black shoe swung across my vision, having sent my head snapping to the side. I was seeing fireworks, and not the cartoon variety that follow a blow to the head. These were the midnight display being launched in salvos from the opposite side of the River Cam.

It seemed the kicks rained down in slow motion, the pyrotechnic flowers unfurling overhead with a leisurely grace, blues and greens and reds so lustrous that any true bloom would hang its head. I floated in a timeless, painless, velvet silence and knew that I was dying. I had let go of fear, and only sorrow kept me company in those last infinitely extended moments. A profound sadness that I had to let this go, the sunsets and sunrises yet to be seen, places unvisited, secrets yet to be unlocked, girls unkissed, lives untouched, songs neither heard nor sung. I even felt sorry for the idiots kicking me. That their lives of privilege were now to be brought low by this murder that forces beyond their understanding or control had edged them into.

Suddenly I was in a brightly lit kitchen. The reflection in a glass-fronted cabinet showed me Eva. That connection she and Demus and I had forged, that tenuous quantum entanglement wrapped about with the strands of our paradox, still linked us across unknown years. Eva and I only glimpsed her reflection, but it told a story. She looked tired. Her hair was almost to her shoulders now. She wore different clothes. Whatever she was doing, she had been at it a while.

'Give it to me!'

'Come and get it, runt!'

In a nearby room two boys were shouting at each other. Something crashed to the ground as they wrestled. Quickly Eva opened the cutlery drawer before her and took out the bread knife. She rooted in her bag through a collection of over a dozen other bread knives and brought out a very similar one. She measured it against the one she'd taken. Her new one was about an inch and a half longer. Without delay she substituted the longer one, put the shorter one in her bag, and left by the door to the back garden.

Eva retreated to the bushes at the rear end of the sun-dazzled lawn and inserted herself among the dark and glossy leaves of an overgrown rhododendron.

A minute passed. Another. And in the next moment someone burst out of the door from the kitchen. A boy of about twelve, his dark hair messy, clothes tugged about, a wild grin on his face. He wiped at his mouth, scanned the garden with beady black eyes set either side of a blade of a nose, then turned back towards the open door.

A smaller figure flung itself after him. A similar boy, but half his age at most, and wielding a long knife. The bread knife that Eva had left as a replacement.

Charles Rust managed a disbelieving laugh before his little brother stabbed up at his face. To his credit, the older Rust managed to interpose his left hand with snake-quick reflex. The blade went right through his palm. For a moment it seemed as if he had stopped the point from reaching his eye, but no, in the next heartbeat he was reeling back, clutching his face, careless of the blood spurting from his hand.

His high-pitched screams became the wailing of rockets spiralling into the air.

'Get up!'

'What?' I mumbled the word as a hand hauled me to my feet.

I found myself eye to eye with Charles Rust on that same Cambridge lawn with the rockets bursting into sparkling blossoms overhead. To be more precise, eyes to eye. Rust wore a black eyepatch. I stared at it in confusion. A large part of me knew he had worn that same eyepatch every time we'd met. He'd even told me the story of how he'd lost it in a fight with his brother . . . Another part of me, however, smaller, and fading like a waking dream, knew that Eva had changed something small but important.

Glancing around I saw the big ginger lout sitting dazed on the grass nearby, nose broken, blood streaming from it. Two more of his punt buddies lay groaning. The rest seemed to have scarpered. Simon stood a safe distance from Rust, but from the missing buttons and torn shirt I guessed he'd stood up for me before my guardian devil pitched in. A circle of shocked guests hemmed us in, watching open-mouthed.

Rust let go of me. 'I know what you did, Hayes. I know you come back from the future and end my brother. I had the DNA results. It's you in those morgue shots. I even know the unmarked grave where you're buried. That little shit owed me an eye, but family rules meant I could never collect. So, I owed you a debt. Consider it paid.' He spoke into a brief gap amid the din of the fireworks overhead.

I coughed and flexed, expecting to find myself in agony, but apart from a bruised arm where I'd landed after Ginger's initial shove, I seemed uninjured. Rust must have stepped in pretty quickly. 'I thought it was your job to make sure I do mine. So keeping me alive just seems like what you're paid to do.'

Rust gave me a nasty smile full of thin, predatory teeth. 'Don't push it.'

I turned to go. I could see the girls in the distance, still sitting just a yard from each other.

Rust caught my elbow and paused before speaking as rockets exploded the night sky. 'I saved you. You need me. So remember that, if you're ever tempted to mess with my past.'

I held up both hands. 'Honestly, I never would.'

With that he let me go. I still felt like I'd been run over by a steam-roller, but the codeine kept my legs moving. If Rust were here, he couldn't be in Bradwell. That timeline had been pruned from the tree . . . or at least, if it still existed it wasn't me who had died there. My Demus had completed his mission and would have already headed back to January 1986, where I would meet him for the first time. Or perhaps he never came here at all. With the paradox removed, his calculations should be sound. My head hurt and I gave up thinking about it. All I really knew was that our daughter had saved us both. Or me, twice. Either way, she'd done well, given the limits to the change she could make.

Simon returned to my side to help me while the onlookers began to disperse, distracted once more by the pyrotechnics overhead. The echoes of the time hammer still reverberated around me, flexing the night as I made my slow pain-filled walk across the lawns, drawn on by glimpses of Mia and Helen still at their table.

The hammer's aftershocks filled both the flashes of brilliance and the darkness between them with possibilities. New tomorrows streamed away from every moment, a billion billion versions of me, each heading into the next heartbeat on slightly different trajectories. I walked through it all, spawning an infinity of futures, just as all of us do every second of our lives. I held tight to myself, to me, *this* me, the one I cared about. Ten yards from the girls I shook Simon off and made my own way.

Helen and Mia had their eyes on the sky now, watching the explosions. Neither noticed my arrival, even when I sat between them.

Shockwaves from the hammer blow tore through me, and this time I let them do their work. Two versions of me sat in the same space and time, one written over the other. One me reached for Helen's hand, and she turned with fire-bright eyes to see me as if for the first time, her fingers curling around mine. The fireworks shattered the heavens with one final crescendo and fell silent. She told me that Piers had gone off with a boy from London. She told me how silly she felt, not ever having realised he was gay. How Piers had been using her to deflect attention from other girls, to stop his friends and family asking questions or trying to set him up with eligible debutants. She'd been pretty enough to be believable, and too common to be drawn too far into his circle. No invitations to meet Mother and Father. Even now she worried for him, how his coming out would affect his chances of the political career he wanted, whether his friends would desert him. I told her times were changing, perhaps faster than we knew, and soon maybe there would be no more need to hide and lie about such things. And as we talked, behind me Mia noticed us, stood quietly and walked away.

The other me reached for Mia's hand and she turned with a smile of relief and concern, hugging me. She told me that her relationship with Sam had been something of convenience to both of them. A place to take shelter while they both tried to make sense of their lives. She would understand if I'd been too hurt to try again, but she wanted to. Seeing me in hospital had made her see how fragile happiness was, and she wanted to try for hers while she could see it in front of her. And behind us Helen rose from her chair and walked away beneath the cloud of her own misery.

I could see both futures. I wanted both. *A* Nicholas Hayes would have each of them. But *this* Nicholas Hayes, my own mote of sentience, could have only one. Eva had given me my limited wish, got me to this moment where the day could be saved, along with all the days that followed. I could untangle the timelines. But there were limits. I couldn't have it all. Whatever I did, someone would be hurt. I would hurt someone.

I wasn't yet seventeen, but I knew enough now to understand that the world was more complicated than mathematics, however advanced, and that there were no perfect solutions to it. Whichever hand I took, tomorrow I would still be ill, tomorrow Guilder would still think he owned me and my work, tomorrow I would have given up on Helen and Eva, or on Mia and Demus.

But that was tomorrow. Two Nicks reached for two different hands. I was the one that reached for Mia's. She turned to me, relief and concern warring across a face that I felt I could love forever. She reached for me. And, following the advice I had once left for myself on a note six months and half a lifetime ago, I kissed the girl.

ABOUT THE AUTHOR

Photo © 2010 Nick Williams

Before becoming an author, Mark Lawrence was a research scientist for twenty years, working on artificial intelligence. He is a dual national with both British and American citizenship, and has held secret-level clearance with both governments. At one point, he was qualified to say, 'This isn't rocket science – oh wait, it actually is.'

He is the author of the Broken Empire trilogy (*Prince of Thorns*, *King of Thorns* and *Emperor of Thorns*), the Red Queen's War trilogy (*Prince of Fools*, *The Liar's Key* and *The Wheel of Osheim*) and the Book of the Ancestor series (*Red Sister*, *Grey Sister* and *Holy Sister*).

7/6/19.